DARKNESS

DARKNESS

Victoria Sadler

"The argument of the broken pane of glass is the most valuable argument in modern politics."

Emmeline Pankhurst

"Oh Liberty! What crimes are committed in thy name!"

Madame Roland
Final words on the guillotine

CHAPTER ONE
The Death

I alone survived. Of all the people that had lived in the block of flats that had been my home, and my prison, for the previous three years, I was the one who made it through. Just me.

My father was the last of the others to die. He died in the night, though he had been in acute pain for days. I stayed awake with him the whole of his last night, kneeling on the floor with his head in my lap. I knew he was dying. So did he. His breathing was stilted, raspy.

"I can't see a tunnel. I can't see any light. No... Wait... White light."

There was no white light welcoming my father into heaven. It was just the light from the phosphorus flares coming through the window, shot up into the dark sky by other survivors. The State was rebuilding. Some of the flares were from survivors who wanted back in, others from bandits – opportunists – looking to entrap the recovery units.

"Mary, Mary. Hold my hand."

I could feel his cold hand through my wool glove.

"Mary. Look after... [yourself]. Keep... [safe]." I've added what I think he said as his voice kept fading out and he hadn't eaten in days. He was too weak to talk. "And whatever happens remember, you were... [loved]."

Then he closed his eyes.

And died.

The dying exhale their last breath. A simple exhalation and their body diminishes, turning in on itself. And then they're gone. I don't believe any more that it's the soul or the spirit escaping. There's no release of the spirit to another dimension. The exhalation is just a function, the internal organs clearing themselves out.

So, no, there is no God. If there was, he would have ensured my father left me with something I could hold on to, something to keep me going. Instead I got nothing. Not even meaningful final words.

You see, my name is not Mary.

My name is Laura.

I don't know who Mary is, or was. Was she a sister I never knew about? Was she an ex-girlfriend? People harbour many secrets. Perhaps she was a young lover from my father's past that he'd kept hidden inside the caverns of his heart. I don't know. And I never will because my father was the last of my family to die.

Well, the last but one.

As with the others, I wrapped my father in a double sheet, binding it tightly like a mummy to make sure the body was secure. You have to do this before the rigor mortis sets in, while the limbs are still malleable and loose.

In this world, in this new world, you can't afford to stand still and mourn. Maybe there will be time for grieving later. Disposing of the body quickly is hygienic, yes, but more than that, it is imperative. It helps you shut down your emotions quickly, cut off the pain. Like ripping off a plaster. Dispose of the body and cauterise your heart.

Handling my father's body was less traumatic than handling my mother's. Maybe I had become used to it – there had, after all, been a few in between. Or maybe it was because I had loved my mother. Who knows? I have no answer. In fact, I don't have many answers these days. I just have a lot of questions.

Our apartment block used to have blazing rows about whether we should dispose of the bodies during the day or at night. Some wanted the cover of darkness to protect them; others feared the cover of darkness would protect those preying on survivors who strayed outside. Given how weak the sun is during the day, I always found this a somewhat futile argument.

Nevertheless, cheeks flushed and veins strained as the neighbours screamed over each other, demanding to be listened to, or at least heard.

It's amazing the rage inside people when they're hungry. These were adults that could barely muster up the energy to join the teams sent out to scavenge for extra food, but they could always find the adrenalin to fight.

I had always voted for daylight, and, as a result, I had always been on the winning side of the argument.

The others, though, they feared the darkness, or rather, what lurked in it. "The scavengers, the bandits," that's what they would shout. "The darkness will protect them." But when pushed, when explained that bandits would be easily outnumbered and outfought, the men's heads would fall and they would whisper, "The women."

Ah, the women...

RAZR.

"If one of them catches us, we'll be butchered..." "They're animals..." "I heard they put men's heads on spikes on the bridges..."

RAZR. The four-letter word that caused the blood of grown men to run cold.

"And Jane, the leader, I heard she cuts off the fingers of all the men she's killed and has them in a pile in her barracks..." "I heard Jane was dead..." "I heard she's still alive..." "Well, if she is dead, I hope they tortured her before they killed her..."

No one from our block was ever caught by RAZR, but we knew they were still out there. We had seen the news reports before the televisions were switched off, and we had witnessed the terror on the streets before the state of emergency was declared. And it was fair to say that if the women were ever to get one of the men... Well, if they were lucky they would be killed quickly.

So the bodies were to be taken outside in daylight hours only.

Some of the leaders in the block then tried to argue that disposal shouldn't be attended to with any ritual, that this new world was no longer a place for sentiment. Factually correct but actually dangerous thinking, especially if you are trying to keep people calm.

Most argued they wanted to preserve a moral code, even in times when the rest of society had abandoned theirs. The argument seemed compassionate but I sensed a lack of self-awareness. It's not about a moral code but about fear. People fear change, they just do. When the world you know has been wrenched from your grasp, you cling to the rituals of the old order. It gives you security. It makes you feel safe.

So it was an odd set of rules – we had to dispose of the bodies during the daytime to minimise risk, but rituals had to be observed, which took time so increased risk.

I didn't care either way. I had to survive. I looked at which way the majority were leaning and voted the same way.

The ritual of disposal continued.

But not everyone could fall into line.

After it happened, The Fall, many simply couldn't cope. A lot of the people in my block started using drugs, almost desperate to lose their minds. My age, older, younger... No discrimination. In a way you could rationalise it. Survival seemed like long odds and maybe they thought, 'Fuck it, what's the point in living any more? We're all gonna die so let's just get out of our minds.'

So they got high.

And the drugs got passed around.

Some learnt to make drugs on-site.

Then the drugs got passed around more openly.

And the addictions started.

And more people got addicted – those that had used before, those that never had.

That was hard for the rest of us. Trying to stay calm, organised, keeping everyone alive, when there was a group who couldn't – wouldn't – pull their weight. They said they wanted to die but it didn't stop them drinking clean water.

Or eating.

Or wanting to use electricity.

Or hot water.

Eventually, those who considered themselves in control decided to prohibit the drugs – though that was a very hotly debated vote. But those who wanted to die continued to survive and for that, they had to take responsibility. It's hard enough to talk someone out of killing themselves without them being on drugs. But when they've checked out, when their mind's splintered, you can't convince them. You just have to make them go cold turkey.

So the drugs were taken away and the makeshift kitchen factories destroyed.

Not that those who survived the come down thanked us for it.

Most of those who survived the drugs couldn't survive the reality. They jumped off the balconies, all at once. Some sort of pact. At least they got what they wanted.

We didn't wrap up their bodies. Their bodies were already outside and back then, Central Command was still running sanitary collections.

And we didn't have sheets to waste.

Binding my father took less than thirty minutes.

It's funny... No, wrong word... It's *awkward* the things that run through your brain when you are dragging your father's body down eight flights of stairs. Like, why was he still so fat? This was a world of food shortages and intermittent heating. How had his big fat tummy survived into this new world?

I had thought that perhaps I could use this to my advantage, drag my father down the cold cement steps on his front, using his belly like a snake's and letting him slither down, his soft fat smoothing his final journey over the sharp edges of the cold stone steps.

But it wasn't to be.

When I dragged him by his feet, all that happened was that his skull cracked on the edge of each of the steps it hit. Each. One.

Smack.

Smack.

Smack.

And when I dragged him by his head... Well I couldn't. His neck wasn't flexible enough. I would have snapped his neck clean from his spine. The steps were too steep.

How much respect should you give a body? As much as you can afford? But how much could I afford? The day may have only just started but the sun was still weak and I had a lot to do.

For those who still believe in heaven, trust that my father forgave me for the treatment of his carcass. I pushed his body off the landing of each floor and watched as it rolled, slid and bundled down each flight of stairs until we got to the bottom.

I heard the cracks of the bones. I wasn't deaf. One of them, I think, was the femur. It was a terrible sound. But I had bound the body well and tightly so nothing came loose this time around. Surprisingly, I had plenty of ties left over. My frugality had paid off. And there was no one else left to save them for.

The incinerator just outside the block of flats was still padlocked. There were no new marks, scratches or chunks cut out of the chains and locks. Either that meant those running the streets had given up or moved on.

I undid the padlock, the only person left who knew the code. It had been the numerical version of the postcode of our apartment block – 6 9 6 7 7 2. Maybe if the scavengers had used their brains rather than their brawn they would have worked that out.

The sound of my father's body hitting the bottom of the tin incinerator reverberated off the walls. I caught my breath. The noise would have travelled much further than this small brick out-house. I didn't have much time. I covered the body with the remainder of the fuel and set it alight.

Fire. The first heat for many long days and cold nights. The heat on my face, the warmth flooded through my sweat-shirts, into the tops of my arms. My blood was warming, flowing down into my thighs. Life from death.

I didn't cry. I don't know why. I should've done. There were so many reasons to. Sadness, shock, self-pity. The vulnerability of being the last one standing. When your parents die, there's no longer a buffer between you and the grim reaper. In a moment, I went from adult to child. A child with no one left to lean on.

My whole body was hot.

The flames were too high, too hot. I had to get out.

I shut the door behind me and clicked the padlock closed. I could have left it unlocked, I suppose. After all, heat was now priceless and who was I to deny a starving, wandering tramp a few moments of warmth? But rules were rules. I had been told to lock everything up before I left, to leave a secure block.

Plus, those drawn to the fire that were not part of the rebuilding might work out that the block was still inhabited, if only for a bit longer. And that would make me vulnerable.

I did what I was told and spun the dials on the padlock to make sure.

The steel gate we'd constructed at the bottom of the steps to the apartment block was a cold, heavy beast. I could feel the frost even through my gloves. My face was chapped from my burning father so the chill of the ice was marked.

I tried to close the gate gently behind me but I couldn't grip the gate tightly enough. It slipped through my fingers and slammed shut with a clanging, metallic din.

I froze.

After the clank came a rustle.

I looked out – out to the trees, out past the pile of refuse.

There it was again, another rustle.

I stepped back into the shadows of the stairwell.

Someone had smelt the fire.

I held my breath.

My cheeks were burning.

A gust of wind swirled up a pile of loose rubbish from the refuse.

Suddenly a group of birds flew up into the sky, crowing as they rose up.

The wind blew through the gates, sweeping up the steps.

An empty plastic bag was blown against the steel bars of the gate, its edges flapping before falling limp to the ground as the wind died down.

No more rustling.

Maybe it had been the birds. Maybe it had been the wind. But if someone was outside, they would get another shot at me sooner than they realised.

CHAPTER TWO
The Exit

The other flats in my block had long been secured, each door within them closed and bolted. All windows boarded up and locked. In truth, the self-appointed heads of the block had ordered most of the windows to be boarded up while people were still alive. If it was judged that you had someone who'd lost their mind living with you, access to glass had to be prohibited.

It had been ugly, breaking in to a couple of the flats to board up some of the windows. There's little compassion in anarchy. And even less democracy.

Robert, the man from next door who'd clinically assumed control of the block, led from the front. I suspected he liked the violence. Power has that effect. A couple of the families tried to prevent entry into their homes but the militia broke in anyway. You can't hold back vigilantes, you just can't.

The violence to get to Brian's mother was the worst. Gillian was in a bad way. She had been showing signs of dementia during the war. The Fall pushed her over the edge.

Like the others, she was unpredictable – throwing valuable food out of the secure area, where it was too dangerous for us to try to retrieve it, and poisoning the water (we think, accidentally).

Robert's response was entirely predictable. You could see it in his eyes. They bashed the door in, the men, even though they knew Brian was right on the other side. The crashing of the door over him and the stampede to get in... No one could have survived that. The blood was everywhere.

Then there were the Allens, who, rather than have the windows in their kitchen and living room boarded up, chose to excommunicate Tommy, their son, to his bedroom. They also agreed to put a lock on the boy's door. On the outside. I don't know whether it was the violence that scared them or whether this was an act of selflessness.

Thinking about it now, maybe it was selfishness, a bit of self-protection. Hard to tell. Human motivations are complex.

I visited Tommy as often as I could, at least once a day, usually under the cover of checking drug supplies in each flat. The isolation made him worse. What had been just endless crying quickly disintegrated into insanity. It's frightening to watch the human brain unravel. And it can happen at alarming speed. Yet, even in its unravelling, it can make perfect sense.

Tommy started talking to himself, withdrawing into a world full of people who didn't exist, where The Fall had never happened. Was that insanity or a coping strategy for the brain?

When he escaped from his room and stabbed himself and his mother with a kitchen knife, the block heads had to introduce a new rule: that the mentally ill should be isolated in separate flats.

That decision almost led to revolt. It was a very rowdy block meeting. Many didn't want to become like animals. They wanted to care for loved ones who became ill.

It was the right decision but a bizarre one considering isolating the mentally ill away from society was exactly what governments had done before The Fall. Put them in hospitals and fool yourself that you're helping them. Out of sight and out of our – and their – minds.

I wanted to complain about their treatment. I should have complained. But I didn't. I didn't speak up. The days of articulate debate were fading into a distant memory and as the numbers in the block diminished, those left just fell into line. I had to survive, I had to. I couldn't afford to make enemies.

But, also, I didn't want them to take my father away.

If I had let my passions rule my mind and spoken out, they would have worked out something was up with him, that I had a vested interest. I had to keep his illness secret.

So when Emily deliberately smashed her priceless vase over her own head, I nodded that security for the sane had to be improved. I agreed with the adoption of restraints, I voted for the restriction of their food allocations and eventually for their total isolation.

I feel guilty about that.

But it meant I got to care for my father till the end. My pliancy with the harsh treatment of others diverted any suspicion around my explanation for my father's sprained ankles (obtained from slipping off the chair when he tried to hang himself and not from when we were carrying my mother's body downstairs). Nor did they question my explanation for the marks on his neck (rope burns from the noose when he tried again, not a rash from house mites).

But as Central Command demanded, we did board up each of the flats in turn as their inhabitants died. Recently, most had died of natural causes. Well, whatever you can call natural in this world. Is dying of cold natural? I cared for some of the dying. Others I didn't.

I didn't go out of my way to care for Robert when he fell ill. Nor was I overly attentive with Tommy's father. And those two had died only recently. Maybe withholding care is a form of murder. Maybe I did kill them. Maybe I didn't. I can't prove their causes of death, I suppose. But the birth of any brave new world is always ugly.

And there is always payback.

They died and I nailed planks across their windows and doors.

My father and I, we outlived them all.

But, in truth, we had become I. I hadn't been able to communicate meaningfully with my father for many months but at least I had done the right thing. At least he had been able to look out of his window in his own flat until the very end. His mind both trapped and free. We were the ones who survived.

I turned the transmitter in the radio on. It would take a while for the link to be made with CC.

I looked out of the kitchen window, out across the dead trees in the parks I would soon have to cross and beyond. The Gherkin had gone, the Shard was destroyed. Only one of the buildings had been spared. The Cathedral dome still dominated the skyline. It was broken – the spire and a section of the dome had been damaged – but the rest hadn't crumbled. It hadn't cowed. No doubt the emergency rebuilding was helping but it was still romantic – the dome that had survived it all.

The line crackled into life. "CC responding. This is the Central Command reporting line. Please identify yourself."

I picked up the microphone. "CC, this is Representative from Tower Block eighty-four in NW1."

"Tower Block eighty-four, please go ahead."

"The block is ready for clearing."

"Tower Block eighty-four, you are reporting an evacuation. Please confirm."

"No, I'm requesting pick-up."

"No pick-up, eighty-four. You will have to evacuate yourself and make your way to HQ."

"Why can't I be picked up? I'm just one person."

"Pick-ups no longer in effect, eighty-four. They are ad hoc and not for personnel. And safety of the roads is considered adequate. Please confirm evacuation."

The radio fell temporarily silent.

It wasn't true that the roads were safe. If the roads were safe, the control orders would've been lifted.

I pressed down the button on the transmitter. "OK. Evacuation today, arrival today. I will do my best."

"Tower Block eighty-four, evacuation confirmed. Please follow instructions as previously communicated and report to the Cathedral. If you are not received in due time a search party may be sent out but they cannot be guaranteed. Use the route prescribed and use caution."

"I understand."

"Copy. Over."

The line clicked. And went dead.

I sat back in the kitchen chair and, for a moment, let myself stare out into the nothingness.

It was just silence.

No sound from my father crying, no boiling water on the stove, nothing. Just silence.

I hadn't heard silence before, not like this.

My mind was not calm though. Why weren't they giving

me armoured pick-up? There was a reason. There was most definitely a reason. And it made me uncomfortable.

I stood up and looked out towards the Cathedral again. I knew it was a lot further away than it looked. I had to get going if I was going to make it by dusk. If I was even going to make it at all.

I'd packed my backpack a long time ago. There had been many hours to fill as my father drifted in and out of consciousness. You'd think it'd be hard to pack all that you need in the world in one bag, to reduce everything to just ten kilos. But my bag was half empty. What use are possessions?

I stood in the living room, backpack on and thought about taking a photograph with me. Or a book, perhaps. What did I want to remember? I looked around the room, scanning the shelves, the walls. The many paintings my mother had completed and hung proudly, framed photos of family holidays and my graduation, my mother's collection of paperweights, the blankets on the ground stained with my father's urine, the planks nailed across the balcony doors...

I turned on my heels and headed for the front door.

You can't survive carrying baggage.

CHAPTER THREE
The First Steps

I drove the last nail hard into the plank I'd placed across my front door. Maybe one day I would return. Maybe not. This hadn't even been my own flat. The one I owned was south of the river. I had abandoned it to be with my parents. I have no idea what happened to that apartment block or the people who had lived there. Maybe they have survived but I doubt it.

Would I ever see that flat again? Unlikely. My future is uncertain and I'll probably not survive long enough to return there, even if I wanted to. Maybe someday a new generation will tear down the board that is probably nailed across my own front door and bring my long-abandoned flat back to life.

Maybe not.

I looked out onto the courtyard below, weeds and grass overgrown. I looked across the floor level. Every door faced out towards the courtyard, and each was nailed shut. I'd done a lot of them. Even those I hadn't done the first time I'd had to redo when the planks started to split. The pollution in the atmosphere – the chemical fallout from the war – still had not dissipated.

There were no happy memories here.

I headed out into the stairwell and sped down the steps, the scuffing of my trainers echoing all the way down the stone steps.

Boards, planks of wood... They weren't going to cut it on the large steel gate at the bottom of the stairwell. CC had already thought of this. In their last drop-off two months ago they had left some heavy duty chains along with the oats. I was more surprised by the oats. There were always oats. Did that mean Scotland was unaffected? Were there unpolluted lands to farm?

The chains were thick and almost unbearably heavy. I wrapped them as carefully as I could around the locks on the steel gate but the clanking was deafening. I jerked my head round with every hit. Had I been heard? Was anyone behind me? My heart rate shot through the roof as I tried to wind faster and faster.

But the clanking got worse. I felt like a target, a sitting duck.

I wound and wound.

The chains smashed against the steel. Head jerked round – was anyone there?

I wound and wound.

The smashing of metal against metal. The clanging. The ringing. "Please stop, please stop," I whispered, tears welling up in my eyes. I moved my head all around.

I couldn't see anything. My vision now blurred.

Clang, clang, clang.

My hands were shaking as I locked each of the padlocks into the chains.

Finished, I snapped right round, pressing the gate into my back.

Nothing.

No one.

My heart was racing.

My breath short.

Left. Right. Ears tuned up to the max.

Nothing.

I breathed.

I pulled the can of spray paint out of my pocket and sprayed a large green circle on the wall by the gate. I inhaled the fumes and placed the can back into the little side-pocket on the backpack. I had no intention of painting again but maybe the aerosol would be useful in other ways.

The block of flats stood on the crest of a hill. London lay before me. It was a great metropolis, my home city. Or at least it had been. Maybe it will be again. There is always hope. But right now, it was dangerous territory.

The city lay in a basin, the Cathedral at its heart. The fires had destroyed much of what remained after the bombings. Since The Fall I'd been trapped in the block of flats behind me. Able to see but never to touch. Yet now I wasn't just free to walk out, I was obliged.

For three years I hadn't been further than the block perimeter. And for all that time I had been desperate to leave, not so much a caged bird but a caged tiger pacing the edges of her enclosure, wanting to roam further than she was allowed. But now, here I was – backpack solid and heavy, gun loaded and hidden under my jacket, and the ash of my decaying father still billowing faint clouds into the air.

This was not how I thought my exit would be.

I looked up to a blanket of cloud smothering the sky. Not white clouds but a dark grey. The heat from the incinerator warmed the back of my neck and legs. There was only death to keep me company if I stayed. In truth, all that lay before me was probably death as well.

I closed my eyes, said goodbye to my father, and took a step forward.

London was cold and the road down to the heart of the city was covered with debris, the mud and stones making it tricky underfoot.

Do you know what silence sounds like?

Maybe you live alone. Maybe you work alone. But these are confined spaces. Do you know what a silent city sounds like or, rather, what it feels like? It's so absurd, so abnormal that it stokes fear in your soul. Every sense is heightened. The crunch of gravel underfoot echoes all around. Your heart jumps at the sound of your own footsteps. The gusts of wind feel like the ghosts of the dead encircling you, swallowing you whole. And your eyes... They flit constantly, side to side, up and down.

At least I could feel my racing heart, my desire to survive.

The houses on both sides of the road were, remarkably, intact. But deserted. Each one I passed had boarded windows. And all had planks across the doors. Some had green circles sprayed on them as well. But most had red crosses. The roofs hadn't fallen in but brambles were creeping across walls, taking over the territory.

In every front garden were the pale stark trunks of trees long abandoned by their leaves. Those not destroyed by the fire had died from the pollution. Whatever had been released into the air had killed them. Their leaves had evaporated and their bark was white and crumbling. These scarred ones remained, their branches grasping up into the poisonous sky like skeletal hands.

Piles of rubbish lined the road but not grotesquely so. In the beginning, much had been collected in an attempt to prevent the spread of disease. Then, when the collections were no longer possible, we were told to burn it. What remained was the refuse when fire was no longer possible, abandoned by those left behind.

There was no sight or sound of others, though I knew they were out there. Where were they? London was supposed to be deserted under instruction from the control orders but why would they have said "Keep to the roads" to me unless they were still there?

And by they, I mean RAZR.

The clear and present danger.

The terrorists.

The enemy within.

The State was terrified by RAZR. We all were. Their success was frightening. And the more the war weakened the State, the more confident they became.

Almost inevitably RAZR had fed off the rioting in the streets, their numbers swelling with every shattered pane of glass. Maybe they caused them too, the riots. I'd long thought that, that they were instigators as well as exploiters. I suspect that's why the control orders were brought in. The orders cleared the streets, yes, and got people back in their homes. But the defoliation of the urban jungle would expose RAZR too.

And that's when it came to a head – the straight-out fight between the State and RAZR. On the streets of London, just a few years ago. RAZR didn't win. But their defeat must not have been total as those control orders were never lifted, and the restrictions on our movement remained severe. The televisions and Internet were switched off soon after that. Who ran the streets now? I was about to find out.

Halfway down the hill, I stopped. All that lay in front of me was a wide open space. The straight road had ended. I was at a junction. My choice was either directly left or directly right. But I needed to go straight ahead, across the brown grass, through the mud and trees towards the destroyed towers in the distance. And to the Cathedral.

I needed to cross the park.

A thin vapour of smoke – or was it dust – hung over the City. The remains of recent fires. I had seen them from the window. Were there still riots? Or had RAZR made it as far as the City again?

The winds blowing up the river had broken up much of the smoke and fumes. But not all.

I looked left, then looked right.

Nothing. No one.

Nature is never silent. And man is only silent when he is trying to be.

I stood still. Listening, thinking, analysing even the most fleeting of sounds.

Then I heard them.

Feet.

Running quickly.

From behind me.

My head spun round.

The dog was on me before I could lift my feet from the ground. Its claws, long and sharp, dug into my neck. The smell of decaying meat dripped from its jaw. Its teeth biting at my face. The claws on its hind legs dug deep through my tracksuit into my legs.

I pushed hard on its neck as I fell back under the weight of its attack. The jaw thrashed at my face. The razor sharp canines brushed my cheeks. The dog barked and growled, unable to get its teeth into me.

Its claws at my hip slashed so deep they must have hit bone as well as muscle. I kept digging my fingers into its neck. I felt its muscles twitch, its fervour weaken. It yelped.

Finally, I got it onto its back. I thrust my knee into its chest. It yelped again as its fight began to leave it. Its head whipped from side to side, and then slowed. And then stopped.

Its eyes closed.

I pulled away, getting myself on to my feet.

Then the dog's eyes flashed back into life. It growled and barked. But as it leapt up with a snap, like a salmon pounding upstream...

Bang!

The gun was in my hand, a bullet was in the dog's chest.

The shot, strong and true, had killed the dog but the sound had ricocheted off the empty streets around me.

It would have been heard for miles.

I had little time.

The dog, now on its back, its legs limp, had left its mark. My left hip and thigh were bleeding. The cuts were deep. And probably infected.

I returned the gun into the back of my trousers and pulled my backpack off.

Using some of my remaining bandages, I wrapped my thigh tightly and quickly. But even with the padded cotton wool, the red began to seep out. I swallowed a couple of thrombin to slow down the bleeding before pulling the bag back onto my shoulders.

I definitely couldn't take the roads now. Any scavengers would be intrigued by the gunshot, not scared. Straight ahead it was.

I took a deep breath – then started running.

CHAPTER FOUR

The Journey

My pace was quick but the wound was stinging. Stinging and bleeding.

My left leg was wet. I didn't want to look down. Too terrified. In spite of everything I've seen and what I still have to do, I can't stand the sight of blood. Is it worse when it's your own blood or someone else's?

The damp was trickling out from under the bandages. Running was making it worse, surely. But I couldn't stop.

I had to keep running.

The long grass brushed against my knees. I broke through to a patch where the grass had already been flattened out. Was this a good thing, to follow someone else's path? It was heading where I needed to go. But it was too risky. I ran on through the grass.

I didn't know what was in front of me. My eyesight was blurred and all I could think about was the blood – the blood pouring from my legs and the blood that kept flooding my nightmares.

She had fallen. I heard the thud. She'd been trying to change a light bulb in the kitchen, up a step ladder. I'd told her I would do it but she didn't listen, couldn't wait. Another woman in her seventies who still thought she was in her forties.

Back then the radio was in the living room, before the reception weakened and we had to move it to the kitchen. I was reporting our medical stocks – antibiotics low, insulin gone. It was the crash of the step ladder – metal hitting the cement floor. And then the thud.

Then the silence.

My head snapped round. My finger dropped from the radio. Frozen.

"Mother?"

Nothing.

My stool fell to the floor as I jumped off it.

The grass whipped my legs as I ran faster still.

The slow motion as the kitchen floor came into view. My heart beat as fast as if I were running through a field. The gasp of shock.

Floating between the sight of my crumpled mother and my brain blocking it out. I wanted to forget.

Impossible to forget the blood. Her body inert, my stifled moan.

I was almost at the end of the field, my back damp with sweat, my leg numb. Running faster to forget.

The end of the park so close.

Sweat flooding through my sweatshirts, through my track-suit bottoms.

The pain, the lack of breath all taking me further away from a hell I had failed to prevent.

I burst through the last of the grass – free at last. I could breathe. I stopped, hands on my knees, head hanging down.

I gasped, I panted. I breathed.

Short, sharp breaths. One. Two. Quick and shallow. Then slowly, slowly long deep breaths.

One.

Two.

Three.

Long deep breaths.

I picked my hand off my thigh. The palm was red and sticky. All around the bite the black of my tracksuit was even darker. I put my hand on it again, it came up even redder. And stickier. The wound was tacky.

I threw my bag on the ground and peeled off my sweatshirt. Then my second sweatshirt. And then my top. It was freezing but I was hot like fire. A river of sweat poured down my spine.

My tops were soaked. I hadn't trained in a long time. Exercising, yes, but not proper training.

I wiped the back of my hand across the dip in my lower back and flicked the sweat off my hand.

Pushing my tracksuit bottoms down, I pulled the bandages away from my thigh and gently tugged free most of the cotton wool. Threads from the pad remained stuck amongst the congealing blood but I left them. I squeezed the saturated pad gently and watched a trickle of blood run down my arm.

I pulled the remaining clean pads and bandages from the bag. I had neither the time nor the inclination to clean the open wound first. Instead the pad and bandages went straight on.

As I wound the gently stretching crêpe round and round, my heart rate began to come down. As did my body temperature. By the time the safety pin was attached, my exposed skin was shivering.

I put my clothes back on and let my focus return to the roads. The silent roads.

I knew where I was. I was standing at the bottom of Regent's Park and the top of Marylebone. The dome was down on the river bank. After the literal jungle of the wild, the jungle of the City lay ahead.

I picked up the bloodied bandages and bagged them. Fresh blood... You don't want to be leaving that out on mean streets.

I walked on.

I had last seen this street from the balcony of our flat. It was this area that had been at the heart of the rebellion – and of the battle that followed. When the lockdown order came, the army were sent in to quell the rioters, who seemed to be in control of the streets. But when the army arrived, not all reacted with obedience. The suppressions were brutal, but they weren't completely successful. People were scared, angry. But they weren't organised.

And into that vacuum walked RAZR.

The riots gave RAZR their opportunity, and they swooped like vultures. We'd heard they had sabotaged the fighting overseas, and now the domestic instability gave them what they craved – the chance to destroy the State completely.

Of course it was them on the streets of London.

They tried to cover it up on the news, the government, fearful of crediting RAZR with success, but you only had to look out the windows to see the scale of the fighting to know it was them. And her. These were organised attacks. Plus, we had all seen the videos on the Internet. Or at least some of the videos – not all could endure the more graphic parts. And there were many eyewitnesses who swore they had seen Jane herself at the head of her attacking forces, at the heart of the action.

Our army used overwhelming force. They had to. Carpet-bombing your own capital city is not a decision you take lightly but can you let the reins of power be taken by those who wilfully murdered their own brothers, their own fathers? What is the point of liberalism if it will not stand and fight?

That was the day we were told to remain where we were, whether we were at our own homes or not. And that night, as the basin of our great city was consumed again by fire, I was with my parents.

My mother and I stood on the balcony watching the ferocious battle, our hair swept up in the back-draught from the low-flying Eurofighters, hearing the screams and the deafening sound of bombs, of gunfire.

"You know, I would understand if you left to join them," she said.

I turned to my mother, staggered by what I had heard. I couldn't think of anything to say in response.

"Don't you think that, my darling?" she added. "Don't you think that RAZR... that they might be right?"

The ground shook, a flash of orange in the distance. Another bomb.

I looked out to the basin then back to my mother. I'd expected to see shame but she looked out defiantly, unfazed by the explosions.

"Mother, those women are murderers."

"Maybe," she muttered.

Another Chinook flew low overhead, whipping up a rush of wind.

"I'm not sure we're much better," she said as her eyes followed the Chinook as it headed to the centre of the battle.

Then my mother looked at me, her eyes surprisingly full of peace, or resignation. "I would support you if you left, my darling, for them. It's worth fighting for, your future. I would understand. Don't stay just for me."

"I'm not going to leave you," I said. "Not for them. They are not the future."

My mother's gaze fell away, down to the balcony, then she looked up and out again, towards the flames.

I had disappointed her.

My mother and I never spoke of this again. I couldn't abandon my mother and father. Not that I had the opportunity to, anyway. The temporary order to restrict our movements that night became permanent. Martial law. Our houses and flats were ring-fenced into blocks – blocks that would become our lifeline and our prison. Wherever we were that night became our home until either we were the only survivor, or death released us.

I stayed in their ring-fenced block and added our names to the register. But many fled.

It was the last news report we ever saw. So many men, mostly young men, wouldn't be locked down and took their chances on the streets. And with RAZR on the streets, that was a big risk.

The boy of one of our neighbours, well my parents' neighbours but I guess now my neighbours too, Josh, burst out of the block just as we were locking down.

His father went apoplectic, his mother lost her mind. She never saw him again after he screamed the walls down in his lecture to her and his father on their passivity, and ran out. His mother broke down when the television sets were turned off, her last opportunity to find her boy amongst all the footage of the rioting.

It led to our first suicide.

Josh's parents weren't on the 'at risk' lists that were handed out by the authorities to each block, but you put ordinary people under extraordinary pressure and anything becomes possible.

The centre of that spontaneous male rebellion, short as it was, took place on the edges of the City. Mother and I watched the encircling from our kitchen. Many joined us. The army crushed them. RAZR had escaped their grasp, but not the men. There was gunfire, there was smoke. Then, a week later, there was nothing.

RAZR was obviously never going to break cover to save them.

But the scars of those two battles, I could now see up close. The tower blocks around me had been gutted from the inside. The glass from the windows long gone, smashed out completely. What RAZR started the army finished. The aim? To make the buildings so uninhabitable, so cold and dark, as to prevent any squatters. Or survivors.

For me, now, this meant that the wind was coming at me from all angles – up from the river, whistling through the streets, from the left and right, flushing out the loose rubbish from the abandoned buildings.

Did it also mean the streets were safe?

I checked my gun.

It was impossible to know for sure what the time was. The clouds above me were still thick. I needed an injection for my leg. Rabies needs only four hours to take hold.

Under lockdown we had to destroy all pets for fear of infections. But also because, in priority between man and beast, only one could eat from the half-empty trough. And there are always those who'd rather give the food to their cats.

It was the old ladies who were the most stubborn.

"They'll outlive me. Why should I sacrifice them?" Lillian in the one-bedroom flat downstairs wasn't having it. It was hard not to sympathise. "I've outlived everyone else. You take Smokey from me..."

Smokey had to go. Unanimous decision by the Board despite Lillian's plea. She did outlive Smokey, but not by much. She tailed off soon after Smokey went to the

29

Victoria Sadler

incinerator. Like a mother losing her will to fight on after her child is gone, the umbilical cord never truly cut.

The lockdown had come into effect so long ago now. I had celebrated three birthdays in that time. Well I'd *had* three birthdays. Could anyone have survived on the streets this long? My pace wanted to be slow, to take in the blown-out vacant alleys and dark cold blocks. But I walked quickly forward.

On this side of the park the streets were sparse, surprisingly so. No loose rubbish, no overflowing bins or discarded refuse piled in corners. It wasn't quite the *Marie Celeste* but it wasn't far off.

Loose gravel crunched into the grooved soles of my trainers. This used to be the most expensive part of the City. Rows and rows of terraced houses. No garden, no front yard. Each front door guarding the entrance to abandoned homes once worth millions. Not any more. Now they were just like the block of flats I hadn't stepped outside of for almost three years – glass covered, doors bolted.

I kept up the pace of a soldier.

But the silence was creating a rising tide of panic within me.

Silence always heralds trouble.

Silence was what followed the thud of my mother hitting the cement floor. It was silence that fell across the City, for only a moment, when the lockdown came. And it was silence that greeted the news that the rebellions had been defeated.

The shock. The defeat. The relief.

And then the fear of what was to come.

Silence means hope has gone.

Silence means you're on your own.

I stopped.

Silence means run.

From a standing start I burst into a sprint. My calves ached and my bag was heavy but it was one long straight road in front of me. I could see all the way down. Straight through to the main road.

My feet pounded the road. The wind whistled past my ears. I could hear no other feet but mine. I had to keep running.

Oxford Street was getting close.

My stomach hurt.

My leg was throbbing.

Sweat poured down the sides of my cheeks and into the corners of my mouth.

So hot.

The crossroads getting ever closer in my sight.

My breath short.

I felt like crying.

My leg was in pain, my body hurt.

Too scared to stop.

The road ahead looked brighter, not smothered in cold shadow.

I was almost there.

I burst through the end of the high street and out into Oxford Street.

I stopped. Dropped my hands to my knees and tried to breathe.

Breathe.

I looked back. No one behind me.

I turned to my left and, hand on my hips, stared straight ahead. As I gulped for air, trying to calm my heartbeat, I stared right down the middle of the road, the long road that ran for a mile.

Oxford Street. The direct artery through London that led to where I needed to be, straight through towards St Paul's Cathedral.

Standing smack in the middle of the road, the gutted building of Selfridges behind me. The road went on for further than my eye could see. Not one abandoned car, no overturned bus. Not one traffic light flickered through its limited rainbow.

Nothing.

Nothing moved. Nothing was moving.

I looked left. I looked right.

Nothing.

No one.

And no sound. No rustle of a paper bag, no screech from a wild cat.

Complete silence.

That meant one thing – time to run.

My heartbeat leapt. Terror and a lack of fitness is a terrible combination but nothing puts the speed into you quite like fear.

I didn't look left, I didn't look right. I wasn't interested in the new river running down my back or the pulsing, bleeding veins in my thigh.

The junction up ahead was coming ever closer into view. I was halfway there.

And that's when I saw them.

The first one came into view from the road on the left of the crossroads. Head-to-toe in army fatigues. Hood over the head. The second joined him from the right.

I stopped immediately. My feet skidding on the road, so sharp was my stop.

I stopped breathing.

Shit.

Up ahead of me at the crossroads...

I had no idea how the hell I was going to get out of this.

I couldn't go forward.

The road to my right, just ahead, my only way out.

Then I heard the crunch from behind.

My head snapped round.

Two men, also in hoods, were standing, fifty, sixty metres behind me.

Shit. Where had they come from?

Could I outrun them? One? Yes. Four? No.

Then came the fifth, and the sixth. One from my left, one from my right.

And all I could think... how many bullets do I have left?

I'd only ever shot a dog.

One step, two steps. They started to move in from the back, from the front, from the sides.

No words. No warnings, no demands.

I was out of options.

"Stop!" The gun came out as soon as I spoke.

I turned to my left, then behind, left again. All the way round. I pointed the gun at every single one of the men.

And all of them stopped moving.

"What do you want?" Sometimes you ask questions even when you don't want to know the answer.

The faint echo of their suppressed, shared laugh.

And then they started moving towards me again.

"What's in your bag?" The question came from one of the men ahead of me, at the crossroads.

I kept turning round, gun always held up. But no matter how quickly I turned, no matter how sure my outstretched arms remained, the men moved in. Either they didn't believe I would shoot or they were too desperate to care.

I didn't even know whether I would shoot.

Until I did.

I shot because I didn't have time to think.

The man must have been about twenty metres ahead of me, standing in the middle of the crossroads.

It all happened in slow motion. I'd stopped, seen him

move, snapped up my wrist and pulled the trigger.

The bang came from the gun and then everything stopped. We all stopped.

We watched as the man took the hit and crumpled to the tarmac.

The blood rushed from my head.

I thought I was going to faint. I thought I was going to be sick.

I felt a trickle of sweat run into the dip of my lower back.

The gun in my hand was warm.

I couldn't move. The man's body lay slumped in the road. His, well, friend, colleague I guess, just stood there near him. Didn't move. Didn't check on him.

And then – whack! – I was smacked on the back of my head.

My knees wobbled, my feet went and – bam! – I hit the ground.

Everything went dark but I could feel my gun with the tips of my fingers. Then crack!

I screamed. The agony of the bones in my hand crushed under the stamping boot of one of the men. The gun tugged free.

A blow to the side of my stomach.

A kick to my shoulders.

My arms shot up instinctively to protect my head.

As they did I felt my fingertips brush my gun again – it was still on the ground. It was my bag they were after. It was pulled and pulled. I felt it rip open.

Another kick to my side.

I reached out, grabbed my gun and threw it under my body.

And then another kick to my side.

Then another.

Then another.

Then another.

34

I felt a bubble of blood come up through my throat.

I needed to secure my gun. I pushed it into my trousers.

One of the men threw himself over me, smothering my head with his body. I thought I was going to suffocate. Another grabbed my leg.

They were after me.

I was lifted from the ground, punched in the face. The blood fell out of my mouth and over my lips.

Thrown back onto the road, hands grappled at my waist, at my trousers.

A kick to my back. Blood came up to my throat again. I could taste it. Sweet, thick.

Another punch brought it out of my mouth.

The next kick was so hard I thought his foot was going to come through my spine, smashing a hole through the centre of my body. I could smell their unwashed clothes, the odour of stale sweat. My throbbing hand, the gun out of reach in my trousers. My stomach bleeding. The ooze in my mouth, my waistband suddenly ripped. Hands grabbing at the flesh on my stomach.

And then I heard the shot.

Then a round of gunfire, from further out.

A body fell on top of me. One of the men.

Another round of gunfire.

Another body fell.

Then an army of feet. I could feel the earth move.

The shouts.

The gunfire.

The men around me fired back.

Another body fell near me.

I was fading in and out of consciousness, unsure what I was feeling, what I was hearing.

It sounded like another crack of gunfire.

35

And then it stopped.
A brief moment.
Then the bodies were pulled off me.
A cold hand hit my neck. "She's still alive."

CHAPTER FIVE
The Truck

The truck stopped. The brakes were so sharp I slid along the floor. A hand grabbed my waist, stopping me slamming full into the van door.

I was still alive. I had been slung on the floor of the truck. My fingers could feel the rubber grip on the edge of one of the soldier's boots. That was the only thing I could feel. The rest of me was either numb or throbbing.

But I could hear.

I could hear men.

Their voices came from above me. Gruff, short.

Then the crack of van doors as they were flung open, slamming against the side of the truck.

A gust of cold air swept through. I could feel that.

The boots around me moved. The squeak of rubber on metal. The shudder of the floor – an army mobilising.

Then I could feel the heat – warm air coming up from the tyres.

"Lift her up." A male voice from outside the van. "Lift

37

her up and take her inside."

Cold, rough, stubby fingers checked the pulse on my neck. "Are you awake?"

I pulled my hand away from my head.

"Yeah she's awake. Lift her."

Arms reached down under my stomach and the men hauled me off the floor. The pain. I screamed in agony. My wounds were reopening. But the men didn't let up. I screamed again. It felt as if my stomach was ripping in half, becoming a ball of blood. But my cries fell on deaf ears.

They started moving, carrying me out.

The light changed as they stepped out of the van. My eyes were still closed but I could sense it – dark to light. The glaring whiteness on the back of my eyelids became blinding.

We started moving up a flight of steps, my weight falling towards my feet as my body was moved into a slant.

There was no compassion for my wounds. Each step up, each jerk of my body, felt like another cut to my side. My stomach felt as if it was trying to wrench itself away from my rib cage.

I opened my eyes slowly. My right one couldn't fully open but I could see the white light, the glare of sunlight reflected on white clouds. And through the blur I could see the guns next to my face, slung over shoulders. And as the haze came into focus, I glimpsed the marble Cathedral steps beneath me.

We reached the top of the steps.

"Can you take your weight?"

My feet were brought down to the ground. I tried to look around, slowly turning my head. A hostile perimeter fence encircled the Cathedral. High wire fence, armed military, camouflage fatigues, stern-faced boys and men carrying guns.

And the noise. Not of life, but of a militarised zone. Engines roaring, shouts and marching boots.

I was the only woman in sight.

Two arms under mine kept me upright.

The blood was coming back to my head. Pins and needles shot up my neck and over my scalp like a wave. My ankles went.

"That's a no. Men, carry her."

The men on either side lifted me clean off my feet, cleaving my stomach from my ribs. I cried out again.

"The doctors are inside."

We moved upwards. Then across. And then the white light was gone.

The cool darkness of the Cathedral interior enveloped us. The soldiers dropped me on to a hard pew by the doors. It hurt. It all hurt. I leant my head back against the cold brick wall. I tried to move my hands. The right one was fine but the left... The snap of pain prevented me. The fingers were probably broken.

The men all moved away, leaving me. Except one, who was handing over the shreds of what remained of my bag to the first woman I had seen for months.

"We picked her up in the centre of town. She was being attacked but we managed to pick up her ID."

I held my one decent hand over my crumpled right eye to let my left one focus. She was thin. Well, we were all thin now. And her long hair was scraped back into a ponytail.

She nodded. "OK, we'll take her from here."

CHAPTER SIX
The Filtration

If I had known what the interior of St Paul's Cathedral had looked like, felt like, smelt like, before The Fall perhaps my comparison would be more meaningful. Perhaps then it would give context to my shock, justification even. But I did not. Only tourists and members of the Royal Family had really ventured inside before. And neither were around any more. Instead I can only tell you what I saw then.

And all I could see was people. Hundreds of them.

I took my hand away from my right eye and slowly it began to open and adjust. It hurt and involuntary tears began to roll down my cheeks as it looked to heal itself but, most importantly, my eyesight was undamaged.

An altar stood at the far end. Above it, Jesus was still dying on his cross. And the saints in the stained glass still looked on, traumatised. But no one on the ground was paying attention to iconography. And most of the pews for contemplation had long been ripped out. Instead the floor of the Cathedral had been transformed into a huge office. Cabinets, desks, computers, screens, lights... And people. More people than I'd seen in over three years.

The hum bounced off the stone walls, rising all the way to the top and out into the sky. I could see the sky through the break in the dome. It was blue, but dark blue. The cloud cover had momentarily broken.

On the underside of the dome, a web of men crawled across scaffolding and netting, working slowly but surely to blot out the sky, one piece of stone at a time. The dome would soon be complete again.

"Move forward." The woman spoke to me. "Movement is good for you." Then she turned her back and went behind the row of tables that ran across almost the whole floor. More a barrier than a welcome.

The woman was in a brown uniform – brown shirt, brown trousers. As were all the other people in the Cathedral – the staff, the officials. I was the only person on my side of the barrier.

On the other side, the woman dropped what was left of my bag onto the floor.

I gripped the swelling bowling ball of my stomach, got to my feet and started shuffling towards the desk. The woman wasn't moved. I suppose the time for warmth in this world had long gone.

I stopped when I got to the desk, grateful for something to lean on. The woman looked at a large, tightly bound folder of papers lying on the table between us. As she did, I could make out her hair. It was dark, black as night on her scalp, down to the elastic band at the nape of the neck. Then, in her ponytail, white blonde. Straw-like. Frizzy. Dry. And dyed. The elastic band – the water mark on the side of the ship, the ring inside the tree. The detail that marked the date when there was no longer any hair dye to be bought.

"You need to register." The woman didn't even look up.

"I reported myself this morning."

"Location?"

"Block eighty-four, six nine six seven seven two."

The woman went to the filing cabinet behind her. The shelves of the cabinet full of black folders, each with a series of numbers down the spines. The numbers were codes. Addresses.

I ran my tongue across the inside of my jaw. Not one tooth broken. I'd been lucky. How vanity grips you.

The woman pulled out a file with '696—' on its spine and turned back to me.

Inside the folder were pages and pages of numbers. Down the left side of each sheet of paper were numbers in black and blue ink. On the right-hand side was the red ink. Words such as 'Nil Return', 'Empty', 'Void', 'Abandoned', 'Closed'. Or simply lines, like this '—'.

The woman's voice dropped to a whisper. But her tone did not soften. "We expected you some months ago."

"I called this morning."

"Yes. But your block has been at close to minimum inhabitants for some time."

"Death is unpredictable."

"Really." Finally, the woman looked at me. But it wasn't asked as a question. "You are the single return? The building was locked and secured as requested?"

"Yes. As instructed."

"We do drive-bys so if there is something you wish to declare…"

"I am alone."

She looked at me. Death moves some, numbs others. Or maybe it had been a while since she saw death. Or she didn't believe me.

"The remaining residents at the last registration were a Miss Laura Lewis, thirty-three, and Mr Edward Lewis, seventy-five."

"My father died this morning, last night. I am Laura."

She looked at me. Nodded, just once. Then she turned to another section of her folder. And there it was – my picture. A copy of my passport photo, the one I had attached to my file. I didn't realise she'd have that. It was a shock. My vision was sharpening up. Even upside down I could see my round face and long hair. The photo was taken a lifetime ago.

The woman looked at me, looked at the photo, looked back at me again, looked down at the photo.

She turned the page. My father's passport photo, right in front of her. A full-size A4 copy, holes punched in the side. She tapped the photo. "He is dead?"

"Yes."

The woman picked up a red pen and drew a diagonal line across his face.

I don't really remember what was said in those few seconds after that. I was stunned by the red line. Until the woman turned the page and my father's image was replaced with pages of numbers and text. "You need to go to the doctor. He will inspect you, complete the tests before you are transferred to an enclave for registration and integration."

"Where are the enclaves?"

I watched her as she wrote 'One. Locked. Verbal Conf' next to 696 772.

"You will be allocated after your assessment. That way." She pointed to her left, past the columns, to a path that led away down the side of the Cathedral. No assistance offered. I started off.

"One thing."

I looked back. "Yes?"

"You had a confrontation on your way here."

I looked down at myself, my bloodied, crushed hand and my ripped clothes. "Yes."

"Did you tell them anything, about you?"

I looked at her closely. For the first time she held my gaze. She was nervous. I saw fear, just briefly. "Who?"

"The women," she said.

"I wasn't attacked by women," I replied. "This was done to me by men."

"Oh." The woman's cheeks flushed.

Interesting. So the fear of the women remained.

I walked on.

The path down the right-hand side of the Cathedral was framed with a row of empty chairs on the left, pushed up against the backs of filing cabinets behind them, and the cold, stone walls on my right.

I started to walk down the aisle. The shuffling wasn't as painful as I'd feared. My legs hadn't been as damaged as I thought. It was my stomach and my throbbing left hand that had taken the force. But my mind was racing – those men, they had been after me as much as my bag.

At the height of the chaos there must have been huge demand for those chairs. Long queues would have wound all the way out of the Cathedral and down the steps. That would've been back when the survivors fled their allocated blocks, back when the enclaves were announced.

The enclaves. The lifeline.

These were the demarcated areas where resources would be focused, arable land cleared and fertilised, and where survivors would be brought together into new communities. 'From these seeds, we will grow once more.' That was the tagline, the spin, the phrase that was used again and again by the politicians. But basically, the government was saying, 'We're giving up on everywhere else. This is the only plan we've got.'

But there were a few significant hurdles. One: we had too many survivors, and Two: the enclaves had not been built. Or even fully identified. Why would they have been? The Fall had taken us all by surprise. We weren't ever meant to lose the war.

That was why we were locked down into our ring-fenced blocks for so long – supporting the blocks with the bare minimum of resources both ensured the number of survivors would fall and would give the State time and means to build the enclaves.

I had known about the enclaves before most, obviously. But back then, before The Fall, they were little more than sketchy ideas, ideas generated from conspiracy theorists and restricted departments in the intelligence agencies. But in a matter of weeks, they went from patronised to funded.

When I was sent away from work for lockdown, the enclaves were still blueprints. Their plots, their resourcing, their supply lines hadn't been finalised. Back then I knew more than I let on, I accept that. But not now, not as I dragged myself across the cold paving stones of the Cathedral floor. I was as much in the dark as anyone else.

Many had gone before me but not all had waited their turn. Some had been desperate to go straight away, abandoning their blocks as soon as the enclaves were announced. They were fearful of the terror on the streets. But maybe they knew they were completely incapable of surviving in their blocks and wanted saving before natural selection could intervene.

We saw the pictures of the crowds on the television,

before transmission was terminated. The reporters called it 'the spontaneous evacuation'. That lurch towards order, to leadership, to control... People fear chaos, fear having to rely on themselves. That has been our downfall throughout history. Our need to be led has always been our undoing.

In the first few weeks, after the enclaves were announced, the queues that filed out of the Cathedral doors had turned into crushes. Too many were trampled to death. And too many were shot as the army tried to keep control.

I remember the applause, the 'bravos' in the block, as we watched the tentative restoration of order. How high the price we are prepared to pay for order. The power we give away.

The Internet was awash with reports from the enclaves by those who'd managed to get over the walls. But I didn't believe them. There are always teething problems.

Then suddenly, inevitably, the Internet was shut down. And with it went all critical reporting. We were told through radio broadcasts that the servers had collapsed. I don't think anyone believed it. Instead it became the case that if you can restrict electricity, you can switch off democracy.

You'd have thought that this censorship would've caused more rioting. But if you thought that then, well, you don't understand human nature at all. Our heads all hung back down and, as a herd, we followed the orders.

At the end of the corridor, under Jesus's left hand, sat the nurse. Well, her desk had 'Nurse' written above it. Do nurses wear brown shirts?

As soon as I appeared in front of her, so did my file, passed to her from another brown-shirted woman who briefly appeared from behind the filing cabinets before disappearing again.

"Laura Lewis?" The nurse looked as if she was in her fifties. A surprise. That demographic had not been given great odds.

"Yes."

"Take a seat. I'll see if the doctor's free."

So opposite Jesus's nailed feet I sat and waited. Jesus's face hadn't changed.

The last funeral I went to was before it all happened. My father was talking as his mother lay in a pine box by his side. As my father talked about regret, Jesus looked down – always looking down – mournful but not broken, punished but innocent. I wonder if my father's faith was as strong when he died. Maybe not. I doubt he'd enough of his sanity left to even understand his faith. Actually, maybe you needed to lose reason to still believe in the hope of salvation.

CHAPTER SEVEN
The Assessment

"Miss Lewis? Follow me."

I followed the nurse across the altar and into the room on the other side. There, in the sanctuary previously reserved for priests, was the modern equivalent – a male doctor.

The little room had been transformed into a makeshift consultation room – one clearly meant to be only temporary but which had become more permanent than expected. You could sense that from the health notices tacked to the walls, the metal hospital trolley crowded with scalpels and needles pushed up against the far wall and the single socket in the corner overwhelmed with plugs for the small monitors and the lamps.

The doctor – an older man, grey hair, deep lines and wrinkles – sat behind a thick oak desk which, somehow, had managed to find its way into the room. Amazing what people think is essential in times of crisis. "So my name is—"

I don't remember what name he said. My brain was beginning to fade. My eyes were heavy and the adrenalin was wearing off. Make up a name if it helps you. I remember he wore glasses though. And that he had five or six lamps littered around his room so no matter which way he angled his head, light bounced off his glasses making it impossible for me to see his eyes.

"Please, sit," he said, taking the file from the nurse and opening it out on his desk.

I slumped down into the only other chair in the room, a church chair complete with a little wooden shelf attached to the back where the Bible and Order of Service went. Neither to be seen in this one though. Disposed, rejected or, like most books in our block, burnt as fuel.

"You haven't reported any illnesses," he said, getting out of his own chair and walking towards the trolley.

"No."

The nurse shut the door behind her.

"You've not been ill? No flu, hypothermia, fever, nausea, rashes of any kind?"

I shook my head.

The doctor nodded. "Open."

I saw the cotton wool bud just in time to open my mouth before there was an awkward bump on my chin. Swab taken, he put it in a plastic bag.

"But you lived in a block of flats."

A block of flats? "Sorry, I don't know what you—"

"Those who come from blocks of flats, as opposed to those areas where separate houses were grouped together as controlled areas. It has been the blocks of flats that have been more prone to disease."

"I guess I just have a strong disposition."

"Constitution."

"Yes."

"No bleeding?"

"Bleeding?"

"From anywhere other than the womb. Through the mouth, anus or any open wounds?"

I wouldn't be alive if I had been. "No. Apart from my leg, here."

The doctor leant over and gave my leg a cursory once over.

"It's a dog bite," I said. "I was attacked on my way here. It's not bleeding any more, but it was. Earlier."

"You have been in the wars." The doctor started messing about on the steel trolley. "It's highly unlikely you've got anything. The virus went over a year ago. We haven't had any more cases in a long time. The quarantine worked."

Not for those who were quarantined with someone who had the virus.

We were lucky in our block – neither my parents nor any of their neighbours were particularly keen travellers. And none of them had family in the armed forces, let alone those stationed abroad. And these were the high risk factors for the virus.

"I was more worried about rabies," I said. "Are you using a clean needle?"

"Every needle is disinfected before reuse."

"In a flame?"

The doctor turned back to me. I had offended him. I didn't care.

"Has it?" I went on. "Has it been in a flame?"

The doctor turned back to the trolley then back to me with a lighter in his hand. Rather dramatically he ignited the lighter and passed the needle back and forth.

I heard the lighter drop back down on to the trolley. I started to pull down my trousers as far as I could given the restricted use of my hand. I didn't even want to look at the needle. I stared instead at the debris of the iconoclasm in the room.

"I've picked the smallest one," he said. "You won't feel a thing."

There had been icons in here. I don't know whether they were smashed in the looting or because people were angry at God. Maybe the two went hand in hand.

There had been a draft ready to be invoked on the State protection of heritage arts. I don't know what happened to that order. Was the cardboard taped over the stained-glass windows in the room the result of that order coming in a bit late? It had been a while since I'd heard anything. And everything I knew before that time was now obsolete.

"Only a drop." The man shoved the needle into my arm.

I gasped. Took a breath, then asked "What about my leg?"

I could feel the needle. I pressed my lips tightly together, holding my breath. Some phobias never fade, no matter how brutal the times you live in.

The needle was pulled out and a folded tissue was slapped on my arm. "Hold."

I did as instructed, though I expect the lack of care was deliberate. I heard the clank of the needle hitting the steel trolley.

"We don't have anything for rabies. Not here," he said. "You'll have to wait till you get to the enclave."

"Look at my bite! I need something. This is serious."

"If you had rabies it would've told by now. You'd be passing out and frothing. You certainly seem as if you've got your wits about you so I would suggest you've been lucky. But I'll test the blood. These are difficult days. We don't have an abundant supply of medicines, sadly. That hand is more of a concern to me, though. Let me look."

He grabbed my hand, turning it over rather roughly in his hands.

I started breathing heavily, trying to push down the daggers of pain that were shooting up my arm.

"It hurts?"

I nodded.

"Well, I don't think anything is broken. The skin is intact. But you've got some nasty swelling. I'll get the nurse to wrap that after you've had your shower." The doctor pulled my folder across the desk towards him. "Your womb... Do you still have your periods?"

My breathing started to slow down. Menstruation. That's quite a question. Would it matter if I answered 'yes' or 'no'? Would that decide my fate? But then, of course, he was mistaken if he thought he had my fate in his hand. "Yes. Intermittently."

The doctor stood up straight and headed to the monitor. "OK, jump on," he said, as he patted down the makeshift bed I hadn't noticed behind me, a couple of chairs against the wall with some cushions on.

"Excuse me?"

The doctor was shaking a squeezy bottle. "Lift up your top and take a seat up here."

"An ultrasound? Why on—? I'm not pregnant."

"Not that. Though it would be a good thing for you if you were." He stopped shaking the bottle. "Miss Lewis, please, take a seat up here. Please."

I looked at the bed, the cushions, then looked at the doctor.

"I want the nurse to do it," I said.

The doctor shook his head. "She's not qualified. She's not a nurse."

"I don't care."

I didn't move. I just stayed rooted to my chair.

The doctor sighed. "Please, Miss Lewis, let's just get this done. I have no interest in you and I am not doing this with any sexual intent. I just need to assess your womb."

I looked down at my lap, the bruising on my leg. My

shoulders felt like lead. I was shattered – and out of options. I could feel the tears forming.

I got out of the chair. My lower back was beginning to stiffen up.

"We'll get some heat on your wounds soon," he said. "You'll feel better with the heat. But let's just get this done."

As soon as I got on the cushions his hands were on me. I twitched as he pushed up my top. The gel was cold.

"What are you looking for?"

He didn't answer as he ran the probe over my abdomen. It looked like a mouse – a computer mouse – but cold. It was not an old model – it was wireless. It was new. I stared at the mouse. It was new.

"The bruising is shallow. It'll go down soon. No deep damage." He ran the mouse back and forth. "Womb is fine."

I was transfixed by the mouse. The new mouse. It must've been made in the past three years. The State had new equipment.

"OK." The doctor took the mouse off me. "Are you ready?"

I sighed and nodded, pushed down my tracksuit bottoms and moved my legs apart.

He pushed the probe up deep into me.

I didn't make any eye contact throughout the transvaginal scan. I could hear the doctor shifting on his chair. He poked the probe to the right and pushed it down heavily on my cervix. My bottom lip trembled. I put my hand up to cover my eyes.

"I know this isn't pleasant. I just need to check your womb lining is healthy. I thought I saw a small fibroid but there doesn't seem to…"

I waited, hand over my eyes, just trying to zone out.

He pulled the probe out. I exhaled and dropped my hand back down.

"You can get dressed now. Your womb is fine. Undamaged." And he walked back to his desk and my file.

"What about my stomach?"

"Well, it's been in the wars. It's swollen. Anything other than soup or porridge will be impossible for a day or so. But it is intact. And your womb is fine."

I got up, pulled my top down and put my tracksuit bottoms back on. I couldn't eat but I would still have my period. How was that a good result?

"We're going to make you have a full shower anyway but the warm water will be good for your stomach. And your hand. You need the warmth to release the muscles, bring down the swelling. But then we'll have to wrap your whole midriff in tight bandages. And the hand. I will let the enclave know and they can take over the care."

"So it's not negotiable?"

"Negotiable?"

"What if I don't want to go to an enclave?" I said.

"You don't want to go to an enclave?"

I thought about it, how to phrase it. "What if there's something else I want to do first? What if I want to stay here?"

The doctor sighed. "Miss Lewis, whatever it is, whoever it is that you're holding on to, please, let it go. Let them go. They probably haven't survived."

I turned my face away.

He went on. "Now that you're here, the wheels are in motion. No negotiation, not once you're here. Your anxiety is understandable. You've been by yourself for a long—"

"Do I get a say in which enclave I go to? Do I get to understand, to decide, to choose?"

He made some notes, never telling me what they were.

"But..." How was I going to explain this? "What if..."

"What if, what?" the doctor said. "Miss Lewis, let it go. Learn to make new friends. Others are here. They have been here a few days, a week or so. They'll be going with you so

54

maybe once you meet them, talk to them, you'll feel more safe, realise you have things in common. Tomorrow morning, that's when you'll be travelling. It's too dark now, we travel only in daytime."

"What? How? What could I have in common with these people?"

"Well, for a start you're all women, about the same age." He turned the pages in the file. What it contained I didn't know. "We've always been guided to collate people from similar demographics together. We can only survive if there is community, you see, so you have nothing to fear. You would've been categorised like everyone else on your health, your background, your social circle—"

"What do you mean, would've been?"

"Well, you've been pre-allocated, haven't you?"

"I was unaware of that."

The man nodded, slowly, unconvinced. "Well, there's still procedure to be followed, if only for appearance. The nurse will take you from here."

CHAPTER EIGHT
The Long Night

I stood on the tiles, cold, shivering a little. Waiting.

The shower room was open, exposed. I looked along the row of shower heads and at each corner for cameras, for tell-tale gaps in the tiling. But I couldn't see any.

Then it came.

I gasped, the water catching me by surprise. But it was joyous. I closed my eyes, feeling it wash over my head, down my skin and over my hands. It was warm. I exhaled.

The warmth softened up the damaged tissue in my left hand. Slowly, I could start to move my fingers. Gently flexing the palm back and forth, spreading my fingers out and back together again. I gently rubbed my hands one over the other, again and again. The water running off them never seemed to clear. I hadn't realised my hands were this dirty. The only progress was that it faded from black to brown.

Eventually, as the water continued to fall, I could see my pale skin begin to emerge from under the layer of dirt that had protected it for so long.

Running water. I'd almost forgotten what it was like to just turn a tap on and for water to flow.

There was no way that the blocks would be denied water – that was part of the rationale in ring-fencing, being able to ensure energy and sanitation supplies despite the challenges. But that supply couldn't be limitless so daily showers went the way of fibre optic cabling and 24-hour electricity.

My head was sore and my neck hurt but under the heat I could feel the muscles in them loosen up. My stomach, though, had longer to go. I could feel the hardening, I could see the swelling.

I swept my hands over my face, over the top of my head.

As I opened my eyes again, I caught sight of something I didn't expect – luxury items. On the shelf ahead of me, just to the right. One shampoo, one conditioner, one shower gel. All branded.

My eyes narrowed. I didn't grab them. Just for a moment, I simply stared at them. The bottles were almost full.

The State had luxuries.

I reached out and picked up one of the bottles, squeezing out the faintly pink gel into my hand. It was lightly scented. Like roses. I lathered up and cleaned myself from top to toe.

And then the water suddenly stopped. As they told me it would.

I reached for the disinfected towel behind me and headed back out to the lockers.

Out in the deserted locker room, a small, neatly folded pile of bland, basic clothing sat next to an open bag. Still wrapped in my towel I glanced at the bin at the side of the room. It was empty. Someone had been in and already emptied the bin of my ruined clothes and replaced my torn bag with a new one.

I looked to the corners of the locker room. Where were the cameras? Were they watching me? I couldn't see any. No tiny holes in the walls.

But you can never be sure.

I dropped my towel rather dramatically in front of the wooden benches with the new clothes on them. Feigning it as an accident, I crouched down and, as I fumbled with the towel, I reached under the benches to just behind the pipes.

It was still there.

I pulled out my gun, wrapped it up in the towel and dumped the pile into my new bag.

The woman – I'm not going to call her a nurse any more – didn't look at me or talk to me as I followed her through the empty corridors of the buildings opposite the Cathedral. I had a feeling she had somewhere to go, some other place to be. As if I was keeping her from a prior engagement.

The corridor was a seemingly endless wash of white walls with a few doors, but occasionally the white walls would break and I could see out into the London night sky. St Paul's bathed in spotlights.

I heard the noise first – the noise of other people.

Then, as we turned a corner in the corridor, I saw them through the glass doors.

Behind the doors, rows and rows of sleeping bags spread across a secure room. And at the far end, a group of maybe a dozen women huddled together talking, some holding mugs.

And between me and the room I didn't want to go in were three armed guards. More men with guns.

The woman turned to me. "On the other side of this door are the other women who are going to the enclave with you. I suggest you make friends. You're going to be with each other for a long time." And then I remembered what the doctor had said, that these women had been waiting for transfer for some time. They had bonded. They had become a unit.

The woman handed the file to one of the guards and then turned and headed back down the corridor.

One of the men held open the door, flicked his head to gesture me in, and as I stepped through, all eyes turned to me. Conversations halted and the women fell into a silence.

I looked away from them, to the side of the room.

At the sound of footsteps coming my way I looked up. One of the women walked up to me and introduced herself. "I'm Abby." A quick glance down and to the right – Abby was carrying scissors.

I nodded at the bubbly young woman with long frizzy hair. Then realised she was expecting a more intimate response. "Laura."

Abby smiled. She was the first person in months, maybe years, who'd looked into my eyes and smiled. It was unnerving. I looked away, out into the distance again. These are not days to smile at strangers with scissors in their hands.

"So it's true, you were attacked on the way here." I looked back and saw Abby's face fall. "Oh, no, I didn't mean anything by it. We saw you arrive, your convoy. You were carried out. Saw you through the window." Abby pointed to the large glass window on the far side of the room. "Your face, ah, are you OK?"

I nodded.

"OK, well, I've been given bandages, new bandages, so I can wrap your wounds again, keep them tight, help them heal better, I mean, quicker."

"I can cut my own bandages."

"I'm just offering my help." I saw Abby recoil, just a bit. I had offended her. "Bindings are a lot tighter when someone else does them."

I relented. Make friends, Laura. Bond. You will need them. "OK then."

She smiled, again. "Great."

As I stood in the corner of the room by my allocated sleeping bag, my trousers around my ankles, Abby taped the cotton wool down over my thigh. "It's not bleeding any more, you'll be glad to know. It's in pretty good condition, really. Considering."

I stood in silence, letting Abby do what she felt she needed to do. Two armed men were also in the room, one at each end. Guarding us or protecting us? It was hard to tell. And the other women, well, they tried to make out they weren't looking at me but they weren't trying hard enough. I knew what they were looking at. I could feel the bruises on my face throb.

Abby started pulling up my new tracksuit bottoms and, as she turned her attention to my left hand, she finally asked what it had been apparent she had wanted to ask me from the outset. "You were beaten up, weren't you?"

"Yes."

Abby's voice dropped down to a whisper. "Was it the men or the women?"

My head jerked, giving away my shock. I calmly turned my head back to look straight ahead, to mask my reveal. "Women? The women are on the streets still?"

"Yes. You must know that. RAZR are winning." Abby pulled up straight as one of the men marched past us, slowing down as he drew near. You could practically see his ear twitch. But he passed on. "You know that, surely. You must know that."

"I thought they had been defeated. Or in retreat, at least."

Abby pulled the crêpe bandages out of her first-aid kit

and started winding them around my hand. She was left-handed. "God, no. Why do you think this place is so heavily guarded?"

I nodded, saying nothing.

"So it was men who hit you."

"Yes."

Abby cut the bandage, fastened it with a safety pin. When you've been isolated for so long, some crave interaction like an alcoholic for a drink. Others retreat. The women opposite me, gossiping and glancing in my direction, were from the first type.

Now I had a question. "Abby, why did you think it was the women who attacked me?"

Abby wound the unused bandages around her hand. "That's just what we hear. That's what we've heard since we've been here. That they think that those women who aren't fighting with them are the enemy, so they're killing them as well as the men. One of the girls over there, the one with the black bob, one of the neighbours in her block ran off to join them. It got back that they had made her into a slave. And the other one next to her, in the stripes, she said that she'd heard that RAZR had no food and that they were starving their soldiers, forcing them to fight for them under pain of death. Isn't that what you've heard?"

"No."

"Why, what've you heard?"

"Only from before. That they treat their soldiers incredibly well. Feed them, arm them, protect them. But that they send their soldiers out to murder indiscriminately, and if you disobey them, they kill you."

"Oh, OK," Abby said. She put the unused bandages in her first-aid kit. "You're finished now."

"Thank you."

Abby stayed in front of me, shifting her weight from one foot to the other.

"What?"

"Can I cut your hair?" She ran her hands through the ends of my hair. "You'd like a cut, right? I mean, freshen it all up a bit."

I took a deep breath. Summon up some patience, Laura. Just go with it. "Sure."

I didn't move for hours. I just sat staring out of the window, analysing, and constantly running my fingers through my new short bob, trying to get used to the absence of my hair.

One by one the other women had fallen asleep. And steadily the pace of the patrols had eased off. The two brown shirts sat on chairs, one at either end of the room, their guns resting in their arms.

It had always been ironic that the Cathedral was in the middle of the financial district. I'd never worked in the City, though I knew plenty who did. And to think people were once desperate to work in places like this, even after the financial crash. But I guess few can ever really see the long-term implications of a financial system only partly rehabilitated.

We never really recovered from that economic crisis.

Every economy was bankrupt, though no government was prepared to confess to that. What it meant was that we had no finances – no finances to fight the war, no finances to fund the solution. We needed money to pay for the full mobilisation of every liberal state if we were to stand a chance. And there was no money to be had.

In a war where the rich nations' wealth is negated, it's always going to come down to who wants it more. And not enough wanted to sacrifice their own blood for liberal democracy. That is the legacy of our time, that we were not prepared to pay the price. And even if we end up surviving this, it will be the legacy for our children and our grandchildren.

Extremists are always prepared to go where liberals fear to tread. And with that realisation, the markets collapsed. Decimated overnight. The value of every company, stock, investment and pension fund was wiped out. The footage from past economic crashes had been of harangued, hysterical traders. But this time it was of silent trading floors. Abandoned.

Next to me, Abby, in her woolly hat and gloves, had her sleeping bag clutched up around her neck. She was sleeping but her face, scrunched and furrowed, looked deep in anguish. That's why I hate the night. Sleep allows the drawbridge of the mind to crash down and all the horsemen that you've kept on the other side of the moat come rushing in.

There was a stillness in the room. Not quite a silence, but an uneasy peace. Occasionally a rustle, a cough or a brush of skin against synthetic fabric. I don't know why I couldn't sleep that night. I was shattered. I should have been out like a light.

From the corner, I could hear the muffled cry of one of the women who was apparently mourning the loss of her boyfriend. I hadn't asked but Abby had told me nevertheless.

I hadn't had a boyfriend for years. I didn't miss him. I expect the doctor thought that was who I was referring to. I didn't care where he was, not at all. The evening he called it quits on our relationship was pretty much the last I heard of him.

It was his incessant tapping of his beer bottle that hinted at what was to come. I'd been late before – I'd been late many, many times before in the few months after the start of the war. My promotion demanded it and it was an obligation I had no issue in fulfilling. But this time a quick kiss on the cheek and a smile didn't cut it.

The noisy bar, the crowds of people out on a Thursday night... Yes, this had all been planned. Along with the expectation that I'd provide him with the necessary excuse to start the ball rolling.

"I don't see why I should accept your apology if you don't mean it," he said.

As he delivered his speech, his eyes constantly wandering around the bar, refusing to look at me, I thought about offering the obligatory protest but, frankly, I couldn't be bothered.

Anyway, he was doing me a favour.

"I think we should call it a day," he added.

"OK" I agreed. "I've got to go back to the office anyway so move your stuff out tonight and just leave the keys on the worktop."

He looked at me, somewhat staggered. "Well, I've got to find a place to stay first."

"Move back in with your mother," I shrugged. "I own the flat and there's no point dragging this out."

His shoulders slumped. "Fucking hell. This job has made you crueller than even I had thought possible."

"Hard," I said.

"What?"

"Hard, not cruel. To be cruel I'd have to take pleasure in it and I don't. I'm just decisive. So, I'll take 'hard' but not 'cruel'."

"Fine," he said. "Hard, then."

Actually not even that was true. I know I'm hard but it wasn't the job that made me this way. I was like this before I stepped foot through their door. That's why they'd head-hunted me, that's what got me promoted so quickly. And that's why they'd given me the responsibility.

64

I sat against the wall watching the other women sleep. Occasionally I caught the eye of one of the shirts watching over us. Does it count as a first night of freedom when you're being guarded by people with guns? My head was saying I could let go, that I was protected. The burden of survival was no longer on my shoulders. But inside, the weight hadn't lifted. Since I'd been within this gun-controlled perimeter I hadn't let my guard drop once.

CHAPTER NINE
The Interception

"OK, listen to me and listen carefully. The convoy is outside, a few yards from the doors behind me." It sounded reassuring but the man lecturing from the front of the room was in army fatigues and carrying a rifle. As were the six men behind him. This was not a drill.

"We are going to transfer you to these vehicles, which will transport you to the enclave. Your estimated transfer time is three hours. Please prepare to file in."

The others foraged around on the floor for the rest of their belongings. Some of those belongings were practical – a couple of blankets, a towel. The blonde in the stripes had a panic when she couldn't find her glasses, which were eventually found. That was understandable, but too many frayed photos were tucked away amongst their possessions. I pulled on my one rucksack and looked out of the large glass windows, out towards the armoured vehicle being reversed up to the perimeter gates.

"It's such a relief to be finally moving to a new home."

Abby was following my eye-line. I looked at her. She was biting her lip. "I just want to start again."

"You feel safe?"

Abby looked at me. "What, you mean all these soldiers? Yeah, of course. They won't let any harm come to us. Some of them I even know, you know, from being here so long."

Abby blushed. I asked nothing more.

One of the other women, the blonde, frowned at me then jerked her head, encouraging Abby to leave me, which she duly did.

"OK, ladies, women. Please file in." One of the soldiers spoke and we followed him out into the light.

The sun was low in the sky and bright. I wanted to look up, to see the sky. Instead I had to block out the glare by covering my eyes with my hand. All I saw either side of me were rifles. Rifles to my left, same to my right. No break in the line as we were marshalled into the back of the truck.

The trucks rattled down the empty roads. There were twelve of us in the back of one, with two soldiers. The soldiers flanked the doors at the back of the van. Another two were on the front seat, driving and guarding. Another eight soldiers were in the truck behind us. Another twelve in the one in front. Twenty-four soldiers for twelve women. This prison van was still transporting prisoners. The world turns, nothing changes.

"... so I know they are in an enclave, I mean, that's what the lady said who, you know, glanced in one of the folders for me." Abby was opposite me, chattering away to the blonde next to her. "But I don't know if, like, the enclaves are allowed to communicate with each other, you know."

"You must be able to, like, email," added the blonde.

"Or phone."

"Right."

Their chattering had been relentless since we left. Thankfully the squeals and the giggling had pretty much gone. But thirty minutes in, I had hoped they would fall into silence. But no.

I didn't get it, how people could go from complete solitude to a desperate embrace of social contact. So many lurch towards it. Yet when they get it, they never seem to have anything interesting to say. I looked away, across to the guards at the end of the benches. Their faces, impassive. Their detachment such a contrast.

The van suddenly shuddered to a halt.

The tyres stopped fast, causing our bodies to jolt down the benches.

That stopped the chattering.

I looked through the wire to my left, out to the front seat. I saw the soldiers cock their rifles.

The soldiers in with us... Their cool expressions evaporated and they did the same.

The truck behind us screeched to a halt.

This wasn't a scheduled stop.

Abby was breathing quickly, clutching the hand of the blonde. The woman next to me let out a whimper. The woman next to the blonde had her hands over her mouth.

The door-slams from the trucks either side of us were followed by the sound of boots hitting the ground, surrounding us. A perimeter.

And then we heard the shouts.

"Formation! Formation! Stay in the van!" They banged on the sides of the van.

We heard the clicks of their rifles.

And then came the gunfire.

"Down! Down! Faces down on the ground!" The soldiers bellowed and we obeyed.

The twelve of us threw ourselves to the floor of the van. I accidentally elbowed Abby in the face.

Bang! Bang! Bang! The gunfire was coming at us.

Strings of bullets punctured the side of the van.

The other women screamed.

"Stay down! Stay down!" The soldiers in with us sounded less certain than before.

Someone shouted out "Who's attacking us?"

"Stay down!"

Two big bangs hit the side of the van, rocking the vehicle.

"We're hit! We're hit!"

And then – Bang! – something landed on the roof of the van.

"We stay here! We stay here!" The soldiers weren't telling us but each other.

Crash! The windscreen shattered.

Gunfire filled the truck.

We all covered our ears and screamed. Everyone. There was no sound barrier between us and the gunfire.

The bullets shattered the sides of the van.

The heat.

The rush of air powered through our cage.

The doors were flung open.

Bang! Bang! Two bullets close by.

I felt the thud of the soldiers' bodies hitting the deck of the truck.

And then we heard it – a female voice. "Stay down!"

More gunfire.

Then it stopped.

"Is that all of them?" Another woman's voice, from outside the van. "Check all of them."

"They're all dead." The first female voice. "All of you, get up." The woman's voice was strong, well spoken.

We stirred on her command, gradually opening our eyes. The women who had been lying on the floor of the truck around me started, slowly, to sit upright.

A woman was standing between the destroyed doors. She had brown hair and was dressed in a black vest. I couldn't see much more for the glare and the shock, but she was flanked on either side by women also carrying large automatic weapons.

Another woman came up to her – stocky, a large scar on her arm. "They managed to link a call for back-up before we cut them off. We need to leave."

"Come on." The woman in the vest turned to her cohorts. "Move them."

She walked away.

The two women with instructions to fulfil slung their guns over their shoulders and started to marshal us out of the van.

Abby was crying. The others around her were shaking, terrified. They were all hauled out. I was the only one still lying on the floor, letting my eyes adjust, trying to register what had happened.

The women, the soldiers with guns, came deep into the truck to speed us up. We were taking too long to file out. "Come on. Move."

As the last woman but one was dragged out, I looked up. And caught the eye of the woman with the scar standing outside the van.

She cocked her rifle into my face. "You too. Up."

I lifted my arms above my head and slowly stepped over the dead men and climbed out.

There were two other dead soldiers on the ground, almost underneath the van. Their heads were red, half fallen away, the blood still ebbing out of what was left of their skulls.

"Move." The woman with the scar – it looked like a knife

wound – grabbed me by the arm and dragged me away, past the soldiers. All of them, dead.

The soldiers in the front seat of the truck behind us, riddled with bullets.

The perimeter of soldiers, fallen and silent.

The woman, dressed completely in black, pushed me in the back. "We don't have time to stop."

She pushed me on, past the truck in front. And she pushed me again when I tried to slow down. The sides of the vans were punctured with multiple bullet holes. And the ground littered with corpses.

In front of our destroyed convoy, the tarmac was new, just laid. There were no trees, just buildings, empty, half-destroyed buildings. Ahead of us were two vans, both filled with women.

The woman started running, forcing me to do the same.

One of the vans screeched off as we approached. The second one waited with open doors.

"Get into this one." The woman bundled me in, barely getting my feet in before she slammed the heavy doors behind me. Half of us were in this one. The blonde, but no Abby.

I saw the woman with the well-spoken voice look back at me from the front seat next to the driver. Dark brown hair and strong arms. The one who had been in the glare. "She's in. Let's go," she said.

And then we were blindfolded.

CHAPTER TEN
The Resistance

The blinding light hit me when they took off the blindfold. I cowered on the floor, eyes scrunched, right hand held up to the light, waiting for my eyes to adjust. The other eleven abductees were all around me and they too had hands overhead in an attempt to shelter them from the bright white light.

Yet there was not a single light bulb in the room.

The brightness came from the sun pouring through the vast skylight above us and bouncing off the white walls, the marble pillars and the polished marble underneath us.

I knew exactly where we were.

The priceless art was long gone – stolen or stored? Who knows? And the huge bronze sculptures, well, maybe they had been melted down before they were saved. But there was no mistaking the architecture. This was the art gallery on the bank of the Thames. Or it had been. Now it was a gutted building, its rooms cold and its structural beauty an irrelevance.

A cold draught swept through the high-ceilinged hall causing the twelve of us huddled on the floor to shiver. But around us the dozens and dozens of soldiers in uniform didn't even flinch.

All women, all dressed in black. Physical, strong.

And all carrying automatic weapons.

Dozens of them, Fifty, sixty... I tried to count but it was hard to do without being conspicuous.

So it was a surprise when the most demure, frail woman from the line in front of us took a step forward and started to speak. "My name is Jane."

Jane.

All of us on the floor sat up that little bit straighter.

Next to me, Abby's jaw dropped.

Everyone's eyes widened, mine more in shock.

"I lead this resistance movement, a female resistance movement, that has been in operation since before The Fall."

We all knew this, everyone knew this. Apart from the ones, I suppose, who thought previous assassination attempts on the most wanted woman in the Western world had been successful.

"We intercept the convoys of women that are being trafficked from the filtration centres to their allocated enclaves."

Jane was, like the soldiers around her, in black trousers and a black top. But her figure was slight and her voice soft. She was little like the images we had seen all over the television and the Internet. Similar face, but, well, thinner. Significantly so. The toll of war?

"The enclaves have been sold to you as the safe areas where the, well, what's left of the population are working to revive, rebuild the human race. I guess in a certain light they're not lying to you."

Was Jane ill? The comparison with the women next to her was stark. They were so strong, so athletic. Jane was a soldier, *the* soldier. An Amazonian woman, or so we thought. But she was so slim, so slight.

73

And then I saw her, standing next to Jane. On the other side from me, partially obscured by the women between me and her. The well-spoken woman who had led the assault on the trucks. The first woman I had seen. The one who had turned back to see I was in the truck before we sped off.

Jane continued to speak. I should have been listening carefully but the woman next to her was impossible to ignore. I kept trying to catch glimpses of her. She was slouched back, leaning against the wall. This woman, unlike the others, did not grip her gun tightly in her hands. Nor was she stood to attention. Instead her gun was loose and her shoulders were relaxed.

"The sharper ones amongst you may have noticed that all of you here fall within a certain demographic. You are all above sixteen but below forty-five. Those who have been waiting at the filtration centre will have perhaps observed that those women left working there are all older than that, older than you."

As Jane spoke, her speech clear and soft, my attention was continually drawn to the woman next to her. This one, not Jane, radiated strength and authority. And power. Rasputin? Machiavelli? Had the State been focusing on the wrong woman?

Jane took a breath, switching her weight from her right foot to her left. "There is no easy way to say this. It never gets easier. You were marked out because, in this brave new world, you have the most valuable commodity on this barren earth – a fertile womb."

Jane let that hang in the air.

All around me, mouths hung open. My heartbeat was pounding but my mouth was closed.

Jane looked up, earnest, passionate. "There are so few of us left. The men of fighting age, well, most of them died fighting.

How ironic. And the elderly and ill were never going to be of any use. But so few women have made it through. Too few to bring up what children have survived. That means we need to start again. And you are what they are planning to start with. The facility that you were being driven to, under very heavy armed guard, exists solely to facilitate procreation."

Jane looked across each of our faces.

Next to me, Abby whispered "Oh God."

I wasn't listening to the propaganda but trying to read the woman delivering the message.

Jane. Jane. There she was, right in front of me. The woman everybody wanted, or rather, everybody wanted to kill. The head of RAZR, a terrorist organisation so efficient, so brutal that the future existence of the State was in doubt. She was RAZR – its architect, its creator and its master.

I hadn't seen an image of her in years, not since the electricity was cut. Her hair was flat and thin, her cheeks hollowed.

I looked at the others on the floor. They were rapt, mouths agape, eyes full of awe. Even the soldiers were focused, not one even shifting a foot. All standing to attention. All except one – the woman still leaning against the marble walls.

I looked back at the woman who launched a thousand revolutionaries. "RAZR is created by women, run by women and fights for women. That includes you and it includes those who have been left behind."

Jane's voice, so uninspiring. So strange. Just as Jane stepped forward, only an inch, I finally caught a clear line of vision to the woman next to her, the power behind the throne. How was it she could get away with not standing to attention?

I narrowed my eyes. Her profile, her dark hair, her physique... Wait.

And then she saw me, caught me looking at her. She looked straight at me. Her eyes focused just on me.

I saw her face full on.

And I knew exactly who she was.

I looked away, feigned interest in what 'Jane' was explaining, a state of play that they'd been expounding for years. "They were going to make you pregnant. All of you. Each of you. And not just once."

I looked back at the woman. She was still staring at me. Her expression hadn't changed. Cold, clinical. I could feel the intensity of her glare, even with all the space between us.

I averted my gaze.

I recognised her face.

I had seen her before.

I knew who she was.

A woman in our group, the blonde who previously thought her glasses were her most valuable possession, choked out "By IVF?"

I caught a couple of the soldiers cast a few glances between each other.

Jane looked surprised, perhaps not realising the question was desperate rather than naive. "No."

The eleven of them on the floor stopped breathing.

Jane took a deep breath. "The infrastructure needed to artificially inseminate each of you is being rebuilt. Most of the remaining medical centres are critically under-resourced."

The woman next to Jane spoke up. "They've told you that they are rebuilding those centres though, quickly, haven't they?" The woman I knew, the voice I had heard so many times before. "But you have to remember, these need to be manned by trained staff and there's not enough of them left. We are here to pull those scales from your eyes."

Next to me Abby started crying.

Jane took up the mantle again. "They will make you

pregnant the only other way possible. The place they were driving you to is an army facility..."

Abby retched.

And then she threw up.

"Can we mop that up?" As the woman next to Jane spoke, no surprise in her voice, a couple of the soldiers moved forward and helped Abby out.

I sat there unmoved, interested only in the power play in front of me.

"I'm sorry," Abby muttered.

"Don't worry," Jane assured her, with more comfort than you'd expect from a leader of an army. "It's OK. You're not the first. We intervened, raided your convoy to prevent you being taken to these enclaves. We have been doing this for some time – identifying the convoys and stopping them. Sadly, we haven't been able to stop them all."

"That's why we were so heavily guarded." I heard the words come out of my mouth when they were only meant to be in my head. "That's why we had so many soldiers with us."

The woman next to Jane looked at me closely. I looked away, not wanting to draw her attention, but I heard her voice. That voice. "The militarisation of the convoys has increased. It will continue to do so. It almost doesn't matter how many soldiers we kill or capture, your wombs are so precious they will guard the convoys with even more if necessary. Men have been geniuses at creating weapons that destroy life but they've never been that great at creating it."

I looked up to see the woman nod to Jane, to get her to carry on. Which she did. "They've been trying. In a facility, we know they've been trying to implant fertilised eggs into animal wombs – sheep, wolves, gorillas – but none took."

Abby was crying loudly now.

Some of the others winced, turned their heads away, pressed their lips tightly together.

"They have been working on an artificial placenta but it doesn't take. Nature's clever, I guess." Jane looked out into the distance.

The woman next to Jane leant in. "The time."

Jane nodded, suddenly aware she'd been rambling.

But this was no longer bizarre to me – I realised what I was watching.

Jane coughed then continued. "This has been a rescue mission. However it was involuntary which is why we've brought you here, a holding place, to allow you to choose sides. Whether to stay with us or go on, to go back to the enclaves. This is a temporary rest for us. We cannot stay, for our own safety. And we cannot take you with us should you decide you want to go back to society, uncivilised as it may be. We cannot have you betray our position. So, believe me, I would join us if I were you. But I cannot make you. The convoy was due to arrive at a stop en route to the facility about noon. That means about now they'll be realising you aren't coming."

Abby was trying to muffle her cries. "Oh God."

"Unlike what you're facing, we are a democracy." I tried to focus on Jane's voice. "We are giving you a choice. We can leave you here, where the reserve teams will find you, or you can come with us. We have enough respect for you to at least give you a choice."

Abby could not stop crying. She was trying to muffle her sobs with her hair, as if she was trying to stuff the strands into her mouth.

"But to stay with us is not an easy option. We are hunted women. Men have not one but two reasons to hunt us down. We are both an opportunity and a threat to them. We never stand still, we never rest. We have plans but I do not have the time to explain that to you now – or the willingness to jeopardise our security. Instead you have ten minutes."

The woman next to Jane held her hand open – five.

Jane looked back to us. "You have five minutes to make your decision. Do you stay or do you go?"

CHAPTER ELEVEN
The Debate

Five minutes. Just five minutes.

Jane and her cabal had left the room but her army remained, the women in black, still encircling the twelve of us. The soldiers didn't even lower their weapons – as much watching us as watching over us.

"Do you believe her, what she said?" I heard Abby ask the group. "Laura?"

"What? Oh." I hadn't realised she was looking at me. "I don't know." I stopped. But none of them said anything else – they just sat there staring at me. "I believe she believes what she said," I added.

"What does that mean?" The blonde sneered at me. "This isn't a time for riddles."

"I just mean, that she believes what she says is the truth. I don't think she is trying to deceive you. But that is not the same thing as the actual truth."

The blonde looked unimpressed. Back to Abby "What are you going to do?"

The tears started welling up again in Abby's eyes. "I don't know." She started to cry and soon they were all at it.

Jesus Christ.

The group collapsed into emotional turmoil. The crying, the wide-eyed fear, the slack jaws, heads in hands... They were all falling apart. How on earth had these women survived this far?

I looked at the guards, looking for sympathy, direction, a helping hand... Anything. But they gave me nothing.

Time was running out. I leant forward and tentatively started to pat Abby's arm. "Hey, hey there. It's OK, it's OK. I know this is hard, I know that, but we don't have much time. Listen to me. Do you know—"

"I'm not going back. I'm staying here." Abby suddenly gripped my arm tightly.

"You want to stay here, in the gallery?"

"No, no," Abby said. "I don't want to stay with these women. I'm scared of them. I'm staying here with you."

"OK. OK." I patted her arm, trying to calm her rising fear. "But I'm not staying."

"You're not?" the blonde and Abby said in unison.

"No."

"But you hate RAZR," Abby cried. "You said they were murderers."

My head dropped, my cheeks flushed. God, I hoped that the women around us weren't taking notes.

"Gail?" Abby said to the blonde.

"I'm staying with you, Abby." And Gail clutched Abby tight like a teddy bear.

"I'm going with them, with the soldiers. With RAZR." One of the others, an Indian woman, looked at me and nodded. "I'll go with you. I believe them." Her soft, calm voice belied the strength of her conviction. "I believe what they are saying."

"Gauiri! Are you serious? Why?" Gail was appalled.

Gauiri shrugged. "Because it makes sense to me."

Gail was spitting. "Well I think that just reflects your—"

"I agree." All faces turned to me but I never broke my gaze from Gauiri, who was sitting with her arms folded tightly in front of her. "I agree with you. I'm going with RAZR too."

"What?" Gail was shocked. "How can you believe her? Jane? She's a fucking terrorist. She's a murderer. All these women are." Gail's rising frenzy was almost palpable. Her eyes darted about, eyeing all of us in turn. "She's lying. Don't you remember the bombings? These women, they murdered the returning troops. They blew up the airports and shot down the planes."

"Exactly." Gauiri remained resolute. "Why would she lie about this?"

Abby was appalled. Even I was surprised. Gauiri had real conviction.

She went on. "These women, they are risking their lives to break up army convoys, to save us. Why would they do that if they weren't telling the truth?"

"Power!" Gail lunged for Gauiri but Abby held her back. "It's all about power."

"Exactly," Gauiri countered. "And I'd rather live under female power than male."

I looked up and around. The guards watched on but they did not move. They must have been able to hear every word. Our row was the only sound in the room. Even the others, those previously lost in their emotional hysterics, were now transfixed with Gail's brewing rage.

"It's a fucking lie, these lies about rape centres," Gail went on. "You can't fucking breed a population through rape. We're probably together because of our age. Maybe we're just going to a place where there are people our age.

That's normal. Maybe it's these women who aren't normal. Maybe they are going to enslave us, make us work in camps. Maybe this is all a fucking trap."

Gail was slowly staggering to her feet. "Maybe it's these women who are going to kill us. Look at their guns. Look at them!" Abby gripped Gail's hand, trying to pull her down to the floor but it wasn't working. "It's these women who are the liars."

The guards didn't even look at each other, yet two of them came forward automatically.

"Don't touch me! Don't touch me!" Screaming, Gail jabbed out her hands, hitting the guard.

More guards closed in, smothering her from either side. In the middle, Gail kept kicking and jabbing. "You fucking murderers! You fucking killers!"

We all remained frozen on the ground. Shocked. None of us intervened.

Gail's kicks started to become less frequent.

Then, from behind the women, the muffled sobs started instead. The guards stood back and Gail dropped to her knees, crumpled and broken, her face red, crying and groaning.

The guards stepped back as calmly as they had stepped forward. They had seen it all before.

We sat there, watching Gail on the floor. This is what war does to people. Before The Fall I'd only read it in books or seen it in films. Shell-shock. Gail lay prostrate, hyperventilating, her eyes wide and open. A violent hopelessness.

Then suddenly Gail burst into tears. Sadly, since The Fall, I was now familiar with this. It's more alarming seeing it in a man though, a grown man. Of all the people in my block – the teenagers, the single mothers, the elderly – the last person I expected it to happen to was my father. The snap. The light switch going off. The sanity tripping the circuit and checking out.

My father didn't come back. I wasn't sure Gail was going to come back either.

I kept staring at Gail. I used to think insanity was a sign of weakness. Experience changes perspective.

Abby leant in, her hand hovering to reach out but too hesitant to get closer.

I pulled her back. "I don't think you should touch her."

Abby looked over to the guards. "Will she calm down?"

One of the guards shrugged.

"I want to come with you." I said it out loud, to the guards, to no one in particular.

Abby grabbed my hand.

"It's OK." I loosened her grip.

"You're only saying that because of what happened to you." Abby looked at my stomach, my leg. The leg had been the dog but I knew what she was getting at.

"I'm not, Abby."

And actually I wasn't. I knew what I was doing. I'm not a fool. I know gender equality is a myth. We'll never have it. It's just a dream, a fantasy. We'll die out before we get equality with men – but I had to join RAZR.

"What about the future?" Abby pleaded.

I shook my head. "This is the future, Abby. Our past is gone." I stood up. "I'd like to come with you."

The echo bounced off the walls, the sound rising up.

"I'm coming with you." Gauiri stood up too.

Then the others did. All of them got to their feet.

All bar two.

Abby looked down at her hands, took a breath, then got to her feet. "I'm coming too."

I nodded at her. She looked terrified.

Gail had not moved from the marble floor. I looked down at her, curled up like a baby.

"Should we move her?" Abby asked.

I touched Abby's shoulder. "Abby, she can't come with us."

"Yes she can."

"Abby, she doesn't want to," I said. "Plus she's ill."

"Exactly, she needs help." Abby crouched down by Gail, stroking her hair. "We can't leave her."

"We have to leave her," I said.

"No we don't!" Abby looked around at the guards. "Help me. Help me carry her."

The guards didn't move but one spoke out. "She's ill."

"Abby, this is an army," Gauiri added. "Gail needs help."

"I can't leave her."

Abby looked at me, pleading, desperate.

I sighed. "OK, let's move her." I moved forward and put an arm under Gail's shoulder, Abby took the other. "We'll move her together, all of us."

Gauiri shook her head. "No. Gail needs help."

"Gauiri!" Abby yelled.

Gauiri looked at the guards. "I know you can't take Gail with you. I know she'll hold you back." Then back at us. "She isn't strong enough. She won't make it."

Abby wasn't having any of it. "No. No way. We can do this. We're all in this together. Right, Laura?"

"Right." I looked at the guards. "Help us."

The guards didn't move.

Gauiri stepped forward and gently ran her hand through Gail's hair. "Goodbye, Gail. Take care."

"We need to go." The guards cocked their rifles. "Let's move."

The others started to walk on as directed. But I didn't. I didn't move. I couldn't. I was stuck there with Gail and Abby.

One of the soldiers came up to me – the stocky woman who had dragged me out of the truck. The one with the scar on her arm. "No exceptions. Your time is up."

I started to loosen my grip on Gail. "Abby, come on," I said.

"I can't leave her, Laura. I can't leave her."

"You can't stay," I replied.

"I'm tired, Laura."

I looked at the other woman. "What will happen to her?" The woman shrugged. "They'll come and get her." Her voice was gruff. "They'll know she's here. They'll find her soon."

I took my arm away from under Gail and looked at Abby. But no words came out.

"Go," Abby said.

I squeezed Abby's shoulder. "You can't stay. It's dangerous."

Abby looked at me, tears in her eyes, and shook her head. "It's more dangerous where you're going." Abby looked at the woman. "Will they find us here?"

The woman nodded. "Yes," she said. "Come on" and she dragged me off, pushing me down the corridor.

After a few steps, I turned round, realising the woman wasn't behind me. I saw her leaning over Abby, hugging her, whispering something in her ear. As I stood there, she squeezed Abby's shoulder and then headed towards me. Words of comfort. That should've been me. I should've had the right words to say.

She came up to me. "Move." And then she jabbed me with her gun.

And as I headed off, I kept turning back. Gail and Abby abandoned in the middle of the atrium, getting smaller and smaller with every step I took.

CHAPTER TWELVE
The Leader

We sat in the trucks in silence. Absolute silence. Split across two trucks, still guarded – only this time by women. We didn't even try to steal a glance at one another. It was heads down and no questions asked.

We were moving at speed across smooth ground. The occasional rattle of the guns against the sides was the only sound to be heard.

None of us had any idea where we were being driven to. And none of us asked. I looked around. We were all sitting on the benches, backs against the sides of the vehicle. The guards were staring straight ahead; the women from the Cathedral were staring at the ground.

This had not gone as planned. And not as I had hoped for either. My one brief alliance had been broken before it even got started. I hadn't known Abby, I didn't ever know her backstory. But I sensed she had placed a faith in me and I had failed her. A tricky balance – to protect yourself yet to also build friendships. I still had to find that balance.

I looked across the truck to Gauiri. She looked shell-shocked. They all did. To a woman, they all looked traumatised.

I looked to my right, to try to see out of the back doors, but the plastic windows were damaged, impossible to see out of.

One of the guards by the door, the stocky one with the scar who had dragged me away, saw me looking out of the windows. She narrowed her eyes. Maybe she thought I was contemplating an escape. I looked back at the floor, trying to take the heat out of a possible misunderstanding.

I had done the right thing in volunteering for this, right?

Suddenly the truck jolted. The gears crunched as we hit an incline. We finally made eye contact with each other as we rocked back and forth. We were now off-road. All of us swaying as the truck lurched from side to side. The speed, though, never dropped.

We exchanged worried, querying looks. Who was going to be the first to ask where we were going?

Gauiri looked at me wide-eyed, as did the woman wearing the striped top next to me. Why me? Why didn't they ask?

I looked across at the guards, my mouth a little open, ready to say something, but their faces said, 'don't bother'. A wall of silence.

I glanced again at the woman with the scar. Clad like the others in her black uniform, she was handling a black M4 carbine US-issue assault rifle, and her face was as black as thunder. Whenever I looked her way, she was already looking back at me. Her focus never left me. I shifted my gaze back to the floor, avoiding the attention. But any time I'd look up, there she was again – staring directly at me, into me.

Our trucks trundled along for a long time. Occasionally the rhythmic bounces and traction would cradle me to sleep.

But each time I jerked awake, there she was again. Cradling her gun, focusing on me.

It was the jolt of the brakes rather than any screech of the tyres that woke me next. We had stopped. We were there, wherever there was. The guards at the end of the truck flung open the doors and we staggered out.

In front of me was a huge field. And not an overgrown one either. It was neat, manicured, and framed by a thick, dense wood on each of its three sides.

And on the field, a brigade of women was in training. Shuttle runs, mock walls, rope webbing just off the ground with women scuttling underneath. These women were fit. They were all my age but really physically fit. They clearly hadn't been kept in confinement. This was an established army.

I turned round and saw the building behind us – a large brick building with sprawling extensions, temporary set-ups and outbuildings. It was a school, or rather had been a school.

I looked back at the woods – we were standing on the edge of the school's playing fields.

The second truck pulled up alongside, its back doors slamming open even before it had come to a complete stop. The armed women leapt down and dragged the rest of my group out.

A woman jumped down from the front seat – the one I knew, the one I recognised. As she slammed her door behind her, she looked at me. Straight at me. Her gaze unflinching and boring deep.

'Jane' appeared alongside her, diminished by comparison.

The woman, that woman, looked at us all. She was counting. "Get them inside. Move the trucks."

The soldiers started ushering us in. I hung back, just a little, looking out over the fields, looking towards the school, scanning the woods and the perimeter of the base.

"Hey." The woman with the scar jabbed me with her gun. "Quit staring. Follow the rest of them."

The others in my group had almost vanished, the last few passing through the large entrance doors at the top of a small set of stone steps. We jogged over – the captor and the captured.

I headed up the steps, through the doors and into the vast entrance hall. Its walls were stripped of any photographs or plaques but you could still make out the dark dust stains that framed the stark cream paint squares where these must have once been. And under my feet were wooden floors.

But in front of me were dozens of women. Dressed head to toe in black, milling back and forth, passing into the corridors that shot off in all directions.

The hum, the shouts… This building was full. Full of people. Or, rather, full of women.

"Right." The one who was focused solely on me jabbed me with her gun.

"What?"

"Right." And she flicked her rifle towards the corridor off to the far side of the hall.

I obeyed.

The busy corridor was long. And convoluted. It would be direct and straight, then suddenly it would shoot off at an angle, then become straight again. Only to shoot off in another direction.

The layout was no doubt an unintended consequence of a school that grew organically over hundreds of years, but as a military base it was brilliant. Like street warfare. Like Northern Ireland or Syria, where the residents knew the myriad of confusing streets and alleys like the back of their hands – and the invaders didn't.

The stocky woman tried to push a sharp pace but I kept

falling off it, weaving past other women, attempting to lean into rooms as we passed. Offices, ammunition rooms, maps on walls... And each time my pace slipped, I was pushed forward once again with a jab of the rifle butt into my ribs.

At the end of the corridor, where the varnish had been rubbed clean from the wooden floorboards, was the entrance to a giant assembly hall. The woman shadowing my every move shoved me in.

The back of the hall was filled with the army while the rescued were huddled on long benches at the front. Tables had been pushed to one side. This room clearly doubled up as a dining hall as well as a place for meetings.

But one thing about this room struck me most of all – it was lit up like a Christmas tree. Every light fitting had a bulb, and every bulb was on. No shadows in this room, not one. Electricity. They had electricity. And they had no issues using it.

That woman stood at the front of the hall, flanked either side by the army. And, to her left, 'Jane'.

The woman stood there waiting, hands in her pockets, watching me enter. "Sit down." She spoke and I obeyed, hanging my head and taking a place on the edge of the bench.

She watched me as I sat down. And then she spoke again. "My name is Jane and I am the leader of RAZR."

The others next to me drew their breath. But this I had already guessed.

"I am the leader of this resistance movement. This woman here who introduced herself to you as me is actually Anne, my sister." Jane gestured towards the slim woman who diminished further into her sister's shadow. "Anne is my flesh and blood. Enough to be mistaken for me and enough to pass any DNA test should she be captured."

Anne bowed her head, let her shoulders drop and gently

cowered into the background. The true balance of power was restored.

Jane, in comparison to her sister, was imposing, suffering from none of her sister's physical weaknesses – shoulders back, hands in pockets, chin up. "My identity is valuable information. There are those in the State who would pay a high price just for a confirmed sighting of me. I could not, therefore, let anyone who may leave this group know who I am."

The woman in the stripes next to me gasped and Jane caught sight of the recognition. "You want to say something? What's your name?"

"Ah, Lucy." Lucy was nervous. I could see the sweat on her forehead. "No, I have no questions."

Jane went on. "But other than my identity, everything we told you at the gallery was true. I have no soma for you here. The resistance can be tough. This is an effective militant guerrilla resistance against the restoration of a violent patriarchal state that has oppressed women since the dawn of mankind. Man has finally achieved mutually assured destruction and now it wants to rebuild the discriminatory State that existed before." Jane shook her head. "Not while I have breath in my body. We will herald in a new world order."

You could see the effect of Jane's demagoguery on the rest of the room. Her army straightened up with every word, their swelling chests bursting with pride. And the rescued women on the benches around me were swept up in the current.

I sat back and watched.

"To a state run by men, for the benefit of men, you are little more than chattel – bodies and talents to be exploited and abused. To me, you are strong, intelligent, an extraordinary resource capable of leading a new age and capable of saving mankind from itself."

She went on. "The State has chosen to classify you. You, all of you. You were all selected for the enclave you were travelling to because of your health, your age and your reproductive capacity. To the system, all of this meant you were ripe for imprisonment; to us, it makes you perfect soldiers, members of a resistance that needs you to be fit, agile and sharp. I want you to join RAZR."

Jane stopped and placed her hand on her heart. "In return, I commit myself as your guardian. I personally guarantee your safety. I will not hesitate to defend you from hurt and I will give my life to ensure each one of you is safe."

Jane dropped her hand. "Where you were heading, where they were taking you, was an E-1 enclave. That means it was not part of the main network. These are laboratories. They were taking you there to rape you. I cannot phrase it any other way.

"What you have not been told, in this age of censorship, is that population rates are low. Exceptionally low. Few of the younger generations survived – unable to survive in a world without modern conveniences and a structured society. And their bodies? Too weak from antibiotics and convenience store medicine to withstand the virus. And the women are not getting pregnant. The policy of keeping residents in restricted areas while the network was constructed backfired. Fertile women passed years in confinement away from suitors. And as the men – or these women – died, opportunities for impregnation diminished. Extreme need has resulted in extreme demands – or maybe not that extreme depending on your level of cynicism."

Jane started walking slowly over to the other side of the hall. "And even the brave new world has failed in its design. Men are dying in battle – overseas, still, and here – or are kept in the army, where women are no longer allowed, so precious are their wombs. So the women and men never met. So the establishment faced a conundrum. And the best response they came up with was to enforce, on pain of death, a systematic programme of forced impregnation of women. And where *in vitro* takes too long or requires medical support the State no longer has resources for, more primitive methods are used.

"So, here's the deal. I will protect you. I have dedicated myself to the creation of a society based on democracy, consensus and human rights. The purpose of this army is to fight for these rights. And to that end, I will ensure that this army is safe, is fed and will have the opportunity to move to the secured zones in the west and the north – places where men and women can build this new society based on your consent. In return, you will help me, you will help each other, in fighting for our future."

Jane looked down at the women at the far end of the benches. "Are you ready for a fight?"

I craned my neck and saw Gauiri and another nod back. I could see the sparkle in their eyes.

"Good," Jane said. "We are winning. The State is on the rocks. They only need one more big push."

Jane then abruptly turned on her heels and left the room.

The rescued women around me were buzzing, their eyes wide and bright. Hope is a wonderful thing to give someone.

And as dangerous as hell.

CHAPTER THIRTEEN
The Preparation

Her name was Andrea. It was probably her real name too as she didn't seem the kind to play games. We'd each been allocated to a squadron. And I had been allocated to hers. Our group had been broken up, dissolved into the pre-existing support divisions and brigades within RAZR, and I was the only one from our group to join hers.

Andrea headed up the elite squad, the squad responsible for supporting Jane in all the assaults and raids. (Noticeably she hadn't used the phrase 'protecting her'). But either way, this was an extraordinarily fortuitous allocation for me.

Andrea had dragged me up to an isolated room in one of the turrets of the building. She'd sat on a low chest of drawers, big shelves filled with discarded computer equipment either side of her. She was rummaging through the pockets in her trousers. I was more distracted by the giant angular 'R' she had tattooed on her left arm. A very strong left arm.

"Do you smoke?" she asked.

"What?"

Andrea smuggled out a packet of cigarettes from one of her trouser pockets and offered them to me.

"I don't smoke. Thank you."

"Good for you." Andrea pulled one out of the packet, put it between her lips and lit it. "I wish I didn't smoke."

"Then why do you?"

She laughed. "That's a good one."

I wasn't aware I had cracked a joke. I forced a smile and sat down on a swivel chair, the only chair in the room. "How did you get them?"

"What, these?" Andrea held out her half-full packet of cigarettes. "We pick them up in the raids." She exhaled smoke in my direction, accidentally I think.

I winced a little.

"Sorry."

"No, it's fine," I said. "I'm just not used to them any more."

"To be honest, I'm not even meant to be smoking... I'm not really allowed to smoke these things. I mean, Jane knows we take them. But don't tell her we smoke them, OK? Though to be honest, she probably knows. I doubt there's anything she doesn't know about us."

Andrea looked at me closely, taking a drag, before turning to the window. Her brown hair was tied up out of the way. She had smooth, clear skin and she was slim. But her arms were strong, really defined. She was fit. This army was not an underfed one, probably not even on rations. "I'm always glad I get the computer ones as it means I get to hide away up here for a bit on the pretence of training you up."

"You don't think I need training up?"

"Not on computers."

"Why not?"

"I've seen your file."

"My file? What file?"

"Well, not exactly seen it. More like, Jane gave me excerpts from it when she put you in my squad. All files travel in the convoys to the enclaves. Nothing serious. It was with you when we picked you up."

That file. "I was part of a data collection team for—"

"Google. Yeah." Andrea laughed and shook her head. "Which in reality meant you were a hacker, right?"

"Ah, more data analysis. All the information we got was obtained through legal—"

"Loopholes, PRISM." She smiled.

"You hate me, don't you?"

Andrea laughed again.

I smiled, genuinely this time.

"Yeah, well, now's the time to make up for all our errors before." And Andrea took another drag of her cigarette. "What happened to your face?"

"Ah." Instinctively my hands went straight up to my face. The swelling had come down a lot both in my hand and on my face but I couldn't cover the heavy bruising and the split skin around my eye and forehead.

"You don't have to be embarrassed. I wasn't trying to chat you up or anything—"

"No, I didn't think you were—"

"I mean, it's just some swelling. I can see it might have been worse—"

"I didn't think it was that bad any more—"

"No, it's just in the daylight I can see it. Just wondered what happened."

"I got into a fight that's all."

"A fight?"

"I was attacked, on the way to the Cathedral yesterday."

"By men?"

97

"Yes. But it's nothing serious. It doesn't hurt. It's not a hindrance. My eyesight isn't affected."

Andrea clicked her tongue against her jaw. "Another reminder that you made the right choice, huh? They don't hurt though, right?"

"It looks worse than it feels."

She jabbed her hand with the cigarette at me. "What about your fingers?"

"Ah, this." I'd pulled the bandages off before we left the Cathedral but the hand was still red and a bit swollen. "This is nothing, just a bit of soreness."

That seemed to pacify her and she got back to her cigarette. "Your file said you were an only child."

"Yes, I am." I dropped the hand and, out of sight, tried to straighten out the fingers. The pain was sharp.

"Do you miss them?"

"Who?" I gently moved my fingers back and forth, trying to warm them up with movement, gain some flexibility, some strength in them.

"Your parents."

"Um, yes. Yes, of course I do. I try not to think about them too much though."

"Why?"

"Well, it won't bring them back."

Andrea took another drag and thought about it, looking at me as she breathed in the nicotine and exhaled it out. "Did you keep anything?"

"From my house? No. Nothing. I don't think it's healthy."

Andrea pulled up the sleeve of her sweater and on her wrist was a tiny conch shell hanging on a thread of black string. "My mum found it walking along a beach a few years ago, before The Fall. She picked it up, cleaned it and gave it to me. 'I know how you love shells, darling.' I mean, I don't.

I haven't collected shells since I was a kid but still my mum kept picking me up a shell from beaches she walked on. I thought she was an idiot, a pain. But that's mums for you." She looked at her shell then pulled the sleeve down and leant back against the wall.

I had made a mistake. Damn. I shifted my feet a little, awkwardly. "Do you miss her?" I asked.

"She's not dead! They're in the secure areas – my parents, my brothers…"

My eyes widened.

"Oh, sorry," she said.

"But… Why… How did you get them out of the controlled areas?"

Andrea raised her eyebrows. "Obedience doesn't save you, Laura. I'm sorry you lost your parents. It's a shame you didn't keep anything. It's important not to harden your heart, you know. I know it's difficult."

I said nothing.

Andrea sat, back against the wall, watching me. "It gets easier."

I nodded, giving away nothing more.

She narrowed her eyes then widened them and smiled again. "You have questions."

I laughed a little – the nerves. "It's just… The electricity. You have it everywhere. Your lights, this computer…" I pointed at the laptop that was on the desk next to me – my way into the elite unit. "We had no electricity in the block. Can't they trace you, you know, harvesting the power like this?"

"You have been out the loop a while." She leant forward. "We took control of the electricity network a while ago. Basic guerrilla warfare – prioritise what you need and target your effort. You don't need numbers for a revolution. Target the key utilities, bring them under your control. Taking control of the power network is a double blow – it benefits us and it takes the State down further."

"The State didn't try and take it back?"

"They tried. We had a few Chinooks overhead for a while, until we pinned them back. It was quite a bitter fight actually, though Jane says the State gave up quite quickly. They chose to ring-fence themselves in the controlled areas instead, to focus their strengths and efforts on securing the enclaves and just let the rest of the country go."

"They retreated?!"

The sharp shock in my voice surprised me as much as Andrea. I sat back in my seat, a little embarrassed.

"Of course. Look at this base. It's a fixed base. You think we'd have a fixed base if you weren't in a secured area – our secured area?"

"So where are their areas?"

Andrea leant back. "We have them pretty landlocked now. Central, Midlands... Up to Manchester. But they do have access to the sea in the east. Though nothing to the west, thank God."

I nodded slowly, as if I was weighing it all up, but my mind was racing. Shit. RAZR had almost taken over the whole island. Jesus. They were close.

"You seem surprised." Andrea's eyes were quizzical.

"No, it's great. This is great. It's just that last time I saw you, heard anything about RAZR, was the attack on London. And that didn't... It didn't seem..."

"It didn't seem like we won."

"Yeah."

Andrea took a drag. "Yeah, we took a hit. We over-reached. We were advancing so quickly and we just thought... Well, we've learnt a lesson. They were divisive, those attacks, but they brought a lot of people on to our side.

Only, well, they were expensive, in terms of casualties. We lost a lot of women."

She sank back into a slouch, gazing out through the window, out into the distance. Lost in thought.

I let the silence hang, wondering what else might be revealed.

She sighed again. And then suddenly perked up. "Jane changed strategy after that."

"To what?"

Andrea reached her arms out. "To this. We take control of pivotal targets and strangle the life out of the State."

"So you've never actually seen these enclaves?" I asked.

She shook her head. "Jane doesn't want to attack them. They're well defended and getting better all the time. There was some debate about attacking them before they became fully developed but Jane didn't like that, thought it was too much of a trap. She's gone for the suffocation option."

"To cut their supply lines – of women and of energy."

"Yes. She's playing a long game."

"So you've never actually seen them."

"And?" She shrugged.

"Well, you might have got this all wrong. The enclaves might be good places. The women... We might be safe there."

Andrea looked at me warily. "You don't believe Jane?"

"Of course I do." I dropped my head and turned towards the computer on the desk. It was a decent model and in pretty good condition. I picked up the keyboard, turned it upside down and shook it. Dust and debris fell from the gaps in between the keys. I put it down, grabbed the edge of my sweater and wiped my sleeve back and forth over the desk till all visible dust was gone.

I replaced the keyboard in front of me and turned on the computer.

I looked across at Andrea, about to ask something but she was just watching me wide-eyed. "Feel better?"

"Sorry," I said. "Old habits. I like to keep everything clean." She nodded.

"So this is where I come in, isn't it? You want me to hack," I said. "That's why I'm useful to you. You want me to hack into their servers, the State's, and monitor what they're doing."

Andrea blew out a stream of smoke, a glint in her eye. "I'd like to think the State was that stupid, but no. Well, sometimes. But we did a lot of damage to them during The Fall. D-dossing, corrupting data... A lot." Andrea nodded, emphasising the point. "A lot. But they wised up and took most of their workstations offline. It was high risk for them, to keep key data stored centrally and offline. Forced them to revert to convoys and physical transfer but, well, needs must."

I thought about it. My forehead furrowed up. So how was I... Oh. "I'm going to hack the local servers actually in their buildings, aren't I?" I said. "You, the army... We're going to attack their buildings just so I can log in and corrupt the data directly."

Andrea took another drag, eyes still sparkling. "Well, not just for you. We do have other reasons for attacking the State. But yes, in RAZR our computer geniuses are also soldiers." She turned to gaze out the window. "Oh look, they're out training again."

I got up and walked over to the window, following Andrea's gaze. Down below the army trained on the playing fields.

A flow of black-suited women were pouring out from the school, spreading out over the field, running and jumping as they moved out. These women were incredibly agile. They spread out into units across the field, falling straight into rhythm, into coordinated training circuits.

"That's what they're training for, another one. Another raid." Andrea was looking on anxiously. "That group over there, the ones jumping over the walls, that's our brigade."

I recognised a face. "That one over there." I pointed at the woman leading the drills. "That stocky one. She has a knife wound in her arm."

"Helen. What about her?"

"She doesn't like me."

Andrea took another drag. "She doesn't like anyone. She completely revolves around Jane. I mean, we all do. I'd take a bullet for her, don't get me wrong."

"For her?" I said, pointing at Helen.

"What? God no! For Jane. We're all totally pro-Jane, but Helen. Actually, would I take a bullet for Helen? Yes. Yes, I would because she would do the same for me, without question, but she's tough to get along with."

"Fanatical."

"Yeah, really." She nodded, taking another drag. "Jane's her alpha and omega. It's a bit fucking intense, but then I guess we are living through intense times. Helen is my equivalent. She leads the other elite squad in the field. Hers are all the firearms and explosives experts. Mine, we're the all-rounders. Nimble on the feet as well as in the mind."

I watched them from the window. I envied their permission to run free, to feel adrenalin. How much I wanted to run, despite the lump in my leg and the hidden damage to my stomach.

"Does Jane do the drills too?" I asked.

"Used to. Not so much now. She trains by herself first thing in the morning and last thing at night. She trains when there's no one else around. But she watches the drills, most of the time. I can't see her though."

Neither could I.

"But she'll be out there soon enough," Andrea said. "I expect she's working on the raids. Actually, I don't know what the hell she works on. But whatever she does, it works. I better show you what you've already been allocated in the raid."

Andrea went to take another drag of her cigarette but it had gone out. She sighed, chucked it out the window and walked over to the computer. "So before you collected data – data on me, data on my friends, data on your friends…"

I sat back down on the chair.

"… my family, your family. And you passed it on, upwards, to the intelligence agencies…" Andrea smiled at me.

I smiled.

She nudged me on my shoulder. "Anyway, back then you might have thought it inconsequential but at the start, when The Fall happened, they used that data to snatch some of us before the announcement came."

I went to say something, to protest. But then closed my mouth.

"What were you going to say?"

I took a deep sigh. "I was going to say that I was just a cog in a wheel, but I know history has left a pretty bloody trail of those who have said something similar."

"All actions have consequences." Andrea leant over me to flick the computer on. "Now's the time to start making amends."

The computer screen came to life, to reveal a desktop covered in files and folders. Andrea starting clicking on them. "In the raid, the next one we're planning, there's a data centre. They'll have a server and we're thinking you can get on to their network. Jane, Helen, me – we're the assault team that's going to get you into the centre and you're going to extract the data. The supplies are at the front of the building, that's where the main assault is taking place. Shauna is leading that. But we're going in at the back."

Images of a building flashed up on the screen – a depot. Schematics. Blueprints. Surveillance photos. Andrea clicked through them – a three-storey building, what looked like an old large retail unit surrounded by a car park, an entrance gate that came off from a roundabout. But now all fully militarised.

Then video surveillance clips. Night vision. How on earth did RAZR get so close to the unit to film them? God, the State was rocking on its heels.

"What we're going in to get is up on the top floor of the main building." Andrea pointed to the screen, her finger touching it as she zoned in on a point. Her face never left the screen, concentrating on the images that flashed up on auto-update. "Alex is leading the second assault here. We're coming in here."

She was fixated by the mission. Friendly but fanatical too. Mental note.

"Up here are the offices. Manned on rotation. Jane and I will get you in. You need to get the information out." Andrea looked at me. "We won't leave you there. We will guard you until it is done."

"What's the information I'm getting?"

"Enclaves. The new population of enclaves being built in the east. One of which is the one we think you were being transferred to." Andrea went on. "It's not just the data we're after but also the supplies on this base. This cell has to be self-sufficient rather than reliant on supplies from our secure areas in the west and north. Double impact again – we disrupt their supplies and get ours."

I looked back at the screen. It was definitely an old out-of-centre superstore. Any branding had long since disappeared. And in this post-apocalyptic landscape, all the shells of mass consumerism looked the same.

I wondered where those rich people were now, the ones who had sat on the boards of those wealthy corporations. I'd like to think they were dead, that they'd been offered no protection, but who was I kidding? They probably had enough money and connections to secure their lives.

"What are you thinking?" Andrea asked.

I jumped, just a little, not realising I had wandered off.

"Ah, just..." I sighed. "I hope the rich didn't make it. I know their millions are now worthless but I hope there's been more retribution than that."

Andrea smiled at me. "Well, even if they got to the enclaves, they obviously aren't safe there now, are they? It's amazing how many injustices can be revenged once the armour of riches can no longer be worn."

Andrea stood up straight. "You know how to get into these systems, right? I mean, look, it isn't my speciality. My focus is to get you in there, keep you safe and get out alive. Just... This is a big one, right? So tell me it won't be wasted."

"I won't let you down, I promise."

"Good."

I watched her closely, trying to read her face. But it was blank. The questions had stopped. "What?" she asked.

"But I don't know Jane, or understand how she works."

"Don't worry. She didn't risk herself attacking that convoy just to get you killed on the first raid."

"Why does she risk herself in these raids? She's so critical. She should be in the secure areas."

Andrea raised her eyebrows then broke into a smile. "You try telling Jane that. Actually, don't."

CHAPTER FOURTEEN
The Night

The women slept. All around me in the dormitory were the steadily breathing bodies of women who'd slipped into slumber.

The room was mostly in shadow but I'd been awake for so long that my eyes had adjusted to the faint light flooding in from the window above me.

I lay still and tried to focus my mind on positive memories, but it kept wandering. I thought about my parents. I thought about my mother. I remember her smiling. I can't remember who had said what but I could see her sitting in her favourite red armchair in the living room, laughing.

I couldn't remember my father laughing, though. I couldn't remember him ever laughing. He was a strange man. Always serious. So introverted. I was never sure what went through his head. He never spoke much.

I don't remember much about my childhood, just fragments. But my earliest memory was of my father. Strange that. We were sitting in front of the television. I can't remember the sofa, the wallpaper or anything like that. I just remember I was sitting next to him, my feet barely reaching the edge of the sofa cushion.

He was watching a football match. I know nothing about football, I couldn't even tell you who was playing. But I wanted to be involved, to show an interest in something my father cared about.

The match was goalless, frenetic but goalless. I started cheering one of the teams, not realising that my father was actually supporting the other. It went well at first. I'd cheer my team. He'd cheer his team. My team would have a few shots at goal. You know, 'ooh, a bit close'. Then his team would have a go. And we laughed. We giggled. And I felt the sun finally shining on me.

But then, towards the end, his team scored. One goal, right at the end. The match finished one-nil. And my father got right up in my face. "One-nil, one-nil, one-nil!" he sang, adding "Sucker!" at me. He was gloating and cocky.

Then he switched off the TV and left the room.

And the sun was gone.

I still don't understand why it was important for him to be right, to beat me. I was only five.

What we remember and what we forget... All the rest of my memories, I don't know if I can believe any of them any more. I can't be sure if they actually happened or whether my brain is creating false memory. And I have no one to ask any more, no one to verify whether what I remember is true or not. Maybe it doesn't matter. Maybe I should just believe what I need to believe and that will get me through.

But I remember having plans, dreams, before The Fall. I remember thinking I would make it to old age. I thought I'd see the world. I doubt that will happen now.

"Don't hang on to idealised memories of your past."

That's what my boss said to me when he gave me the file. "That's the path to suicide. Don't indulge it."

I didn't open the file there and then. I knew what was in it anyway.

But that moment, in my boss's office, was no trick of my mind. I remember him calmly outlining what I had to do while, outside, the world was turning upside down.

Human nature in a crisis, in chaos, is harder to predict than you might think. You make allowances for riots, religious fervour, mass suicides, looting, hysteria, emergency crews abandoning their posts, security service personnel taking arms up against the State... But not all of that comes at once, not straight away.

Defeat overseas had been *de facto* for some months by this time. When large numbers of brigades were quarantined because of the virus, particularly those from North Africa, there were problems. Protests and petitions. But even stopping the boys from coming home didn't bring the system down.

Nor did the announcement of emergency measures.

Nor did the steady imposition of curfews and the increased frequency of energy blackouts.

When the supplies started to run out, that's when the walls started to crumble.

And that was the day I was called into the room.

That delay, the bizarre few weeks when people still went to work, still went on with their lives, despite the unfolding crisis, bought us time.

Unfortunately, it also bought time for those planning against us.

The window by my head wasn't completely sealed. A cold draught was coming through the bottom of the wooden frame, chilling the crown of my head. I looked up and out. What would it be like to be outside at night again?

I scanned the mattresses. The women were definitely asleep. No guards inside the room, although I suspected there'd be some outside.

The woman next to me snorted, snored a bit and rolled back on to her side. I looked up at the ceiling, up into the nothingness. Chinooks. Andrea had mentioned Chinooks. There hadn't been any aircraft in the skies since the Battle for London. Well, I hadn't seen any. So, that meant... What did that mean? Were the overseas quarantines now lifted? Was the doctor right, had the virus passed? Was the State close to being fully operational?

And if they were now back looking for the domestic terrorists that meant... That meant that flights overhead could be surveillance from the State.

I sat up. And then carefully, slowly, I got to my feet.

The window frame was old, meaning it might creak if I pushed it open in a rush. I pushed hard against the glass in the frame, giving it the stability it needed, then gently but deliberately pushed it up.

The breeze came in quicker than I had thought it would. I darted through the open window and, as my feet touched the ground on the other side, I closed the window behind me.

It was cold but I felt a flush of heat from the adrenalin rush.

And a pull from my bruised stomach.

The muddy fields stretched out ahead of me, the trees that surrounded them blacker than the night sky above me. The breeze shook through their leaves, across the grass and washed up over my skin.

The shiver, the delight... To feel cool air on the skin again. And to hear the still of the night. We had let go of so much of what it was to be human just to survive.

Underfoot was gravel. I looked down. I looked up. No sign

of any guards but they had to be out there, for sure. I scanned the walls of the school and the edge of the woods. Nothing.

I tiptoed across the gravel and on towards the edge of the field, to the woods.

Going to the woods was risky – a snapped twig or rustle of dead leaves underfoot would give me away but I was desperate to test the limits.

I stepped off the gravel onto the stone path, then headed quickly towards the mud.

The mud underfoot was damp. It had rained recently but not today.

I pressed my feet down into the ground. I could feel each crumpled blade of grass between my toes as my feet sank, just a little, into the earth. I was cold but I was happy.

I stood there for a moment, shivering, wiggling my toes. I exhaled, my breath forming in sheer clouds from my lips. I looked up at the night sky. I couldn't make out any star or cloud. No moon either. Just darkness.

I looked left, looked right, but I couldn't see any soldiers, any sign of a guarded perimeter. Where were they? Back up at the main road?

I headed to the woods, towards the first trees I'd seen with leaves in years.

The shadows of the woods were freezing. I looked around. Nothing.

And then I looked up. The sky was so empty, so dark.

My eyes flitted back and forth across the sky but still nothing.

My neck hurt. I took a deep sigh and looked back again across the field and to the school. It was silent.

Could I run? It crossed my mind, as I stood there on the dirt, to risk it. But what would I run to? I had no idea where I was. And I had to stay.

A few metres inside the woods were the remains of a dying oak. I wanted to touch a tree. I wanted to feel in touch with nature again. I walked over. I stood in front of it for just a moment, my eyes running over the dry, scaly bark, following its myriad lines. Then I lifted my hand slowly and then gently touched the tree.

My fingertips first. Then I pressed my palm down.

Its thick trunk was rough. Some of the bark flaked off in my hand and my fingers traced the grooves of the fragments. I dropped the pieces to the ground and touched the exposed, pale splintered trunk. Pollution can be incredibly beautiful.

And then I leant in, leant onto the trunk, let the tree take my weight.

I took a moment and closed my eyes.

I felt calm. At peace.

I felt free.

I pushed myself upright again – I had a reason to be here. I opened my eyes and looked up at the sky.

I could now see the odd twinkling star. The cloud cover had broken to reveal the universe still growing and dying, indifferent to our troubles on this tiny rock.

I scoured the sky for tell-tale signs of vapour trails, of moving lights but I couldn't—

"You don't need to go looking for trouble in this world, it will find you."

I snapped my head around as fast as my heart leapt into my throat.

There she was, only a few metres from me.

She had got close.

My eyes widened. "Oh, sorry, ah, I just, ah… haven't been allowed outdoors in a long time, even just to touch a tree, or feel mud."

Jane laughed, not softly but quietly.

Over her shoulder I could make out a couple of patrol guards heading towards us.

I stood rigid. It was chilly but there she was in her vest and trousers, seemingly impervious to the elements.

She didn't take her eyes off me.

"You've been locked up a while," she said.

"Yesterday was my first day outside my block."

Jane nodded, once. "Then this must be paradise for you."

We looked at each other. Neither smiling.

My heart was racing.

"Can't sleep?" she asked.

I managed to croak out "Monsters" from my dry throat. I laughed nervously.

Jane didn't laugh.

"I was just curious, you know, I was just…" And then I tailed off.

"That's good," Jane said. "I don't judge a lack of knowledge – I judge a lack of curiosity." Jane looked at me closely. "You have nothing to fear from me."

My skin had become like ice and I rubbed my hands along the top of my arms, avoiding her gaze.

The two women arrived. They looked alike. Sisters? One of them gave something to Jane. It was a handgun.

It was my gun.

Shit, it was my gun.

My mouth fell open but nothing came out.

Jane turned it in her hands. "It's a good gun."

She looked at me. But nothing came out of my mouth. Nothing.

My mind was blank.

Jane studied me, closely. "It makes sense, to have a weapon with you. But there's no need to carry a gun with you here, Laura. You are safe here."

113

Her face seemed calm, unthreatening, but there was ice behind her eyes.

She turned to head back towards the school. "Don't wander too far, otherwise the monsters will get you," she said. And then she walked across the field towards the buildings, taking my gun with her.

The two women in black boots, full black jackets and assault rifles remained where she had stood, watching me.

I looked back up at the sky.

She knew my name.

CHAPTER FIFTEEN
The Army

In front of us were rows and rows of AK-47s. Hundreds of them. Packed in so tightly I couldn't see a spare slot on any of the racks.

Andrea and I were in the munitions room. At the end of the room some of the women who'd been in my convoy and others from the army were sorting out new uniforms. New black shirts to replace the old.

"Do you know what these are?" Andrea nodded towards the racks.

"No," I lied, giving Andrea my full attention.

"These are AK-47s. We use them because they're cheap, they're light and they're impossible to break. Any idiot can learn to work an AK. You've only got to look at America to see that. Have you held one before?"

"Helen had a different gun."

Andrea rolled her eyes. "She picked it up in a raid. She likes to keep it close to her. Anyway, you can use one of these."

I nodded. "Where did you get all of these? Isn't it hard for you to get weapons? Did you make them?"

"What?" Andrea laughed. "Fuck, no. Why waste time and resources making guns when you can just buy them dirt cheap from the Russians?" She picked up a rifle and pushed it into my hands. "The Russians will trade anything for a case load of vodka. Their whole army is rogue. Jesus, they'd give you a submarine for one more bottle of the stuff."

"Why didn't you get a submarine?" I asked, as she picked up another for herself.

"Their submarines ain't exactly reliable." Andrea pulled out the case of the rifle in her hand. "Now, this is the case."

And so I followed Andrea's guide to the disassembly and reassembly of an AK. Really, it's simple. You could teach a child to do it. Well, obviously there are people in the world who do. No wonder it had come to this.

I fumbled where I needed to, despite it being so easy. It was impossible to ignore Andrea's deft handling though. She had evidently been a soldier for a while. The clicks and clacks of her reassembly were almost rhythmic.

Then I too was suited and booted in black. Andrea found it funny that I wanted to change in private. I made my excuses, putting it down to shyness.

I caught sight of my reflection in the pane of glass in the door on the way out. I hadn't seen my hair short, not since Abby cut it. It's strange running your fingers through your hair only for it to suddenly stop when you're so used to it continuing on. Short hair, black boots and a vest top. I was part of RAZR now.

I turned away from my reflection. A transformation can shake you.

"I know it's not ideal, the raid being tonight, but show

them what you can do." Andrea was leading me out of the ammunition room, through the corridors, to the back of the school. Out to the playing fields. "They just want to make sure the running alone won't kill you."

Andrea laughed. I touched the tough ball of bruised tissue in my stomach. I had to make the grade.

"What did she say to you?" I asked.

"Who? Jane? Nothing really. So these rooms here are for surveillance." And Andrea pointed into a few of the rooms as we passed by, rooms where women sat at wire taps and computers. In another, a group of women were hunched over printouts.

"And this one here—" Andrea nodded her head towards the next room where a row of women were sitting in front of computer terminals. "I don't know what they do in there, to be honest."

"Andrea, you're changing the subject." But she didn't reply as she walked on. So I added, "I suppose she told you about my gun."

"She did, yeah." Andrea looked at me. "You should've told me."

"Sorry."

Andrea stopped me, letting two women pass by before she began talking again. "You can't keep secrets here, Laura. It doesn't work. It just doesn't. We're not here to hurt you. You have to trust us."

I nodded. "OK."

"I know why you're scared but don't ever try to wrong-foot Jane, not ever. Trust me on this. I'm here to help you."

I nodded.

Helen was standing in front of the large group that had been brought together to be drilled into line for the assault.

"My name is Helen." She straightened up as she said her own name. "The purpose of these exercises is to sharpen up your agility, increase your heart rate and blow out the cobwebs."

Most of the others had been here for a while. I recognised a handful of the others from my convoy, one of them was Gauiri. She was completely focused on Helen. Plus, there was the blonde, and the one who wore the stripy top. They all stood, arms folded, focused on Helen.

"High knees all the way to the trees and back," said Helen, pointing to the trees at the far end of the field.

And so we started off.

The ball of damaged tissue deep in the pit of my stomach hurt. It didn't like the movement. I bit down on my lip and continued. But the high knees were killing me. I made it to the trees just about in line with everyone else, but there was no way my stomach and my leg could take any more. The way back to Helen and Andrea became impossible, my knees barely making it horizontal. All I could do was jog.

The others got back while I was still only halfway across the field. I stopped. They were all looking at me. I caught Andrea's eyes. Shit. I was in trouble.

I jogged slowly back.

I was greeted with momentary silence.

I looked at Andrea. She looked away.

Helen walked up to me, her gaze boring deep into mine. She stood right in front of me, as close as possible. I didn't move. I didn't avert my gaze.

She lifted up my top. I didn't look down. I just kept my eyes on everyone else as they stared at the bowling ball I'd been nursing.

Helen looked at Andrea. "She'll jeopardise us all."

"I won't," I said. "I'm fine."

"We don't have a choice," Andrea said to Helen. "She's on the raid. She made it to the trees. That's good enough for me."

"I'm not interested in your territorial bullshit," Helen spat back. "She's a liability. I'm not protecting her."

"Well I am. My squad, my responsibility. Laura is fine. Fuck off with your bullshit aggression."

Helen strode towards Andrea.

Andrea dropped her folded arms and fronted up.

Everyone else took a step back. I took a step forward.

"Don't you fuck with me." Helen was straight up in Andrea's face.

I grabbed Helen's arm but she pushed me away.

"Ladies." All heads snapped round.

And there she was. Hands in pockets, flanked by two guards, walking towards us. "Are we having trouble?" Jane asked.

Her two guards were the same ones who had brought her my gun. The sisters.

Helen turned to Jane, backing away from Andrea. She pointed towards me. "It's this one. She's more injured than she's told us."

Jane looked at my face, then down to my stomach. Reluctantly, I lifted my top again. She stepped forward and touched my skin, gently, tenderly. She pressed against the bruise. It hurt but I didn't wince.

"These are recent." Jane looked at Andrea. "You should have told me."

"She didn't know," I interrupted. Jane looked back at me as I dropped my top. "I didn't tell her."

"What happened?" Jane asked.

"I got into a fight, on the way to the Cathedral."

Jane looked into my eyes, no emotion betrayed.

"A group," I added.

Jane had blue eyes, but incredibly pale. "Of men?"

"Yes."

"And yet you are still here," she said. "Not many lone travellers survive an attack in the City."

"The army arrived. They intervened."

Jane was standing so close. She didn't back out of my personal space at all. "What was the army doing on the streets of London?"

"I don't know."

"Were they there just for you?"

"I don't think so. Why would they be?"

Jane nodded. Once. "Any other secrets?"

I thought about it, about not mentioning it. But it was her eyes, boring deep into me. I took a few steps back then pulled down my trousers and exposed my bite, unwinding the tight bandages that had been covering it.

The gasp around the group was audible.

"It's just a dog bite," I said. "It looks worse than it is."

Helen turned to Jane. "Rabies."

And then the group followed suit. "Rabies... Rabies..."

I caught Andrea's face and she was noticeably paler.

I pulled up my trousers.

"We should dump her," Helen went on. "She's a danger to the group."

The group murmured. I could sense them starting to pull away from me.

But Jane smiled. "Should we now? You haven't got rabies."

Helen was appalled. "How do you know?"

"Because this is Britain, not North Africa," Jane said. "An army of rabid dogs weren't in the bombs that got dropped. And they weren't in the planes and boats that brought whoever was left standing back here. We don't have rabies in this country."

"How can you be sure? You're not a doctor," I snapped. "I was meant to be getting injections at the enclave."

"Indeed," Jane said. "But use your brain, Laura. You're a smart woman. Why would the State tell you you needed vaccinations when you don't need them?"

My head was reeling. I shrugged. "I don't know." I racked my brain. What was Jane's angle? What was her angle? "My womb. Ah, over-protection, over-zealous protection of my womb."

"Tender is the State. Well, that'd be a first," Jane said. "No, they told you you had rabies and that they would treat it as it fosters a misrepresentation in your head that they care. And it fosters a dependency too – you need those vaccinations so you never stray, fearful you could develop rabies. It makes you stay with them, stay linked to the State. It's bullshit. There's nothing wrong with you. I'd bet my life on it. But if it makes you feel better, Anne's got some rabies injections in the medical centre."

I looked at Andrea. She still wasn't looking at me.

I started back towards the school.

"Wait," Jane said.

I turned back to face her.

"Any other secrets, Laura?"

I shook my head. "No more secrets."

Jane kept staring at me. "Then I'll see you on the raid."

"Pull down your trousers," Anne said. "Let me see."

I did as instructed. In truth, I hadn't looked closely at the damage since the filtration centre. Even on the playing fields I hadn't looked down.

We were in the gym – a beautifully empty high-ceilinged building on the perimeter of the school. Only it was now the medical centre. Anne had organised the space with a military neatness, with rows of empty beds filling the room. On the wooden floor under the beds, the old painted netball court lines could still be made out.

I watched Anne's face as she inspected my wound. She didn't give much away. "It's nasty but you'll live. We'll put you on a series of injections, just in case."

"Who's we?" I asked.

Anne's laugh bounced off the walls. She was nothing like her sister. "Well, one day I'll have a team."

Anne turned to her cabinet and I looked down at my leg. My thigh wasn't good. It was a bloody, dark red and the bite marks had turned black.

As soon as Anne turned back to me she slipped the needle in her hand straight into my thigh.

I gasped.

Anne laughed again. "You'll have to get used to this, I'm afraid. You'll be getting more over the next month."

"I haven't got rabies, have I?"

"No. Just really nasty bruising. If you had rabies you'd be dead by now. But we'll do the course, just to be sure. We've got the drugs so we might as well use them. Antibiotics are the bigger problem. Antibiotics are useless now so be grateful you haven't got an infection."

Anne withdrew the needle and returned to her desk. "I don't know how you're going to manage tonight though."

"Adrenalin," I said.

Anne looked back at me, smiling. "Well, you're braver than me. Have you ever been in a battle before?"

I shook my head.

"Oh," said Anne. "Well, I'm sure you'll be fine."

CHAPTER SIXTEEN
The Calm

It was dark. The sixty of us assigned to tonight's raid had left the school, or rather the camp, some time before. Like the others, I was dressed all in black with thick boots. And now I too was cradling my own assault rifle.

There were five trucks in the convoy, a squadron in each. Jane was in the front truck with Helen's unit. I sat with Andrea and her unit, my allocated unit. I say my unit but Andrea had barely said a word to me since the field.

I could feel the sweat in my palms, under my arms, on my forehead. I tried to focus on the floor of the truck, hoping it would calm the twists in my stomach.

The rifle felt awkward in my hands. It was so light. So, so light. I looked down at it. It felt like plastic, tacky to the touch. It didn't feel heavy enough to kill. I missed my gun.

"Hey, Laura." I looked up to see a broad-shouldered blonde on the bench on the other side smiling at me. "You'll never get to heaven with an AK-47."

Her cohorts laughed at the joke, especially the slim one

next to her. Cropped dark hair, bright blue eyes and cheek-bones sharper than any blade.

I hung my head down again.

"Back in your box, Mandy." Andrea opposite me brought the laughter down.

I looked up at Andrea. She held my gaze briefly before looking away again.

"I'm only teasing," Mandy said to her before turning to me. "I'm trying to break the tension. You look white."

"I'm not scared," I said.

Mandy nodded. "Sure. You'll be fine."

"I'm Alex, by the way." The brunette with the cheekbones next to her waved at me.

I brushed off the drops of sweat from the top of my lip.

"You don't need to worry," Mandy said. "I'm sure you've been through plenty enough already. I'm sure there's nothing in a battle that will scare you."

I nodded, saying nothing. Avoiding eye contact.

"So," Mandy said. "What's been the worst?"

I looked at her. I didn't understand.

I glanced across at Andrea but she gave me nothing.

Mandy tried again. "What's the most terrifying thing that's ever happened to you, before this?" Mandy seemed to have found in me a new toy to play with. "Come on."

I shook my head, catching sight of the R tattoo, like Andrea's, that Mandy had at the top of her arm. Only hers looked carved in, as if by a razor.

"That's not gonna cut any fucking ice with me." The truck laughed as my best attempt to hide away crashed into Mandy's irrepressibility. "Come on. What have you got?"

I shook my head again. "My life really has been pretty dull."

The truck booed and laughed. I even had an empty

magazine thrown in my direction along with shouts of "try again" and "bullshit".

Andrea leant forward. "It's easier if you just play along."

A brief jump as the truck sped over a bump. The convulsion of movement swept through the truck but still they kept their attention on me.

I took a deep sigh.

"Well, it's not particularly terrifying," I said, "probably not to you. It's a bit funny, I guess but, ah, the worst thing was when I first saw a dead body."

I nodded, but they said nothing, expecting me to continue.

I looked out the back of the van and sighed again. "My gran had died. She had been living with us. I don't know why. I don't know if it was because she had no money or because the cancer had made her so weak. I was only about twelve so I've no idea. But she was living with us, we had a big house at the time and my gran stayed in the front room so she didn't have to climb the stairs."

I paused, staring into the distance.

"She died and my mother wouldn't let me see her afterwards. They kept the door to the front room shut. I had to sit in the kitchen when the undertakers came to take her away. They were all speaking so quietly – my parents, the undertakers. But I could hear my mother telling them I wasn't to see her as they carried her out.

"The rest of the day I couldn't even go into the room, even though they'd taken her away. I was just too terrified. I didn't even want to touch her things or help my mother with her clothes. It was if they'd all become tainted."

The truck was silent. I was lost to my memory. "I started panicking about being left in the house when my parents wanted to go to the undertakers so I tagged along. But when we got there I wasn't allowed into the office to discuss, I don't know, procedures, I guess. Or arrangements. I had to sit outside on this really old wooden bench in the hall. It was wobbly and it hurt my back. I got bored just waiting there so I went for a wander. I found some stairs at the end of the hall and I went down them."

Another wave went through the bodies as we sped over another bump. No noise in the truck except for me. "I pushed open the large wooden door at the bottom. It was a very large door, I remember that. I don't know why I kept going but I did. I pushed open the door and, God, it was so cold on the other side. A small, stone room. The walls were just uncovered bricks. No heating, no paint, no furniture. Just a dark, stone cold room. And there, on the other side of the room, was a wooden box. The wooden box."

I looked up. Realised everyone was staring at me. "Sorry, this is boring to you." My cheeks started flushing.

"Go on," Alex said.

"Well, I let the door go. It must have been on a spring as it just slipped out of my hand and slammed shut. I didn't think anything of it at first. I wanted to see what was in the box. I don't know why because it was so obvious. But I did. I walked over and the box, the coffin, was open. And there she was. It was her.

"But they hadn't touched her. They hadn't done her make-up or dressed her. She was still in her nightie and seemed to have been just flung into this box. Her eyes were closed but her mouth had fallen open. Her cheeks were hollowed out and she was grey. Her skin was just this really dark grey and it had shrunk into her skull. And she smelt. I could smell the urine. They hadn't cleaned her. I touched her. She was dead cold. Freezing. Not even ice is that cold. Shivers shot through my hand, up my arm and through my own body. I felt as if I was being possessed.

"I freaked out. I started screaming and screaming and screaming. I ran to the door but it had locked itself and I couldn't get out. I screamed and screamed, banging on the door. But they didn't hear me. The cold in the room... I was only wearing a thin dress and I was freezing. I screamed so much that I started crying. I was giving myself a fever. My head heated up and my tears were burning. I screamed for an eternity until eventually someone heard me and they unlocked the door and let me out."

I'd finished my story but I'd whipped myself into such a state that I was on the edge of the bench. I looked at the women and then laughed in awkward embarrassment. They sat in silence. I slid back until I was up against the side of the truck. "I guess it's kind of funny when you think about it."

I looked back at the floor.

Silence in the truck.

Then. "Well," said Mandy. "War is a shit load easier than that."

And the whole truck burst into laughter.

I smiled and blushed.

I looked up smiling, and caught Andrea looking at me intensely.

I bit my lip but thought, no, I should keep reaching out. Make alliances. "What about you?" I asked Mandy.

"I used to swim with sharks," she said. "Great Whites. Hungry ones too. I was a conservationist diver."

"Any tourist could go cage diving," I said, a little cocky.

"Who said anything about a cage?" Mandy grinned. Then she lifted up her top and there, slashed across her stomach, the scars from a giant shark bite.

My jaw fell open.

Mandy dropped her top. "You'll be fine, L. Just remember, it's harder to kill people when they're looking straight at you. Always shoot from behind."

"She'll be fine," Andrea said, then turning to me, "You may even take to it."

"I doubt it."

Andrea smiled. "You'd be surprised by the monsters within us."

Suddenly the radio unit at the front of the truck crackled into life. "Up ahead. All pull over. I have to speak to you there."

Her voice was unmistakable. And it also gave me an opportunity to dig a bit more.

"Why is Jane is in the front convoy?" I asked. "Isn't she over-exposed?"

The truck became noticeably quieter.

"Shouldn't she be more protected?" I continued.

I looked at Mandy, and she duly replied, "Would you follow a leader who placed her safety above yours?"

CHAPTER SEVENTEEN
The Speech

The truck pulled up and we filed out.

I had no idea where we were and could see very little in the darkness. I think the convoy had pulled up alongside a large field. The terrain certainly looked wild and overgrown. It had been a while since any people had been here.

Out of the trucks the army in black filed out, only the brief reflections of moonlight bouncing off their skin. We walked out into the field, the tall grass rustling against our trousers, and came together in a huddle only a few metres away from the trucks.

I stood at the back, observing, thinking, trying to get my bearings. To my right, not that far away, I could see the glistening of water, not flowing but ebbing gently. Was that the Thames? A lake, maybe? No, it was a river. I could make out a riverbank on the other side.

Jane strode through to the middle of the group and jumped up onto a plinth of some kind. The statue that had probably stood there before was now long gone. What anyone would want with a statue, I don't know. These are strange times. Maybe it'd been valuable, worth stealing. Or maybe it'd been one of the few pieces that the Heritage Arts Task Force had managed to save before—

Wait.

I knew where we were.

River, plaque, field… This was Runnymede. Jane was on the memorial plaque for the Magna Carta.

Then I realised I was the only one not paying attention. Around me each woman was completely focused on their leader. Even Mandy was in reverential silence.

Jane looked out over her army, then spoke. "What we are going to do, what I have asked you to do tonight, is another step towards our goal of replacing this violent repressive State that was not built in our name."

She was still in just her vest, seemingly oblivious to the chill in the air. There was no shuffling in the group. They all stood silently. They were all listening.

"We've come to free our world from tyranny, not to replace it. We are freedom fighters, not terrorists. We do not dance on the graves of those who seek to destroy us. Instead we celebrate the emancipation of those who have been enslaved.

"We go with one focus only – to liberate. But we will cut down all those who seek to stop us. And we will do so ruthlessly, without regret, without sorrow."

Jane's voice was strong and clear. "Our enemies have chosen to fight us. They have chosen the path of rape, murder and violence. They will pay for those choices. But never forget this is our country they've hijacked and this is our heritage they've perverted.

"We follow in the footsteps of millions who have fought and died for freedom in this country. We are the inheritors of Boudicca, Magna Carta, of Cromwell, of Pankhurst."

I couldn't look away. Her delivery was flawless. "Do not destroy what we seek to reclaim. Destroy the men, but tread lightly on the ground. There is still good in this country. And behind those bars, many good people cower. Trapped, coerced into slavery, waiting for us to free them. We will meet that expectation.

"And amongst those who guard them are those who harbour doubts, of that I am sure. Give both a chance to live. Treat the defectors with the compassion we treat each other. They will be scared and uncertain."

She paused, looking across every single face that was turned up to her. "Know that future generations will know that the light of liberation was brought to them by you. Act with honour. But for those men who love only violence and murder, they will meet their match today. Do not fear to kill these men. Show magnanimity to those who surrender. But do not hesitate to strike down our enemies.

"Do not kill without purpose. This is not Dresden. This is not Fallujah. We are not men. Judge your enemy. If he is hungry, we will feed him. If he is thirsty, we will share our water. If he so much as touches a hair on your head, we will kill him without mercy."

I could feel my pulse race.

"I want to bring each one of you back alive. But amongst us are some who will not make it through this war. I may not make it through this war. But that does not deter me and it should not deter you either. Freedom is the greatest of causes. If liberalism wants to survive, it needs to get up off its knees and fight. There is no need for sorrow, for fear. Know that we fight together for the rightful destruction of the corruption of our country.

"Our victory is not a question of if, but when. Every resource has been dedicated to this. And we have many resources.

"They are already frightened. They fear us. They have made preparations for us. We will be resisted. But their preparations will not be enough. It will not save them. We are stronger than men in heart and in mind.

"Power isn't willingly given, it's forcefully taken. Irrelevant of race, creed or religion, man has always ruled woman and that control has always been partnered with violence. But all empires must fall. Gather your strength. Our business now is with men."

The women cheered.

I cheered.

We cheered.

Jane leapt down from the plinth and marched towards her truck.

Mandy turned to me, hugged me. "Good luck," she whispered in my ear.

She caught me off guard, but as she released me, I saw all were doing the same, shaking hands, hugging one another. "Good luck… Good luck… Stay strong…" Mandy slapped Helen on her tattoo and the two embraced.

Andrea hugged both of the sisters, who were in Helen's squad, and then turned to hug Helen too. "Stay strong."

Then Andrea turned to me, slapped my arm and hugged me tightly. "Good luck. But we won't need it." As she released me she caught sight of Jane heading back to the trucks. "Come on. We're on."

CHAPTER EIGHTEEN
The Storm

The trucks drove down quiet roads, neither speeding nor crawling. In the silence of the night, any sound would reverberate for miles. The shroud of the darkness could only cover sight. The lack of sound was imperative.

Now we sat in silence in the back of our truck. A tense silence. We were close to our target. We were on the edge.

Mandy was in the zone. Total tunnel focus. She was sitting on the edge of the bench, eyes wide. Alex, the one with the cheekbones, was the same. Andrea was staring constantly out of the back. I could see the rapid rise and fall of her chest.

My gun rested on my lap. I touched it rather than held it, trying to ensure the rising tension didn't show itself in a tight grip. Keep the hands loose, keep them mobile. I flexed out my fingers, slowly, keeping the joints warm, loosening them out.

Then the roads changed. Smooth surfaces replaced with jolts and bumps. A physical wave rolled through our hemmed-in bodies each time the wheels hit a hole but no words were exchanged, nor many glances either.

I couldn't see any of the other trucks out the back. They must have been in front of us. I turned right to try to catch sight of them ahead through the windscreen, but there was nothing to see.

I tried to breathe calmly. My skin was shivering. I couldn't even feel any heat from the engine. But I could taste the dust in the air. Dust coming up from the roads, which was causing my mouth to dry.

Suddenly our truck stopped. No squeak of the brakes, no sharp intake of breath from anyone other than me.

Andrea pushed open the doors and jumped out.

I followed her, as lightly as I could.

As soon as my feet hit the ground, she closed the doors behind me.

The truck moved away as quietly as it had pulled up.

It was as dark outside as it had been inside the truck. And as cold. But I could see enough. We were in suburbia. A residential road. Houses boarded up on either side. And underneath one of the large, moulted oak trees at the side of the road stood Jane and Helen.

Andrea grabbed my arm and we jogged over.

"Hey," I whispered.

Jane nodded at me. Helen glared. I felt my cheeks flush. No words allowed.

Jane and Andrea nodded at each other and we were go.

The trucks had already vanished.

Jane headed up the street at a jog, Helen following in her shadow. I fell into step behind Andrea.

We were running up a street with a slight incline. There was no sound at all. Past the houses to a crossroads.

All I could sense was the lump in my leg. The vaccination was solidifying the muscle around the wound. I could feel the skin stretched tight over it, so taut it felt as if it was about to tear. But I ran on.

Jane didn't stop. Straight over the junction and into the next street.

Low-rises. Offices. Blocks with about a dozen floors. And car parks. All abandoned.

Barely a scratch or sound from our boots on the tarmac.

Jane vaulted over a low wall in front of her and into a car park, barely breaking her step.

Helen and Andrea followed. I did my best to do the same.

Andrea looked back at me, checking I was keeping up.

Rifle slung over my shoulder, I managed it fairly gracefully. My left hand had almost completely healed. But the cement wall brushed my stomach. I could feel the bowling ball inside. Still hard and sore. Anne had wrapped it tight and I refused to allow a wince to cross my face. I pulled my legs up and over and down to the ground on the other side.

From the shadows, Jane pointed up. We were under the building, closing in on the target.

Jane picked up the pace again, but this time faster.

We ran across the underground car park, vaulted over the wall on the other side and out into the next street.

More offices on either side.

We ran straight down the centre of the road. Not on the pavements, not in the shadows. Straight down the middle. The dark sky loomed overhead – we didn't need the shadows to camouflage us. The fear lay on the sides of the roads, on the pavements, where the rubbish collected.

Because rubbish meant noise underfoot.

I pulled my rifle forward, carrying it in my hands like Jane, like Andrea and Helen in front of me.

I could barely see Jane out front. Instead I was running behind Andrea. I could just about make out her ponytail but little else.

One foot in front of the other. Running fast.

Jane followed the painted centre line just about visible on the ground all the way down to the next junction. And that's when she dived behind a wall in front of her.

The three of us shot down to the ground beside her, sheltering behind the wall. Waiting.

Jane shot her hand up.

We were there.

This wall was the external perimeter. On the other side a superstore. Well, what had been a superstore. Now the army depot. Our target.

For a moment I couldn't hear anything but my breathing. My heart was beating so fast. Why could I hear my breath? I never normally breathed this loud. My rifle felt so light, like a toy. My hands were sweating.

I was frozen, back up against the wall, next to Andrea.

It was then I started to hear the noise.

The area behind us – the building and the vast car park surrounding it – was militarised. The sound of men, the slamming of truck doors. Trucks were being unloaded. Patrols were being made.

And I could smell the petrol.

Jane crouched next to us, peering over the wall. I could see her making calculations, though I couldn't tell what it was she was planning. Hopefully what was in front of her was what she expected.

We didn't move for a while. Why weren't we moving? We were meant to wait at the back of the superstore, not by its perimeter wall. Andrea, Helen and I watched Jane. She was still crouching, still looking, still calculating.

Jane looked across at us. Her eyes glowing, her jaw tight. She put her hand up, then palm down. We had to wait here.

Shit. They were more prepared than we'd anticipated.

Jane never moved from her position. Something was on the other side of the wall, something she hadn't expected. She jabbed at her lower back. Andrea slung her rifle over her shoulder and pulled out a pair of wire cutters from the pack on her back.

We waited. Time was ticking on. Our trucks would soon be there. Soon the assault would start.

We were in the wrong place.

Helen looked at her watch, watching it, waiting for the moment.

Jane's focus never broke from the target.

I focused on calming my breath. I had to ensure my cool wasn't just a mask. I didn't move, fearful of the clichéd snap of twig underfoot that could sabotage our silence. I could feel the cold cement of the wall through the thin material of my top. I was shivering. Nerves. Adrenalin. Fear.

Andrea had her hand on the wall, ready to climb.

Helen next to Jane, looking at her watch, ears pricked.

Jane, head cocked, listening, waiting.

Suddenly a flash lit up the sky, like a sheet of white lightning.

Followed by a thunderous crack and a second flash.

Then, BOOM!

The deafening sound of the explosions.

The ground shook.

"Now." Suddenly Jane leapt over the wall.

In a human wave, Helen, then Andrea, then I followed.

On the other side, between us and the back of the superstore, was a towering barbed wire fence.

Without hesitation, Andrea was straight up to the perimeter fence. Snap, snap, snap, snap… As she cut, Helen and I held open the fence, yanking the hole wider with every cut. Jane crouched nearby, gun up.

There was gunfire but not from our side of the building. In the distance. On the other side.

The night sky flashed a brilliant orange.

A deafening crackle ripped across the sky.

And then…

BOOM!

A massive explosion rocked the building, shaking the ground under our feet. I almost fell.

Through the wire I could see armed men running towards the explosions. We saw them but they didn't see us. And I could hear the screams, the shouting. The gunfire.

Andrea stood aside and slung the cutters back into her bag as Jane raced through the hole. Then Helen. Andrea grabbed the other side of the cut wires and jerked her head, urging me through. I did as I was ordered.

Dozens of vehicles lay between us and the back of the building. Jane and Helen were already weaving their way through. I got a jab in the back, Andrea pushing me on.

Gunfire filled the air, the smell of fire from the front of the building.

The sky flashed a brilliant orange. A beautiful vivid shade heralding terrible destruction.

And then another burst of orange.

BOOM!

Hails of gunfire followed another explosion.

The distraction was working. But at what cost?

More gunfire.

Another flash of orange above us.

BOOM!

Andrea jabbed my back. I saw Jane weave past the last truck and run to the back wall of the building, starting to climb as soon as she hit it. Up the back of the building, like a spider.

I hit the wall and just thought, shit. There was so little to grab on to. Some pipe fittings, a chip in the brickwork, the window ledge above me. That was it.

I looked up. Jane caught her foot on a pipe and propelled herself through an open window. Then her head appeared again through the window and she tossed down some rope.

"Get moving," Helen hissed as Andrea came up on my other side, both of them taking lookout positions.

BANG!

The explosion rocked the wall. I could feel its structure weaken. The flash of orange was immense.

The ground shook again, my legs trembled.

The gunfire. The smoke. The shouts from the soldiers...

I looked up, grabbed the rope and started to climb, hauling myself up as my feet spun like a hamster in a wheel trying to get some grip on the bricks.

A series of explosions out front.

The crack of gunfire filled the night sky.

The shouts from the women, the bellows from the men.

Almost there, I grabbed the bottom of the window ledge. Then I felt her grip me under my arms and, with a powerful yank, Jane pulled me up and in to the building, my stomach bashing against the window frame.

Inside, Jane threw my body to the ground and returned to the rope, pushing her feet against the foot of the wall as she held on to it for dear life, the tension straining with the weight of first Andrea and then Helen. I scrambled to my feet and took up position on the other side, gun up, on lookout for both outside and in.

Inside the building, the white corridor was deserted, the echo of the firefight out front bouncing off the walls.

Helen and Andrea crawled in through the window.

Up ahead, there was a turn in the corridor. Jane had dropped the rope and was at the turn before I could draw breath.

The other two followed her. As did I.

We stood at the turn, waiting. Jane looked round the corner. Then she sped out.

We followed.

And again at the next corner.

And again at the next.

We made our way deeper into the building. And with every step, the explosions sounded louder, closer. The walls rattled.

Jane stopped at the next corner.

We heard an army of boots pass by. I sat, back against the wall, heart racing.

Then Jane walked out.

I looked up, thinking that it was the signal to move but Andrea raised her hand. Stop.

I peered around the corner.

The ceiling was a series of squares – exposed metal bars in a large grid formation. Jane was already halfway up the damaged wall as I was still trying to take it all in. As she got to the ceiling, she dug her feet into two corners of one of the squares, her hands gripping tightly to the other two, using pressure against the metal bars to keep her firm.

Jane was facing down to the floor. She hung there, her black uniform and her dirty skin stark against the bright white paint.

Andrea pulled me back.

We held our breath.

Then we heard the boots.

The uniformed guards raced past underneath Jane, oblivious to the spider hanging above their heads waiting to drop her web.

The three of us hung back, out of sight, waiting for the moment, waiting for the sign.

She was letting a lot of men pass underneath her.

Then another squadron of men jogged round and that's when she dropped.

Suddenly. Right into the middle of the squadron.

In the blink of an eye, Jane stabbed everyone around her.

She pulled a pistol from one of the men's trousers and shot those remaining at point blank range.

In seconds, all the men were dead.

And all with barely a sound.

I stood there, stunned. I almost dropped my gun.

Jane ran forward.

Andrea grabbed me. I gripped my gun tight and we ran on, following Jane and Helen ahead of us.

We were going to achieve our target. We were going to do this. It was round the next corridor, the data entry point.

Then she stopped at the corner.

The hand went up.

Andrea and Helen crouched down, guns ready.

I copied.

Jane's hand slowly came down.

Slowly, Jane passed her rifle to Helen. What was she doing? I looked across at Andrea but she wasn't remotely startled. Her focus was solely on staying crouched by Jane's feet.

Helen took the rifle.

Jane pulled out a gun, a pistol with a silencer, from the back of her trousers. And then, silently, slowly, she walked out into the corridor.

I had to see this. I crept forward. Helen put her hand up but I wasn't interested.

At the end of the corridor were two soldiers. Both of them facing in the other direction, towards the sound of the assault out front.

And creeping up on them from behind, gun pointing

directly out in front of her, one boot carefully, quietly, in front of the other, was Jane.

She was outnumbered and outgunned. If they turned round she was dead. The noise alone would attract others.

She kept walking. One step, then another.

We were all holding our breath.

Next to the soldiers was the data entry booth. I could see the smoked glass at the side and, through it, the flashing of computer lights.

The two soldiers, in assault vests and holding rifles, hadn't heard her, hadn't sensed her presence.

Still Jane walked towards them so slowly, minimising the range, improving the odds, trying to do this as silently as possible for as long as possible.

Buying me time.

I wasn't breathing. There she was – one woman. No bullet proof top, no armour. Just trousers and a vest top, gun up, walking as clear as day down the white corridor towards two men who were stronger than her, armed with rifles.

One of the men started to turn round, then suddenly he caught sight—

Too late.

One shot straight into his head and another straight into the head of his companion.

Jane sped forward. Andrea and Helen ran out to flank her but she was at the room before they could get to her. Jane fired three bullets into the booth, then looked at me. "Come here."

I ran towards them. Heart in my mouth, not even remembering the last time I drew breath, sprinting past the bodies in the corridor.

In the booth, two more soldiers slumped in their chairs.

Helen kicked one of the bodies off its chair. "You have three minutes."

But as I sat down, Jane corrected her. "You have less than that. We're running late."

Andrea, Helen and the leader of the most dangerous resistance movement on Earth took position outside the booth. I pulled the pre-formatted USB out of my bag and put it in the side of the computer terminal.

As the screen came to life, I wiped my arm over the work surface and pulled the keyboard towards me.

I recognised the mainframe, I recognised the software. That hadn't changed since I last saw it. But the paths, the network paths... They were different. Not what I expected.

"Laura?" Jane looked at me. "Problems?"

"No."

I flipped through the paths. Telegrams, posts from the front line, admin. Too many unprotected network drives. Shit, State security was loose, but where were the confidential drives? I had to come up with something. I had to be able to produce something from this effort. I trawled through the drives, one after another, but nothing seemed credible. Identity logs. Death logs. All historic.

Shit.

But then I found it, a drive that was protected. Just one.

Whatever was on that path, I wanted it.

I scrambled the access code, causing it to override itself.

And in front of me flashed up a screen of folders – 'stocks' 'EMEA Reports' 'MENA logs' 'MENA cables'...

And 'RAZR Pro'.

"I'm in." And as I said this I hit the extract facility for the whole drive.

The images flashed across the screen as the zip on the USB stick pulled copies in. Briefs, reports, photos of army front lines, images of destroyed villages, of destroyed cities – some of them British, some foreign...

Then suddenly photos of the dead flashed across the screen. Corpses. Bodies strung up in town squares. Next to them British soldiers, British men in uniform. Thumbs up next to piles of bodies, men in uniform kicking decapitated heads around like footballs...

Then blueprints, landscape shots, barracks... The redesigned parliamentary assembly rooms, I recognised. The network of underground tunnels under Westminster. Photos of buildings being built, photos of buildings being destroyed...

What the hell were these reports?

The extract finished.

Should I release the trace? Should I leave the trail, the marker? The sign that would prove to the authorities that I was here, that I was back, that I had infiltrated RAZR?

I looked across at Jane. She was already staring at me.

"You done?" she said.

In that moment I made a snap decision.

An explosion rocked the floor, momentarily distracting Jane. I released the trace.

"Time's up." Andrea snatched the USB from the terminal and dragged me out of the booth.

But just before we ran, Jane turned back into the corridor, pulled out a grenade from the belt at her waist, drew the pin and threw it back towards whatever was chasing us. And towards the data entry booth.

"Run." Then she flew back at us, dragging us forward as fast as she could.

BOOM!

The explosion rocked our legs. Andrea fell to her knees but Jane pulled her up. Helen was ahead of us, smashing out the rest of the glass from a window.

Suddenly, I saw them behind us, two men running towards us, cocking their rifles.

The others were all facing the window.

"Behind you!" I shouted.

I raised my AK and fired.

A hail of bullets. The two men fell dead.

Andrea turned and saw them. "Good shot," she said. I saw Jane glance at me and nod.

Then she looked out the window. Down then across. "On to the roofs," she said.

Jane crawled out of the window, clutching the wall as her feet edged along a pipe.

Helen bundled me out.

Beneath us, the trucks and vans were wrecked – destroyed by bombs and gunfire. But the roofs of many of the bigger trucks were intact. And Jane was headed towards one of them, out to the left.

I followed Jane out along the ledge. A nail ripped clean off one of my fingers as I desperately clung onto chips and holes in the brickwork. Now I was scared. Really scared. We were so close to getting out of this alive.

Jane dropped onto the roof of a truck.

I followed.

She caught me as I tripped over my own ankle. She looked deep into my eyes. She wasn't shaking. Her hand was strong. I could feel the heat coming off her body.

Andrea and Helen dropping onto the truck broke the intense moment.

Jane ran ahead, jumping from roof to roof. We followed. The injured men underneath oblivious to our presence just a few metres above their heads.

I was breathing heavily now.

From the roof of the last truck, on the edge of the secured area, Jane threw herself at the barbed wire fence. She crawled up it at speed.

My stomach hurt. My finger was throbbing. My heart was pounding so hard I thought it was going to burst through my chest. I threw myself at the wire and clung on for dear life. I had to climb. Climb, climb, climb!

Suddenly Jane was right in front of me, on the other side of the wire. Her face was so close to mine I could feel the heat from her breath. I looked at her. I was done, I was out of energy. Suddenly, she was on the move again, back up to the top of the fence. She ripped off her top and wound it tight around a section of the barbs. Then she scuttled down so she was below me on the fence and pushed me up over the wire.

I nearly fell down the other side, my legs too shaky to give me much support.

Andrea touched down right next to me, helping me to my feet.

In the darkness there was a truck, at the roadside. Andrea opened its doors and threw me in. Once again I was on the floor of a truck. I felt another person jump in – Helen. Then Jane leapt in and slammed the door behind her.

We sped off into the night.

I rolled onto my back, gulping for air, and slowly I started to haul myself up into a sitting position.

Jane, now in just her trousers and bra, smiled. "You did better than I expected."

Andrea was smiling too.

And Helen wasn't.

CHAPTER NINETEEN
The Win

The women were raucous. Bawdy, boisterous and alive. The sound of their singing and laughing bounced off the walls in the large hall where Jane had first revealed her true identity. Heavy, rough wooden tables had been dragged in for the food, but the used plates now lay shattered on the floor, along with the remnants of the food. And in their place was the mud and marks from the boots that were now jumping up and down on them.

Drained bottles of vodka lay strewn around, the alcohol from within them now filling each and every mug and glass being raised.

The women flung their arms around their returning comrades who shared their increasingly exaggerated war stories. Some throats already hoarse, others just finding their voice.

Those on patrol, however, remained on alert in the darkness of the perimeter. But those of us inside, those sixty of us who had gone into battle – and those sixty of us who had returned – were letting loose.

Or at least the rest of them were.

I winced. Then groaned.

Anne had doused my ripped nail in turpentine and was scavenging with a needle through the open skin to clear out the debris and dirt. "It needs to be done." This, after she'd already cleaned out the bite on my leg using the same method.

From over my shoulder, a friendly arm slung itself around my neck. "Ah, your first war wound." Mandy's face came into view.

Anne laughed but my cheeks flushed. "I know others have worse injuries but—"

"Actually, they don't," Anne interrupted.

"Really?" Mandy said, one hand on my shoulder, the other holding a beer with a pungent aroma.

Anne nodded as she dropped the needle to her tray and started winding the bandage around my fingertip. "Clean. Shauna got a burn, a nasty one, but nothing serious, from some back-draught—"

"Yeah, she showed me," Mandy added. "Dark black burns on dark brown skin. Her skin's camouflaging itself."

The look on Anne's face... Not sure whether to laugh or be offended.

Mandy slapped me on my back and tried to shove her beer into my hand. "No, no. Really. Not for me," I said.

Mandy recoiled. "You don't drink? Fucking hell L, we need to talk. There's no rationing in here."

"I'm just uncomfortable celebrating death, even if it is the death of men."

Anne added, "Her father only died recently."

My eyes widened. How did she know that?

But before I could say anything, Mandy slapped me on the back again. "Death is coming for us, whether we fear it or not, so don't waste your time fearing it."

"You'll be better off with alcohol." Anne nodded towards my hand. "Numbs the pain better than any anaesthetic."

Anne, whenever she spoke, would look up at me, then she'd drop her head back down again. She began to pack up her medical kit.

"I'll come and drink only if Anne comes and drinks with me," I said.

Anne looked rather shocked, Mandy raised her eyebrows. "Hell, well, we don't normally get the pleasure of the boss's little sister, but fuck it, let's have a drink."

And so we did.

And then we had another.

And another.

Anne barely left my side, but far from a ball and chain, she was an opener for me, a way in to understanding this army, most of whom I still didn't know. Every soldier recognised her – and each one had a different reaction to her. Some were in awe, standing just that little bit further away whenever she approached, regardless of the fact that she was more embarrassed than intimidating.

Others whom she'd nursed would show her their old, ever-fainter scars. She'd ask about pain control and they'd bat her concerns away. But none of these women slung their arms around her, hugged her or slapped her on her back. And she was aware of that. I caught that drop of her head every time one of the soldiers would come over and complement every hug they gave me with "you're the new hacker," or "so you were the one they were smuggling in?" But for Anne, just a respectful nod of the head or a display of her excellent medical skills on their scars and burns.

I put my hand on Anne's shoulder, nodding at her glass. "You've run out of drink."

"Oh, I know. I don't think I need—"

"Come on." I threw my arm around her waist and steered her towards the table where the jugs were. "You've been here longer than me so I was expecting to see you with more, ah, is stamina the right word?"

"Tolerance."

"Yes, tolerance. Sorry." I held up the vodka jug. Anne shrugged, I poured. "So how long have you been here?"

Anne raised her eyebrows and pointed at the ground with her hand.

"No, not here as in here at the school, but, you know, here as in RAZR." I was almost shouting, trying to make myself heard over the din of singing and chanting going on around us. But Anne nodded that she understood. "You weren't there at the start, were you?"

She took a few glugs from her mug before giving me the story. "Sometimes I feel I've been in RAZR all my life."

"Really?"

"Of course. Everything we stand for I've always believed." Anne threw her arm wide but her legs wobbled and she fell against the table. "Sorry. I was trying to show – with my arm – that the others, some of these guys, women rather, maybe about a couple dozen of them, like Andrea and Mandy, they've been there, here, since the beginning. A lot of them worked with Jane overseas. I guess I can't really say too much about all that. But, you know, they were."

"And Helen."

Anne shook her head. "No, Helen joined later. A couple of years ago."

"Jane trusts her life to someone she only met two years ago? After she became the most hunted?"

Anne shrugged. "Jane worked with plenty of men for many years and look what they did."

Touché.

Anne's head wobbled slightly. She slowly brought the edge of her glass to her mouth, but didn't take a sip. Didn't even tilt the glass. It was as if she was steadying herself with it. "I don't really know for sure what Jane did overseas actually. I never asked. Even if I had, she wouldn't have told me. Or maybe she would have, I don't know. But I don't really want to know. And you know, I could see it in her face back then. Donetsk, Mosul, Misrata... These were dangerous places. She would come back, between each mission, and I'd see the darkness in her eyes. The shadows starting to form."

Mosul. Yes, I knew what she had done in Mosul. I had seen the files. The Misrata file was confidential but I had seen it. Obviously. But Donetsk? When was she in Donetsk?

"Drink up," I said. And we both took swigs.

I looked at Anne. I was losing her. Her eyelids were heavy and she was getting lost in her own thoughts. "She worked it out before everyone else, you know," Anne said. "She's quite smart, medically speaking."

I shook my head. I didn't understand.

"It wasn't public knowledge back then but she saw the rashes, the red lumps over the men and she knew."

Oh, now I understood. I nodded. "The STD."

Anne nodded, but with more difficulty. "It was immune to antibiotics, that was what was paralysing them. Literally. The need for access to sex for a male army... That has always caused problems. And the Islamists had ensured all the women near the front lines—" Anne swept her arms and lost balance again.

"Were infected," I said as I reached forward and helped steer Anne so she was leaning against the table.

"Yeah. And had the virus."

I took the glass from her. I had to keep her cogent. "Pretty clever when you think about it." I was trying to direct the conversation but Anne kept drifting off. I needed to keep her talking. "She did the right thing, you know."

Anne looked straight at me and nodded. A solemn look had fallen over her face. "Yeah, that was, well... Jane did what she thought was necessary."

"I thought what she did was the right thing."

"Really?" Anne was wide-eyed, like a puppy.

"Yeah, of course. She did the right thing. Those men, they trained all those local men to fight and instead all they did was abuse those girls and decapitate women for sorcery. She was right to execute them all."

Anne nodded. "That was a lot of men though. Some of them were only children."

There was real doubt in Anne's eyes.

"I know," I said. "But in war there can be no half measures. If you're going to kill, you have to kill them all. You know that, don't you?"

"No, I do." Anne took another gulp of the vodka. "It's just that, it's quite hard being that close to ruthlessness."

I jumped out of my skin as a slap hit my back. "Hey." Andrea. "What are you two gossiping about?"

I froze. But Anne saw no need for silence. "Jane."

Andrea rolled her eyes then slapped me again. "I'm sorry you had such a crap memory, you know, of your grandmother."

"Oh, that. Thank you but sorry, I know I shared too much."

"What?" Anne said.

"Laura here got locked in with her gran's dead body as a kid and it freaked her out a bit."

"Death scares you?" Anne asked.

"I'm a bit better with it now."

Anne laughed. "Well, this is one way to get over that."

"I felt bad listening to you," Andrea said.

"Why?"

"Because my first memories are all happy ones."

"Really?"

"Yeah." Andrea reached over to the table and picked up a half-full glass. "My earliest memory was when I won sports day when I was a toddler."

"What did you win?" I asked.

"Everything."

"Ugh," Anne said. "Just like my sister."

I had to laugh.

"Why are you shaking your head?" Andrea said to me.

"'Cause, I don't know, I just thought everyone in this movement was damaged in some way."

"Oh, thanks." And she finished off the drink in the glass.

"I think what I was trying to do was, you know, bond with the others by sharing a bad memory. But you're not, are you? You're not damaged," I said.

"Well, some of us are," Andrea said, and she smacked her empty glass down on the table. "But that's always the kind of shitty assumptions people make about angry women."

"Daddy issues," Anne added, leaning heavily against the table.

"Exactly, Daddy issues," Andrea nodded. "That the angry women are the extremists, the ones without a sense of humour. You know, probably sexually abused as kids, parents alcoholics, Dad beat the shit out of them, boyfriend forced them to have an abortion, whatever. That society really was fair and not all men were cunts. I've never had a termination, love my dad, but, fuck me, you know what, I'm still fucking angry. Society fucked us over in a million ways and every fucking man benefited from sexism. Every single fucking one. Anyway, I'm getting angry now so I'm going to stop." Andrea looked past me. "What the fuck?"

"Touch my burn, touch my burn!" One of the shortest women in the army flung herself between us. Her top lifted up, she grabbed my hand and pushed it against her stomach.

"Oh my God, it's so hot." Her skin was on fire. The heat it was still producing was intense.

Anne, however, was unimpressed. "You know, Shauna, you really should have kept the bandages on. It's not good to—"

"Oh Anne, I swear we'd all be diseased and dead without you." Shauna flung her arms around her. And there it was, Anne's first hug from someone other than me.

Shauna was a bit younger than Andrea and me, more Anne's age. Her dark hair was cropped close to her head. Her big brown eyes though were wide open. She was hyper, wired. High on only adrenalin and alcohol? Maybe. She grabbed her nurse's hand. "Look! Feel! Feel my war wound. Maybe one day, Anne, we can get you a battle scar all of your own."

"What?" Anne squealed with delight as Shauna rubbed her palm over her stomach.

"Showing off again." Andrea high-fived Shauna. "Just cause you were let loose today, don't think you can run it all without me."

"I don't see your scars!" Shauna bellowed at Andrea. "Too precious to fight the big fights now, huh?"

And the two of them bawled with laughter.

Anne's hands hadn't moved from Shauna's stomach. "Your skin is so rough, so dry. Your scars are like the ridges of the Grand Canyon."

"Cover up your stomach Shauna." And the laughter died instantly. Helen had crept up on us. "It's unbecoming."

Anne pulled her hand away.

Shauna pulled down her top.

"And watch the drinking," Helen added.

"There's no need to be a bitch, Helen," said Andrea, hand on hip. "The patrol outside is fully staffed and was planned to cover this."

"Defences should never be lowered." Helen glared.

But Andrea didn't look away. "The women in here are fine. And safe. We can't be on a war footing every minute of the day. That'll kill them faster than a badly defended perimeter."

Helen sneered and walked away, over to the door at the end of the hall and out.

We watched silently as she exited, our buzz deflating.

But then Mandy arrived. "Oh Helen, that hound!"

"Hound on a leash!" Shauna howled.

And then Mandy started barking like a dog.

We giggled and high-fived each other.

All except one.

"Hey, ease up," Anne jumped in. "Without her, my sister would be vulnerable."

Mandy slung her arm around her. "Anne, if there's one thing we've learnt it's that your sister ain't fucking vulnerable. She's a terrible force that lays waste to everything in her path. That's why we love her."

"That's why we follow her," added Shauna.

And the group banged their glasses together and cheered.

"We can love your sister without loving that one." Mandy whooped as she high-fived Shauna, and spilt her drink all over a woman who happened to be passing by.

It was a soldier with long, red hair.

"Hey." The redhead shoved Mandy. "What the— Handle your fucking drink."

Mandy staggered back a step, letting out a rather sarcastic "oooh" as she did. "Winter! I'm impressed. I didn't know you had it in you."

"Fuck you," Winter snapped.

Mandy fronted up. "Hey, if we get to change your name to Summer does your fucking freezing arse bitch attitude thaw out or are we stuck with it for life?"

A mixture of laughs and drawn breath shot round all the women standing nearby.

"Go back to acting like a man," Winter sneered.

Heads around us turned. Even more sarcastic "ooohs" could be heard.

Except from Andrea and me, who both straightened up.

More heads started turning towards our group.

Mandy stepped forward. "Honey, the only thing I like in a man is submission. Just 'cause you're missing their attention, don't take it out on me."

And with that, all the noise evaporated from the room.

Shauna laughed, enraging Winter even more. "Hey, fuck you bitches." Winter lunged at Shauna but Mandy leapt between them, taking the brunt of Winter's hard shove.

Mandy staggered, spilling her drink. She dropped her glass and pushed Winter from her. "Don't you touch Shauna!"

"Oh, she's all yours, right?"

"Don't panic, sweetheart. It isn't contagious."

The brewing storm was the only sound in the room.

I put my hand on Winter's shoulder. "Hey."

"Don't fucking touch me!" she screamed.

"Hey, hey, hey." Andrea put her hand on Mandy's chest.

Winter pushed me off her and headed to Mandy. "Just keep your hands off me, dyke."

"You're not my type," Mandy spat as she threw a punch at Winter. But she missed.

Andrea pushed Winter backwards.

I leapt forward, pushing Mandy against the wall. "Hey, hey! Let it go, let it go."

"But she's a fucking bitch to be saying that," Mandy was

snorting, fighting me, but I had her firmly against the wall.

Behind us, all I could hear was Winter's "Fuck your clique. Fuck your clique."

I looked over my shoulder and could see Andrea had managed to pin Winter back.

Mandy was snorting like a bull.

"I know, I know," I said to her. "But we're a team, a team. It's just hot air." Mandy shoved me back but I leant in again. "Let it go."

"OK. OK!" Mandy shrugged me off.

Opposite, Andrea marshalled Winter away too, watching her as she made her way back to her own brigade on the far side of the hall.

The room was silent.

I took some deep breaths. I looked over at Andrea, she nodded back to me.

I turned back to Mandy, put my hand on the back of her neck – and this time she didn't shrug me off. "It's OK. We're all on your side."

And as Mandy walked away, Andrea came over. "Nicely done."

"I hope you told her what for," Shauna aimed at Andrea.

"We're on the same side," Andrea said.

"Hey!" Mandy shouted. "What happened to the party? Put the music back on."

And the music came back on. Mandy leapt on the nearest table, picked up a glass and shouted "It's time to drink!" and the whole room cheered back.

The scuffle was quickly forgotten, lost in an alcohol-induced haze. Even my own grip on the reins was loosened. With every arm slung around my shoulder, with every lyric of the chants I learnt, the bricks in the wall I had built around me became that little bit looser. I was happy. I could feel it, a lightness in my heart, in my mind and in my feet. Elation and happiness washed through me.

I remember the alcohol. I remember my vision coming and going. I must've been drunk as I don't even remember when Mandy decided she was going to tattoo an R onto my arm. But I do remember being seated in a chair and she was doing it. And it wasn't hurting. I ran my fingers over it. The skin was tender, but not raised. The women all cheered and slapped me on the shoulder. We were all smiling.

The air was filled with sweat, with shouts and with laughter. The air tasted sweet with victory. We were singing, loudly. Mandy was revitalised and led from the front, standing on a chair, drink in hand, conducting the crowd. Arms over shoulders, hugs all round.

The buzz, the flutter in my heart, the adrenalin in my veins… It was joy.

I spotted the sisters who had found my gun up against the wall. I suspected they had gone in knowing what they would find. I had to build bridges. I staggered over to them. "Why aren't you joining in?" I asked.

One of them turned away. The other nodded out into the floor. "Because you're in Andrea's group."

I looked over at the centre of the room. I don't know why, I could barely make out my own hands so fuzzy was my own eyesight. And I didn't even know which squadron everyone belonged to anyway so I had no idea what I was looking for.

I looked back at the sisters. "There's only ten of us in Andrea's squad and there's about thirty people on the floor."

The sisters didn't move.

"What's your name?" I asked.

The one who had spoken looked at her sister, who was still looking away, then back to me. "I'm Rachel. My sister is Becks."

"I'm Laura," I said.

"We know," Rachel said.

"I'm too new to understand any of the cliques and groups and I'm too new to know anyone to talk to, really, so come on," I said, grabbing Rachel by the arm. I dragged them out into the middle of the floor and, slowly but surely, the divisions started to thaw.

In the centre of the throng, Mandy grabbed me. "It's like life, isn't it? It's like life in the veins. I love this place. This building has an energy." Mandy threw her glass in the air, cheering the building. "It's victory!"

She leapt on to one of the tables again, dragging Alex up with her, conducting the crowd with each wave of her arms. And standing underneath her, we all responded. And each song was greeted with cheers and raised glasses.

I smiled, staggered backwards, but caught myself before I fell and wiped the sweat off my lip. I needed water. I turned towards the door, to head for the jugs. But through the crowd I could see her homing in, coming straight for me. The hound.

CHAPTER TWENTY
The Plans

My head was spinning. And there was ringing in my ears, shrill and piercing.

I wasn't sure where we were going. The school was still a bit of a maze to me. I kept looking over my shoulder for guidance from Helen but there were no words. Instead she kept walking straight ahead, forcing me to do the same.

And every time I looked around I noticed the gun over her shoulder. It wasn't in her hands, she didn't have it up at my back. But the gun was still there.

The final corridor Helen marched me down was on the second floor, a wing I hadn't visited, or even knew was there. Unlike the hall, this part of the building was silent. Dark and silent. So much so that when we turned the corner of the corridor, it was a surprise to see sentries on guard duty.

Helen stopped by the sentries and nodded down the corridor, towards a soft light coming from a room at the far end.

I walked slowly towards the light, calming my breath and pleading desperately for the spinning in my head to at least slow down. I had to get control of myself.

I stopped at the entrance to the room and took a few deep breaths, waiting for my pulse to calm. Then I walked in.

The room was wood-panelled, lit only by candles and lamps. Each of the four walls was covered with maps. But these were not what grabbed my attention, for there, in the middle of the room, was Jane. Standing alone, behind a thick, large wooden table covered with papers. Hands in her pockets, looking straight at me, waiting for my arrival.

I took a few steps in, staying against the wall furthest from her. I was sweating. I stood still, allowing my focus to sharpen.

I had no idea what she wanted with me. Her gaze was impassive.

Above Jane's head hung a plain wooden cross that betrayed this room's original purpose.

I looked up at it for a moment, then back down at Jane. She was watching me all the time.

"I picked the room because it was quiet," she said.

I nodded. My pulse started to speed up again.

"You did well, in the raid."

"Thank you." I didn't know what else to say.

There was a silence.

Then she said, "You weren't fazed?"

"No. I mean, yes. No, not really. It just all happened very quickly. I remember... It just all happened so fast that I'm not sure what I remember actually. It was hot. It was hot, like, I don't know, maybe I'm a bit unfit." I laughed nervously. But it didn't crack the tension in the room.

"Most who have sat behind a desk their whole life are scared of gunfire," Jane said. "It's instinctive to want to run the other way. Yet you're worried about fitness."

I looked down at the floor. Bring your brain under control, Laura. Sober up. I took a deep breath and brought my head up again. Jane hadn't moved. Her hands remained in her pockets and she was still focused only on me.

On the wall behind her was a map of the south-east of England. There were pins in the map. A number of them were concentrated into groups, others were spaced out towards the coastline.

"What you retrieved from their network was critically important," she said.

I looked down at the papers in front of her. And as the images and plans came into focus, I started to recognise them – they were the plans, the photos that I had seen on the computer screen in the raid.

"Do you understand what it was you saw, these images that you extracted?"

I stepped towards the desk, staring at the photos of the bodies, the human heads in rows on the ground, and the lines and lines of dead women.

"I saw maps and plans," I said. "Those were the enclaves, weren't they? What you sent me in for, what you brought me in for. But there was other stuff. Other photos I didn't recognise…" I pointed at the desk. "These ones of death."

Jane nodded. "The data included what I expected, but also what I was hoping for. What you saw were photos of prisoners from the battlefronts in the Middle East and North Africa. Only these prisoners are dead."

"I thought we had retreated."

"Retreated? You mean, you thought we were defeated. We were. But things… You really don't know this, do you? They didn't tell you in the filtration centre?"

"Tell me what?"

Jane looked at me, closely. "That the Islamists got hold of the bomb."

I froze.

"From Pakistan." Jane carried on. "They attached it to a short-range missile, a missile we think they bought or exchanged with the Russians via the Urals."

"I thought the Russians were on our side."

"What Moscow wants rarely translates on to the battlefield. The Russian army has always been rogue. This is what happens when a state starves their army – the army rebels. But, anyway, they sold the Islamists a missile. The missile and the bomb were passed through the caliphates until it got to the Mediterranean coast. Libya."

Oh God.

"The missile was fired at France. An interesting choice, perhaps, as you'd expect them to go for the Germans. But to France it went. The whole of the south of France was lost. It's still shut down. No one went in and no one came out." Jane shrugged. "North Africa's gone but here in the West, we never cared that much about Africa, did we? But it means what we had left of our military had to go back in, with the Americans, to stop more trades, disarm all bombs. Special forces. Then infantry. And that is what these are." Jane picked up a pile of images from her desk. "The rapes, the beheadings, the torture... Our scorched earth policy."

"Maybe the images are fake."

"You think that?"

My gaze shifted away. She was still focusing solely on me. I didn't know whether she was trying to read me or intimidate me.

They weren't fake. I knew that. I felt that truth in the pit of my stomach. "I don't understand why they take photos."

"I hope you never do." I saw compassion in Jane's eyes, and a sadness. "I really do."

"This is what you feared to find?"

163

Jane gave a rueful smile and started leafing through the plans in front of her. "Feared? No. This is what I expected. I want these images because I want to distribute them. What I wasn't expecting were these."

Jane picked up a pile of photos near her and scattered them across the table. Women. Pregnant women. Tied to beds. Strings of them, unconscious, lying on mattresses. Women on the ground surrounded by men. Pictures of hospital beds, of medical centres. All the beds filled with women. Then pictures of dead women. Women having operations. Women with tubes in their mouths. Women in chains. Women in pain.

I picked them up, but couldn't focus. I didn't want to. I dropped them back on the desk and stood back again. "I thought you were lying when you told us."

"Really?"

I corrected myself. "No. I mean, just mistaken."

Jane tilted her head. "A mistake is an error of judgment caused by carelessness. I am never careless. Not in my reasoning, not with the lives of my women. I don't make mistakes."

"OK." I could feel my head beginning to spin. A little nauseous.

"Hope will destroy you," Jane said. "Believe me. Believe what I tell you."

I looked at her. Her gaze, so penetrating.

"Believe what I say," she said, softer than before.

I stood there, I don't know how long for. I glanced again at the photos. "So what are we going to do?"

Jane picked up a blueprint. "This is what came from your download. It is the plans for a base that even I didn't know existed. I thought the fertilisation of women was just in the enclaves. This is a new medical facility that's been built but it's not yet fully secure." Jane dropped the plans to the desk. "So we are going to attack it."

"Why don't we just attack the enclaves?" I said. "I mean, if you really believe this, then go for the jugular."

Jane remained unmoved. "Because I don't play fast and loose with the lives of my soldiers. The lives of those women dancing downstairs are as valuable to me as those in that facility."

I looked away, ashamed.

"I wasn't joking when I said the enclaves are secure," she said. "They are more secure than any military facility I know of. They are secured with as many soldiers as inhabitants. Right now, the female womb is the most precious commodity on earth."

"Could be disinformation, that plan," I said.

"Could be. But the facility is in a place where there has been a lot of traffic over the past year. I've seen references to it in other papers we've stolen, communications we've intercepted, but I've never seen a technical drawing for it."

"What does this mean?"

"It means it's new. It's vulnerable."

"Only by comparison."

Another rueful smile crossed Jane's face. "Yes, by comparison. But 'by comparison' is good enough."

"So, what do you want from me?"

"From you?" Jane shook her head. "Nothing. I wanted to show you what you found. Because it's impressive for a first time haul."

She looked at me, always looking at me. Always reading me. My stomach leapt to my throat. "Yes. I suppose it is."

"And you know how to handle a gun," she added.

"Yes." I smiled. "That was a lucky couple of shots."

"There was nothing lucky about that shot."

"You mean, shots."

And suddenly the temperature in the room plummeted.

A glacial shift.

"Your arm was completely still," Jane said. "The bullet flew, must have been about a hundred yards."

The bottom fell out of my stomach. I felt my legs begin to tremble.

"Yes, definitely a hundred yards," Jane said. "Straight through his head. A clean hit. Impressive for someone who says they've never used a gun."

The room started spinning on a tilted axis.

My balance went.

I swayed, grabbing on to the desk.

The maps on the walls, the files on the tables – they all fell in and out of focus.

I had been seen.

Jane had seen me, at the crossroads.

Jane had been there.

"You saw me? You were there, in London?"

Jane said nothing.

"Why didn't you help me?" I said. "Why didn't you save me?"

"You didn't need saving."

"I was scared."

"You didn't show it." Jane started picking through papers in a brown folder in front of her. "You fired a single shot. A single shot from a Colt. That's a State authorised weapon."

"They gave it to me as part of the militarisation of the blocks."

Jane looked at me, then nodded. Once.

"We saw the army arrive. Once we saw them we knew we couldn't intervene. We weren't at full strength. We were only a small team out on reconnaissance. But you weren't in danger."

I could feel my heart pound in my chest. My pulse accelerated. A knot beginning to form in my stomach.

This resistance movement was supposed to be on my side.

I snapped. "You didn't help me. And you want me to stand next to you, to protect you, even though you've just told me you didn't protect me? How can I trust you? How can you trust me now, now that you've told me you chose not to protect me?"

My fingers were grabbing the edge of the desk. I had collected enough of my composure to feel the splintering of the wood and the sharp sides of the papers.

Jane was unfazed. "Laura, I will always, always have your back. We knew the army was close and I would not have let them hurt you. Whatever we do and wherever this ends, I will lay down my life to protect you. I will never leave women to suffer their fate at the hands of men. That is the responsibility I have chosen and one I am strong enough to carry."

Jane's voice was soft but deliberate. And contrived. The punch in the stomach followed by the mothering and the comforting. Classic abuse tactics. Foster dependency, foster pliancy.

That's when I saw it. A pen just inches from my fingertips. Sitting there amongst the papers on the desk. I no longer had my gun but a pen would do. It was dark enough, the sentries and Helen just far enough away. I could do it.

I made to grab it but it fell away from my fingertips. I lunged for it but it fell to the floor.

Jane's hands grabbed my shoulders. Then slowly, gently, she pushed me upright. "Let me get that," she said quietly. "I wouldn't want you to hurt yourself."

She bent down to the floor, picked up the pen and put it behind her, somewhere in the darkness.

I exhaled slowly, weighing up my options, steadying my feet. Then I asked, "Where did you get my file? Where did you really get it from?"

"It was with the convoy," Jane answered.

"I didn't see my file in the truck."

"It wasn't in the vehicle you were in. Files and personnel are carried together but separate in case something should happen to one but not the other. It was in another truck. All your files were."

"That doesn't make any sense," I said.

Jane remained silent.

I went on. "All files are held in the filing system. They have to be. They can't be transferred from the repository. It's the central resource."

"Your file was travelling with you because you were being permanently resettled."

Jane waited.

I waited.

Neither of us moved.

"Why did you ask me here, ask me in here, now, to see you?" I asked.

As always, Jane paused before she spoke. "During the extraction, you wouldn't have any reason to believe that we left a trail, would you? That any element of their network responded to our presence?"

I shook my head. "No. The extraction was too quick."

Jane nodded. "OK."

"Plus you threw that grenade afterwards," I added. "Which destroyed everything."

Jane looked back down to her plans.

I stood there, not moving, not leaving. "What else does it say, in my file?"

Jane had already moved on, leaning over a file, a piece of paper in her hand, but there was no hesitancy. "It says you were the only child of Ruth, a retired cancer research specialist, and Alan, a construction engineer. That tells me you were brought up by people with values and focus. Your degrees in computer science and the fact that you were head-hunted shows me that you were talented from a young age. Talent and principles – an alluring combination to a recruiter like me. And your file says your mother died three years ago from significant blood loss caused by a head injury. And that you survived alone, with your sick father, far longer than the State expected. That tells me you're resilient and calm. And loyal. Each of those traits is desirable. In combination, they make you an asset."

I nodded. "Can I go now?"

Jane nodded but I could feel her eyes following me out of the room.

I walked past Helen, who had remained outside, down the corridor, back past the armed guards.

I was processing it all. What had been said. What hadn't been said.

And the fact that we both knew my file hadn't been in that convoy.

But then again, maybe she didn't have my file at all.

Not my real one.

Because if she did, she'd have killed me on the spot.

CHAPTER TWENTY-ONE
The Biology

The bleeding started in the night. The sensation was so alien it woke me up. The twenty-eight day cycle had long since been abandoned by my womb. Lack of food? Lack of exercise? The pollution? The stress? Who knows. Maybe all of the above. But after about a year, it started coming when it wanted. Twenty-three days, twenty-two days... Then it stretched out to thirty days, thirty-four days until eventually either me or my womb lost track of time, lost track of the days and predictability went out of the window.

I got to the bathroom but I was too late. Washes of blood stained the inside of my thighs and even though my leggings were black, I could see the blood glistening on them. I searched the communal bathroom, went through some of the lockers, but I couldn't see any tampons or towels. Nothing.

I stole a pair of clean, black leggings from the line at the back of the room and stuffed as much tissue as I could get away with between my legs. It would have to do.

I couldn't sleep after that. I was distracted, even obsessed, with each flow from between my legs. Constantly checking the tissues. The blood was a bright red.

Anne was one of the women who shared my dormitory room. It seemed cruel to wake her just for a tampon. She was in a deep sleep, curled up under her blanket with her hood pulled tight around her face.

I killed time by washing my stained leggings in the sink, watching the water turn red. All the time, conflicted between being mesmerised and relieved, but also annoyed that the flow had started in the early morning of my next raid. I didn't need the stress.

Anne had to have supplies. After all, she had rabies injections. I hadn't seen a tampon in over a year. Maybe longer. Probably more like two years. Supplies had become elusive in the blocks. The blocks were meant to be efficient communities to manage the rations. But when the virus hit UK shores, they became gilded prisons. No one was allowed out.

Our rations used to contain tampons but then their inclusion became more infrequent. That's when the accusations started, some of the women getting to the drops and stealing them before they were distributed.

And then, when the supplies went from limited to non-existent, we were reduced to primitive methods. The red tent rose again. Women never left their rooms, cut-off, cast adrift until the bleeding stopped.

Chloe, though, had got lucky. Hers had stopped completely. It had frightened her at first. After a block meeting to instruct residents on first-aid techniques, she dragged me out the back.

She'd been having an affair with Steven from upstairs. I'd known that. In fact, a lot of the block had worked that out. How his wife hadn't, I don't know, but that's the level of denial people can live in. Anyway. Against the rules she'd been using contraception. Not that there were explicit rules as such, it was just that no contraception was ever delivered to us. Which is, by and large, the same thing. But it turned out she had stockpiled the pill from her last visit to a family planning clinic. Before all of this happened. And although they were all well past their use-by date, she didn't think it mattered. "But now I'm pregnant."

She'd cornered me in the backroom, with the washing machines, while the others were bickering next door.

"Are you sure?" I asked.

"I'm not on. I should be due. I'm at the break on the pills – nothing."

"Sometimes they can go completely."

Chloe didn't take any notice. It was impossible to calm her. "What if I'm pregnant? What if? You know we have to tell CC if someone gets pregnant. Then they'll take me away."

"At least you get to leave the block."

Her jaw hit the floor.

"You want to get out of the block, don't you?" I added.

"No!" Chloe realised she'd shouted. Her voice fell to a whisper. "Once you leave, you don't ever come back. Julia from the other block, she got pregnant—"

"You've been speaking to people in another block?"

"Of course I have. Well, I was. Julia and I tagged notes to stones and threw them over the road. Steve can rig radios. He's been able to tune into the radio frequency of other areas, but that's between you and me." Chloe's pace was furious. "Anyway, Julia missed her period. It disappeared for three months. She thought she'd just joined those with no periods but she couldn't hide the throwing up and then her stomach began to swell and they carted her off. I never heard from her again. What if that's me? What if that's me? I can't be taken away!"

Chloe started picking off the socks from Lillian's washing line and pairing them off. Compulsive distraction.

"You might not be pregnant, Chloe. Really. Just because your period is a few days late doesn't mean—"

"Laura! It's four months late!"

Silence.

"Shit," I eventually said.

"Right. I'm in the fucking shit."

But she wasn't. Her periods did come back a few weeks later. Not for long though.

The scare wasn't enough for Chloe to give up Steve. His wife discovered the affair and the boiling water that she threw over Chloe burnt her so badly that her skin never healed properly. And open wounds get infected. And this is no world for infections.

Chloe's was the first body we incinerated that was younger than the average age in the block.

"Laura."

My head jerked up. I don't know how long Anne had been standing there. I'd lost myself too long in my thoughts. "Sorry. Miles away."

"I saw the light on," Anne said.

"Oh, sorry."

"No, don't be. I've got things to do anyway." Anne leant over the sink, seeing my wet leggings. "Wait. Do you have your period?"

"Yes," I said. "Why? Is that a problem? I was trying to clean up. I was going to ask you for some tampons. Obviously these are going into the wash but I didn't want—"

"Oh, Laura," said Anne. "I don't have any, not even for me." Anne pulled her hood away from her face. "Well I do have some but they're restricted. I have very few. The cotton crop was poisoned from the bombs and the gas and so, well,

173

a tampon would kill you now. We're trying to grow cotton crops in greenhouses in the secured areas but it's taking time and—"

"What do you mean, restricted?"

"Well, Jane has priority. Obviously."

"And she has her period now?"

"And then Andrea and Helen. Then the rest of Jane's elite defence unit. We can't have them incapacitated."

"But they don't all have their periods right now?"

Anne shook her head.

I was bleeding again. I felt the flow. "Can't I have the ones you've got?"

Anne's cheeks flushed and she started pulling the cords on her hoodie. "I have to keep them for Jane," she said quietly.

Andrea wandered in, still half asleep, and looked pretty surprised to see a brightly lit bathroom with people in it. "What's up?"

"Laura has her period," Anne replied.

"Oh."

"I can't go on the raid without a tampon," I said. "I can't fight a war with tissue stuffed between my legs."

"No, you can't," Andrea said, and then she looked at Anne – but not with the disapproving look I had hoped for.

"What?" I said. "What does that look mean?"

Anne opened her mouth but before she could say anything...

"It means, no, you can't come on the raid," Andrea said.

"What?" As I stood up straight I felt a heavy flow.

Alex wandered in, scruffier even than Andrea. "Hey. What's up?"

Andrea and I were just staring at each other.

"Laura's got her period," Anne said.

"Oh," said Alex. "I'll go and reshuffle the grenade allocations after I've had a shower." Alex picked a towel from the piles on the shelves and headed into one of the shower cubicles.

Anne took a step towards me, then I saw her double-check herself and back off towards the door. "I'll see you later." And with that she slipped past Andrea and out the room.

The sound of the rushing water from the shower broke the silence between me and my boss.

My head dropped. I'd lost this stand-off.

Andrea put her hand on my shoulder. "The distraction, the impact on your concentration, would be enough to jeopardise the whole brigade. And what we use for periods would limit your movement. And, you know, if your flow is bad, you'd be leaving a mark like Theseus's string. They'd track us down in a second. There will be more raids."

I looked at Andrea. "I want to go."

Andrea touched my arm. "I can't take you with me. Anne will need help in the medical centre so stay by her side. She likes you. She will need you tonight."

Anne, clipboard in hand, counted the syringes in her cupboard, mouthing out the numbers as she tapped each one with her fingertips. One, two, three, four, five... Then, satisfied, she unclipped her pen from the top of her clipboard and wrote down the number.

Pen clipped back on, she moved on to the crêpe bandages. Then the scalpels, thread and needles. The bags of saline solution were in a separate cupboard. Next to it was a fridge, which Anne opened. It was filled with bags of blood. Bags and bags of blood.

I turned away.

"Laura, you are funny." Anne had a little chuckle. "It's blood. The same thing that is currently flowing from your womb."

I looked back to see Anne continuing much as before,

unaffected, reconciling the details on each pack with what she had on her piece of paper.

I looked away again until I heard the tell-tale noise of the fridge door being closed.

In here, Anne seemed a different woman. This was her domain, everything as she had designed. She walked with her head up, holding her clipboard close to her chest as we crossed the floor.

The room was bright and airy. The large windows and high ceilings filled it with daylight. The metal bed-frames had been secured in parallel lines across the floor. Anne and I checked each one for clean mattresses and sheets, folding down all the corners and checking all the pillows.

Then in walked Jane, unannounced.

My blood ran cold, but Anne's smile widened and her eyes sparkled. She ran towards her sister.

And for the first time I saw Jane embrace someone warmly and hold them close.

Jane didn't stay long, luckily for me as I felt awkward standing in the middle of the vast empty room, trying not to watch the only other two people there.

Jane had her back to me so I could only see Anne's wide eyes and smiles as she nodded at her sister. Jane was doing most of the talking, which was annoying as I couldn't see her face to read her lips. And I couldn't hear her either.

Then she turned to me, briefly, before touching her sister's arm and leaving.

Anne watched her go and I slowly walked over. "I keep forgetting Jane is a sister."

"Most do." Anne smiled.

"I'd imagined it would be easier getting blood from a stone than a smidgeon of sisterly love from her." Then I caught Anne's eyes. "Sorry."

Anne turned back to her desk, shuffling papers. "Everyone thinks they know my sister, but they don't. She leads two lives – a leader and my sister. To judge her on one and not the other is to dehumanise her."

"I apologise. But no one other than you can comment on her role as a sister."

"True."

"Or daughter."

Anne said nothing.

"Your parents are dead, aren't they?" I asked.

"Yes. They died a long time ago, before The Fall. It was just me and Jane when it all started to happen. And I guess it's still just me and her now too."

"What do you remember?"

Anne went quiet, looked down at her hands. "I don't really have any memories of my father. We never really saw him. He was always at work. And whenever he was at home, the odd weekend or whatever, he was always angry. Really angry. Like a simmering pan of boiling water. One that just barely had the lid on. I stayed out of his way. I kept to my room all the time, studying, reading, working on my grades. Anything to avoid him."

I let Anne lose herself in her thoughts. Mean, perhaps. Would a friend be more consoling? But the next question... It was too good an opportunity to miss.

"Did Jane act differently?" I asked.

Anne's reaction was slight – but I noticed it. Her eyes fell down and to the right. "Jane stood up to him." It was said quietly, but firmly.

I said nothing more, knowing that no further questions were needed.

"I'm not blind," Anne added. "I know she's not perfect. Well, she is, but... You know..."

"I know, what?"

Anne looked at me. "She is unique. She is a hero. She is to me, and to others."

"Must be hard, living in the shadow of a hero," I ventured.

"No, it's a relief actually," Anne said. "Though I often wonder who her hero is. Who is there for her? I guess that's why she prays."

"Your sister *prays*?"

Anne smiled. "Ah, that's something you didn't know about my sister. That's why she works in the chapel."

"Jane believes in God?"

"That surprises you?"

I thought for a moment. "But she's so anti-establishment. She's anti-everything. She's so... logical."

Anne shrugged. "Guess you don't know her that well then."

"You don't think it's out of character?"

"When you're the one shouldering the burden, who else can you turn to?"

CHAPTER TWENTY-TWO
The Red Tent

I'm not sure which I heard first. Was it the raised voices? The crying? Or the screaming? For a moment, the faint line between my reality and my nightmares became blurred. Then I realised the sounds were around me. My consciousness flowed back. I had fallen asleep on one of the beds in the gym. I started to slowly open my eyes.

Then I shot up like a bolt.

They were rushing into the room, into the medical centre. The whole army.

Soldiers dragging in screaming comrades, their torsos ripped apart.

One was clutching the stumps at the end of her body, both her legs blown clean off.

The women poured in, a harrowing, bleeding flood.

I leapt off the bed.

The army continued to stream in. Massive head traumas, shattered limbs, arms ripped off, blood drenched cloths held to broken heads... Wave upon wave headed towards me.

I caught Winter just as she was about to fall out of Rachel's arms. We dropped her onto my bed. Her thigh was ripped open and there was a deep cut in the side of her stomach.

"She got caught on the barbed wire." Rachel, too, was bloodied, though whose blood it was was impossible to tell. "It ripped through her."

"What the hell happened?"

"Exactly what we expected." Rachel was looking round. "Where are the drugs?"

Winter's groans were getting fainter. We were losing her.

"I'll get them," I said, despite having no idea where the hell they were, or if we had any.

I bolted in the direction of the nearest store cupboard, but the room was heaving. Filled with casualties in agony. There was enough light in the room to make out the mix of blood and mud that was beginning to flood the floor.

"Get her on here." To my right, Mandy and Andrea were shouting at someone unseen about a patient I couldn't make out.

The cupboard doors had been flung open and those who could still walk were raiding it for everything they could find. I headed straight towards it, pushing past sweating, bleeding bodies.

To my left I heard a woman screaming before catching a glimpse of her through a circle of bodies. She was clutching her stomach. Becks and Helen were fighting her to get her to pull her hands away.

No time to stand and stare.

I had to reach deep into the cupboard to pull out something, anything, from the scraps that remained. I needed anaesthetic, I needed bandages. There was neither. I grabbed a pile of ragged towels from the pile by the wall and sprinted back through the crowd to Rachel and Winter, ripping the towels into strips as I skidded across the floor.

"Lift her legs," I said as I spat a tattered end of one of the towel strips from my mouth. "We've got to keep her legs up, slow the flow of blood."

Rachel held her legs up and I wound and tied, wound and tied.

The smell of blood filled my nostrils.

"Winter, Winter... Winter, honey, stay with us." Rachel was shaking as much as she was shaking Winter.

I wound and tied, wound and tied.

Screams from behind...

I pressed down on the last of the ties and began to clean out her wound. "This will hurt," I said.

"Don't tell her," Rachel snapped.

I quickly reached into the wound and teased out pieces of bark. One twig was in deep, I really had to dig in. The blood didn't even register. Adrenalin is an incredible anaesthetic.

I wrapped the strips tight and firm. Tears rolled down Rachel's face, but she was quiet. She gently brushed her hands through Winter's hair, placating her, calming her. Keeping her conscious.

Winter suddenly screamed.

Rachel looked at me, terrified.

"At least she's conscious," I said. "Drop her legs." I looked away, took a deep breath then turned back and reached into the stomach wound, pulling out the pebbles and loose debris I could find. It was gruesome. I could feel Winter's tissue slide through my fingers.

She was clean. And then, between us, Rachel and I started to secure her wound.

And just as we finished...

"Get her the fuck off there." Helen pushed Winter off the bed with all the force only a bully can muster.

I caught Winter, but Rachel turned and shoved Helen. Helen shoved Rachel back, harder. Whoa.

"What the fuck…" But before I could finish, I saw Jane behind her, with others, carrying in a woman I didn't know. Her stomach was… It was gone. Blood pouring all over her torso, her intestines spilling out.

I held Winter close, but barely noticed the patient in my arms.

They put the woman on the bed. It was impossible to look away. Andrea and Helen immediately flanked Jane's side. The operating equipment was thrown on to the bench next to her. And then Andrea and Helen started to work feverishly on the woman.

Jane moved to the top of the table and cradled the woman's head in her hands but she was unconscious.

Blood from her stomach hit my face.

Anne pushed through the group to get to the table. She was holding a full syringe.

Winter came round in my arms and threw up. Rachel rushed over to help and we lay her flat out on the floor.

I stood up just as Anne jabbed the needle into the woman's arm. And it was only then that I realised it was no gunshot wound. No. And it wasn't her intestines spilling out. No. For there, being cut from her, was an exposed, bloodied foetus. The woman's womb, not her stomach, had been cut open.

And the foetus was big.

Jesus. Christ.

It was her womb. Jesus. Oh my God, it was her womb.

There was a baby. Not even a little foetus. An actual baby.

I'd never seen this woman before. She wasn't in our uniform.

Andrea sliced what must've been the umbilical cord and pulled the baby free.

The baby started squirming in Andrea's hands. It was still alive. Good God, it was still alive. Just.

I jumped up to catch some bloodied towels before they fell to the floor.

The woman groaned.

The others began to work on her. Towels were pressed down on her but she was dying. As was the baby Andrea now held in her arms. She looked across at Jane, as we all did.

"Kill it," Jane said to Andrea. "Then bury it."

I staggered back. The floor was soaking. I looked down. I was sloshing around in a flood of blood.

"Aaargh!" Winter screamed as I trod on her hand.

"I'm sorry." I bent down to her. I had forgotten she was there.

Rachel shoved her arm underneath Winter's legs. "We need to move her."

"What the fuck happened? What the fuck is going on?"

"Just lift her," Rachel snapped at me.

A flash of anger shot through me. The stampede around me continued. I pushed my arms right under Winter's back and we lifted her clear, securing her a safe place in the corner of the room.

"Rachel, what the fuck is going on?"

Rachel pulled the flask from her waist, unscrewed it and gave it to Winter. "The raid, it was on a facility where they were holding women, a high-value target. But it was heavily defended. These women were being held down. Just…" She just trailed off.

A hand grabbed the straps of my top. It was Andrea. Her hands were blood red. But the foetus was nowhere to be seen "Winter's fine. Help me." And she dragged me back to the bed.

The woman on the bed was still alive – just – but her body looked beyond repair. Anne was frantically trying to get the right dose of whatever into another syringe and administer it.

"You are going to hold her stomach together," Andrea said, "and I am going to sew." I nodded but my hands didn't move. Andrea grabbed them and placed them on two pieces of flesh, squeezing the two ripped sides together. "Hold this together. Tight."

I did. And as I did, Andrea sewed. Quickly.

Jane brushed her hand across the woman's forehead. She was conscious – how, I don't know – but her gaze was of someone passing into the shadows.

Jane stroked the woman's cheek.

The freed prisoner looked up at her, the wonder in her eyes giving the impression that a soft halo of light bathed Jane's face.

And then she died.

Anne touched the woman's wrist, her neck. And nodded at Jane.

Jane looked at Andrea. "Finish her. Don't leave her like this." And then left.

I didn't leave Andrea's side. I held all the pieces of the dead woman's body together as she sewed. The silence between us was impossible to break.

Until it had to be broken.

Andrea's hands began to shake, her eyes were wide, as if shot out on springs.

"Here, let me take the needle." I reached out just as the needle slipped out of her bloodied hands and into the woman's exposed flesh. I could just about see enough of the sliver of metal to pick it out from the blood.

"Sorry." The crack in Andrea's voice was marked.

"Just hold the pieces together. It'll be fine."

And I sewed.

Our silence continued but the noise, the heat and the smell in the room was overwhelming. The woman's body was still warm – the blood still flowing from the wounds in her lifeless body. I'm not ashamed to say I'm not sure what was sewn to what, or whether she was whole before Andrea and I left her side. But when Anne came round and told us "enough is enough", we let her go.

I touched her arm. She was not yet cold. Her head hung limply, down to the side, eyes closed. Her face was pale but as I looked down her body... There was no way she could have survived that much blood loss.

"We killed her," I said.

"No. She did this to herself," Andrea croaked out. "We released them all from their chains but a couple of them, including this one, just started stabbing themselves, screaming 'get it out, get it out'."

"How can you keep stabbing yourself?" I asked.

"She was very heavily drugged," Andrea said. "Not by us."

Suddenly I caught a glimpse of her legs. "And this."

Andrea and I leant in. I swiped away some the surface blood on the woman's thighs and there they were, hundreds of red bumps. The sprawling rash.

"Shit," Andrea whispered. "She had the STD."

I closed my eyes and prayed to whatever God may exist that somehow that woman found a peace in death that she was denied in life.

I froze in the middle of the storm. I don't know where Andrea went. She had dissolved into the mayhem.

Soon Anne found me and pulled me over to a bed where a pregnant woman was lying. Her face was badly scarred, her arms covered in bruising and needle marks. She was in a bad way but she wasn't dying. She wasn't passing in and out of consciousness.

Anne nodded at me. "Pay attention to her."

My mind was overwhelmed. It took me a moment to work out what was wrong. There were people dying around me.

In the next bed, one of the soldiers was being prepped for an amputation. Why was I being asked to—

And then I saw the knife in Anne's hands.

And I knew what was about to happen.

I looked down at the woman. "Are you OK? Did they hurt you?" I asked.

The woman couldn't move her head for fear of reopening the deep wounds on her face and neck. They were still red. God how it must've hurt when they did that to her.

"Get it out of me." The woman whispered. "Get it out of me."

Suddenly Jane appeared on the other side of the bed. She nodded at Anne. "Cut."

"Wait," I said. "There's nothing wrong with her."

Jane looked at me, then back at her sister. "Cut."

I pushed Anne's hand with the knife away from the woman's belly. "This could kill her. She's not dying."

"Get it out. Get it out." The woman started moving on the bed.

Jane held her down and snapped at me. "This isn't up for debate." At Anne, "Cut."

"No!" I shouted.

"Don't argue with me!" It was said with an anger I hadn't heard from Jane before.

With no anaesthetic, Anne carved deep into the woman. Her flesh peeled away from the knife, separating like orange segments.

The woman screamed. I ran to the top of the bed and held her head still while Jane grabbed her hands. "Squeeze my arm," she said to the woman. "I don't care if you dig your nails in and shred my skin – squeeze my arm."

Anne slit open the womb.

The woman screamed in pain. I held her shoulders down. Alex appeared at the foot of the bed to hold down her legs.

Anne reached in and pulled out the foetus. She held it rather awkwardly in her hands as Alex tried to cut the cord. But the scissors were blunt. Alex tried a snip, then a bigger cut deeper into the joint of the scissors, but no luck. She began to hack away at the cord with the join in the scissors, trying to free the dead foetus from the womb. The bundle in Anne's hands was a bloody mess.

Jane was focused on the woman. The fingers of her left hand were on the woman's neck, the fingertips of her right on her wrist. "Her pulse isn't strong." The woman was no longer wriggling. She was pale, sweaty, feverishly whispering. Her eyes were closed. "She's falling into a coma."

Jane was right.

Anne didn't know what to do, stuck with the bloodied foetus in her hands. I moved round the table, starting to piece the woman back together as Anne took the foetus away, to where I don't know.

"Keep her conscious," I said. As I took control, I could feel Jane's attention focused on me. I didn't look at her though. I just kept sewing.

"It's weakening," Jane said.

I finished sewing but the woman was fading. "She needs CPR," I said.

Jane and I both moved forward, our hands going straight to the woman's chest. Jane looked at me closely. "You know CPR?"

She moved away.

I clambered on top of the table, on top of the woman, placing my hands over her heart. I started pushing. One-two-three-four...

The crowd around the table was mute and inert. Jane's hands stayed resolutely on the woman's neck. "The pulse is strong."

I stopped. Pressed my hand against her chest and leant in

till my ear touched her lips. She was breathing. Thank God, she was breathing.

She would pull through.

Her head convulsed and I pulled away just as it fell to the side and she threw up.

Her wound was still bleeding but she was going to make it.

I hauled myself down from the table.

The group reformed around the woman as I staggered back. They tended to her wounds and did what they needed to do.

Jane looked at me impassively, then turned and moved to another of the wounded.

I staggered over to the sink with the bloodied equipment to clean and sanitise it. But as soon as I got there, I just collapsed, my head hanging down, the metal utensils clanging against the steel of the sink. I could feel the sick rise up in my throat but nothing came out.

It was the faintest of whispers that snapped me back.

"Do you have a probe in there?" Anne leant in and grabbed one of the instruments. She was covered in blood. "It's Shauna, come with me."

One of Shauna's legs was shattered. The other had a deep cut. So deep that as Anne pushed the probe into it, inches of metal disappeared into her thigh. And as Anne pulled each of the bullets out, the blood flowed quickly after it, pouring over Shauna's black skin.

"Hold this." Anne pushed the probe into my hand and took a long sharp needle in exchange.

Mandy was there, desperately worried. "Maybe we should leave the metal in there," she said.

"It will poison her blood if we do." Anne didn't even break her pace as she replied.

Shauna looked unconscious. Mandy began to pat her forehead. "Stay with me, Shauna, stay with me, girl."

Jane suddenly appeared. Momentarily, we stopped. Jane looked at us. "Continue."

Anne started to move more quickly, the bullets hitting the metal dish in a rhythm.

Mandy melted away as Jane placed her hands around Shauna's head, keeping it still as her sister worked.

"Press harder."

I pushed the clean sides of the wound together as Anne instructed, but the blood flow was not slowing down. There had been many bullets. Her blood could already be poisoned. Every single one of them had to come out.

We were fighting a losing battle. The blood, Shauna's blood, was flowing like a river. Her arteries had been shattered.

Mandy returned and used towel after towel to wrap the limbs, to mop up the blood. But it wasn't enough. The towels changed from white to red in seconds.

Shauna groaned.

Mandy rubbed her friend's arm. "It's OK, Shauna. It's OK. I have you now. You are safe. Anne has cleaned your wound. You will be fine."

I glanced at Mandy; Mandy looked at Anne; Anne averted her gaze.

"Will I be OK?" Shauna whispered. "My leg—"

"Your leg is fine. It will heal," Anne whispered.

Jane looked at Anne.

Shauna had her eyes open, but barely. Jane moved around the table so that she was directly facing the patient. "Shauna, you are not going to make it. You have lost a lot of blood. I am with you now. You are here with us again. And I'm not going to leave your side."

Tears started to roll down Shauna's cheeks.

Anne turned her head, she too was crying. Mandy pulled her arms over her head.

Jane went on. "You are a hero, Shauna, you are my hero. What you did in there was a great thing. Helen is charged with my personal safety, not you. Today, you saved my life."

Shauna nodded. Then her head convulsed with that involuntary spasm that comes when choking back tears.

Jane's voice dropped to a whisper. "You are my hero." Then she leant forward and kissed Shauna's forehead.

Jane continued to hold Shauna's head close to her.

Shauna's breath began to slow. At first it seemed like she was just calming herself down. But then her breath became very shallow.

Then raspy.

Then nothing.

Jane laid Shauna's head back down on the bed.

I dropped my head.

Anne started crying loudly.

Jane left.

Mandy fell on Shauna, holding her tightly.

Anne ran off and as she did, I grabbed Alex as she passed by. "Who are these women? What happened?"

Alex was holding bloodied tools and heading towards the sink. I followed her. "These are women from the enclaves," Alex said, throwing the equipment into the sink. "They were being held outside of the enclaves though, in a facility, a medical facility, to monitor their births. It's not normally done. We're guessing the enclaves are struggling with facilities more than we thought. We're not sure. I don't know. I don't know, OK?"

"What the fuck happened, Alex? These women are dying."

"Don't lecture me!"

"I'm sorry. I'm sorry."

Alex crumbled, leaning heavily on the side of the sink. I put my arm around her. "It's OK."

Alex looked up, tears streaming down her face. She gasped for air, trying to compose herself. "These women... they were all strapped down... They were prisoners... We had to get them all. We wanted to... get them all but..." And she tailed off.

"They were defended better than Jane thought, weren't they?"

Alex shook her head. "Something else." Then she crumpled and burst into uncontrollable tears.

I stood there holding her.

The screaming echoed through the room. Around me the floor was filled with the wounded and the dying.

So much collateral damage to get these women.

I looked around at the chaos, the heavy smell of blood, sweat and rotting flesh was thick in the air.

I needed out. I left Alex and staggered out of the back of the building. The rush of cold air. I closed my eyes, put my hands on my knees and hung my head, waiting for the convulsions to bring up whatever was left inside.

But nothing came.

CHAPTER TWENTY-THREE
The Whispers

Dawn. The light from the sun was trying to break through the clouds. A faint attempt to lift the darkness.

I stood outside, I had to. The putrid smell in the medical centre was suffocating. The taste of death on the tongue, the smell of flesh beginning to rot in the nostrils. So intense that even the polluted atmosphere outside was like a gush of fresh air to the lungs.

I looked out over the playing fields – there would be no training this morning. I could see the shadows of the patrols on the perimeter though.

A squad came out of the main building and headed down the drive to relieve those who'd done the night shift. The returning squad would get a shock on their return to the building.

Or maybe they wouldn't.

Maybe this was the norm. Maybe they were already versed in the casualties of conflict. Maybe this is what had been happening all along, all those years I was in the block. Maybe I was just naive. Maybe this was simply war.

From behind me, I could still hear the noises from the hospital, from the ward, the gym – whatever we were calling it. I had been in there all night trying to save the women – saving their limbs, saving their wombs, saving their lives. It's frightening how quickly you can numb yourself. In one night I had performed four abortions and cut two destroyed legs from a woman I didn't even know the name of.

And I hadn't cried once.

I was scared of what I was becoming. It's monstrous not to be affected.

Anne had cried. She had cried all the way through one woman's termination. We didn't know her name. I think that's what bothered Anne the most. The woman was weak anyway. Her odds weren't great. Her arm showed too many punctures.

"We don't even know her name. What's her name?" Anne was gripping the knives tight in her hands. She was getting hysterical.

"Fucking hell, I don't know, Anne. Just help her." Andrea was holding the woman's head still.

"But you can't just keep saying 'stay with us, stay with us'. She might not make it. She deserves to be called by her name if she doesn't make it." Anne had tears in her eyes.

I touched Anne's arm. "We still care, Anne. We still care, even without a name. But there are bigger issues here." I looked up at Andrea. "Andrea, if we can't bring her round, how the hell do we know this is what she wants?"

"She was fucking raped. Look at her fucking arms." Andrea was quickly losing it. We were crowded round one of the beds, around us was chaos.

I shook my head. "We can't seriously cut this woman's womb and kill her baby without her consent. This is murder."

"This is fucking reality!" Andrea screamed.

Anne started crying.

"Get it out. Get it out." The woman started murmuring. She started shaking her legs. "Get it out, get it out." Louder and louder.

"See?" Andrea said.

"No," I replied. "This woman is heavily drugged. This isn't consent."

"I want it out. I want it out." The woman started thrashing on the bed.

Andrea glared at me. Anne was frozen.

"What is this? Why have you stopped?" And there she was again. The ice in the fire. Jane looked around the table. We all straightened up, fell back just a little. "Someone answer me."

"I... we can't give this woman a termination," I said. "Not without her consent."

Jane looked at her sister, who said nothing. Then Andrea, who also said nothing but at least held Jane's eye contact.

The woman started writhing again. "God, please. Take it out. I don't want it, I don't want it."

Jane looked at me, but I shook my head again. "This woman isn't thinking clearly."

Jane shot round the table and gripped my neck. "Stop finding excuses not to listen to a woman when she speaks."

I gasped, shocked. Jane's grip was tight – and getting tighter.

Anne whispered. "Her pulse is elevated."

Jane released my neck. "Do as she asks," she said. And then she disappeared into the mass of sweat and blood that filled the room.

The law had been laid.

Shaken, I ran the bromine lotion over the woman's small protruding belly. Anne tried to cut but her hands were trembling so I had to take her place, though I wasn't much better.

I nodded at Andrea, who held the woman's head tightly, nodded at Anne, who took the woman's arms, and started to cut.

I started to stroll along the gravel, moving away from my crimes. The gravel crunching underfoot betrayed my escape but I don't think anyone was listening. And if they were, I think we had all exhausted our will to shout and berate.

But I wasn't the only one seeking solitude, time to work out the car crash in their head, for there, crouched up against the side of the school, cigarette in hand, was Gauiri. Shattered and stunned.

And she had heard me. "Hey," she paused, mouth open, wanting to say something else but unable to find the words.

I waited a bit to see if she'd finish her sentence. But she didn't. So I nodded and added my own "Hey."

I didn't know what to say either. In a short time we'd seen a lot, probably none of it we were expecting. So we just hung there for a minute or so, in an awkward silence, Gauiri smoking on her cigarette, me standing nearby looking out over a muddy field at nothing in particular.

"Thank you for saving Polly," she said suddenly, confusing me a little.

"I don't... Do I know a Polly?"

Gauiri shuffled herself on the gravel. "She was the one with the long black hair, in a plait." That wasn't registering with me. "She had a head injury, across her eyes." She ran her hand across her head, where Polly's cut had been.

Yes, I remembered. "It was fine. It's just what—"

"If it hadn't been for you and Anne, she would've lost that eye, wouldn't she?"

"Probably, yes." I looked at Gauiri. She had aged quickly. "She's in your squad, Polly?"

Gauiri nodded. "I was meant to be... We had been sent..."

she stopped and took a deep breath. "Last night, Polly and I were meant to keep secure... keep open one of the exits from the building, to keep a clear alley for the squads inside pulling out the women and putting them into the trucks." Gauiri shook her head. "I don't know what happened. I didn't... It wasn't Polly, it was me. I didn't keep checking behind her. They crept up on her, no gun, slashed her from the back."

"I'm sure it wasn't your—"

"Yeah, it was." Gauiri's cigarette was right down to the butt but she seemed oblivious, miles away. "And all I got was a fucking sprained ankle."

I thought about what to say, trying to get the right words. "A lot of things went wrong last night."

"Yeah, they did." Gauiri realised her cigarette was done and threw it into the gravel. And then took another one out of her packet. "Too many." And then she dropped her voice. "They think we were betrayed, you know. That's what they're saying."

"Betrayed?"

"An informant. We were sprung."

The heat rushed to my cheeks. I didn't move, didn't flinch. "Really?"

"They knew we were coming," Gauiri added. "Someone from within our ranks told them, that's what they're saying."

Was that me? My trace? The trace I uploaded onto their server. That was me. Had they worked out what I had downloaded and guessed? Wait, that was a big guess if they thought Jane would attack that base. We extracted a lot of information that night. And Jane blew up the room. Had the trace even survived? Was that information a plant?

"I think they might be right, though," she added, pulling me out of my thoughts.

"Who told you that, that there was an informant?"

Gauiri shrugged. "They're all whispering it."

"I'm sure that isn't true. That target wasn't disclosed till the last minute. It's just... Everyone's just feeling... on edge. That's all."

"I don't know, I really don't. You weren't there, Laura. It felt like an ambush. They came out of nowhere. Becks and Rachel, they were inside, part of the team bringing out the women and they said the men were waiting for them. It was lightly defended, in some areas, then when they started bringing the women out, bam! They came from all sides."

"What happened?"

She shook her head. "I don't know for sure, I was on the outside. Andrea and Mandy were bringing the first women out. They saved me, they saved Polly. They killed them all, the four or five men who ambushed us. They saved the women and killed the men. I couldn't do either." Gauiri folded into herself, head down to the knees. "I don't think I'm cut out for this, Laura. I think I'm going to request an out."

"An out? There's no out. You made the decision."

"There has to be an out, there has to be. I don't care. Maybe it isn't like this in the territories, the west and the north, away from this army. I'm in the wrong place. I wasn't built for this much blood."

"How did you all get away?"

"Jane. She's just... She started an electrical fire, covered the air vents and blew away all of them. Is that even possible? I don't know. The whole thing detonated up into the sky and we got away. Her brain... It's incredible."

"That means we killed everyone who was inside that building."

Gauiri nodded back towards the gym. "But look at those women, Laura. If I'd still been inside, I'd rather be dead than alive."

"What makes you believe there was an informant and not just, you know, that we underestimated the defences?"

"Something Mandy said." She took a drag. "When she put one of the women in the convoy. We were under fire, it was noisy, the screams of the women… But I heard her say, 'we've been double-crossed'. Then Andrea shut her up straight away. But that's what they've been saying, in there." Gauiri nodded again towards the hospital. "And that's what I saw as the convoy pulled away, the army being caught in a firefight, a firefight we weren't expecting. That was meant to be a new facility, lightly defended." She looked up at me. "I don't ever want to see a sight like what was in there again."

And then, from round the side of the building, Jane appeared. Just two guards with her. She didn't look at us or even glance up. She jogged out past us, on to the field, and started her exercises. High knees for one hundred yards, then sprints and jogs up to the trees and back again. Her hair was clean, her clothes were fresh.

Gauiri and I, still bloodied and bruised, stood in stunned silence at the edge of the field, witnessing first-hand the cold blood that pumped through the veins of Our Great Leader.

Andrea was sweating. We both were. Impossible not to when working this close to fire.

We were digging. Shovels in hands. The only two left who had enough energy or will for the thankless task. Out the back of the hospital, digging a pit as deep as we could, as quickly as we could.

I'd tried to change the towel between my legs before we started but there was no point. There were no clean ones left. Instead I'd thrown my bloodied towel onto the mountain with the rest and used a dry strip of sheet I found on the floor. Whether it was clean or not, who knows.

Andrea dug in rhythm – shovel hit the earth, shovel pushed in, heaved out full of dirt. I kept trying to catch her eye. I knew that she could see me. But she kept avoiding me. Despite the three-foot-high walls of dirt surrounding us, there was enough light left for me to make out how pale she was. One night, it seemed, had been enough to drain much of the life from her face.

"Did you ask her, when she told you?" I eventually asked. "Did you push back?"

"I don't know," Andrea snapped. Before adding, "I can't remember," just that bit softer.

I let the tension fade, just a little, took a few more shovels of earth out, before trying again. "Because what she's asking…"

Andrea stopped, breathing heavily. "I don't even have any fucking cigarettes." She banged her shovel – hard.

I stopped too and leant against my shovel. "She wants to attack this convoy, this one they've heard about on the wires, doesn't she? She wants to attack the convoy when it arrives at the main rest-stop out near the east coast."

"Yes."

"This is high risk."

Andrea was impassive. "She says it's vulnerable."

"So are we."

Andrea said nothing. She hadn't even turned to face me. A sign of doubt. She was avoiding confrontation. If you're not afraid, if you're sure, eye contact holds no fear.

"Did you prepare the computer virus?" Andrea eventually asked, turning towards me at last.

I nodded. "You asked me, I did it. I wouldn't let you down."

Andrea nodded, avoiding me again.

"But I still disagree, Andrea. This is an emotional decision and an emotional decision in war is always the wrong one."

Andrea pulled out her shovel and kicked away some stones near her feet. "She wants a retaliatory strike."

"What happened, Andrea, the night before last?"

Andrea raised her eyebrows, kind of shook her head. "Truth is, I don't know. If I did, I'd be in a better place. That's never happened before, never."

"Caught out?"

Andrea just went on as if I'd said nothing. "Jane's more angry than fazed. She doesn't show it though, you know. She has this white rage. Pure ice. Like a deep freeze. She didn't mean to grab your neck like that. Just. Oh, I don't know. I just want to tear up this building till I find who it was." Andrea started digging again. "I watch these women now, and I wonder who it is, who it was."

"There can't be a rat, Andrea. If there—"

"You weren't there." She stopped suddenly, turning to me, turning on me. "You weren't there. The target was announced late. They wouldn't have been able to deploy those troops so quickly if they'd just seen our convoys. It was a tip-off. They were waiting for us."

Andrea wiped her brow.

I looked at the ground. It would soon be night. We'd have to stop digging and just fill the grave up. Fires obviously make it impossible for an army trying to stay under cover in a period of vulnerability.

"I hate men," Andrea said.

"I don't believe every man is involved in that, Andrea. It's animal behaviour."

"Are you seriously defending men?"

"Hey," I put my hands in the air. "I'm not naive. But there is a difference between an army in the field and State policy. What makes you sure that this is State policy? That it isn't just a brigade out of control? This is the army we're talking about. You treat men like animals, they start behaving like them. I saw those photos of what they did in the Islamic State, of what they did in Libya. They just brought that home with them. Violence, yes. Terrible, yes. But not institutionalised."

Andrea shook her head. She looked broken. "Does it matter, Laura? Does it matter? Either way, whether it's the State or the men, the result is always the same."

I dropped my shovel and walked over to her. "It matters because if I'm right, we can stop this suicide mission. This attack on this convoy, this rest-stop for returning soldiers... You and I both know it's designed to kill as many men as possible. This is an emotional mission and you can't run up a suicidal mission for all those that are left standing."

"She's rationalising that we are strongest when we are on the attack."

"Is that what she told you?"

"Are you questioning her?"

"Aren't you?"

Andrea scowled. "No."

I stepped back. An open door closing quickly. But I had seen doubt in Andrea's eyes, I had seen it. I went again. "But, Andrea, this is vengeful. We are vulnerable. We are attacking this convoy of returning soldiers from overseas... How are these men even culpable in what happened to those women?"

Andrea looked me straight in the eyes. "But if even one of them is, I want to be there to kill him."

And the door closed again.

Maybe the time for alliance-building had passed. Maybe the loyalties to Jane were just too strong. Maybe I really did have to strike out on my own.

CHAPTER TWENTY-FOUR
The Night Before

Jane had dictated our response should be swift. Was it because her blood was up, or because minimal preparation time would give minimal opportunity for any saboteur in our ranks to warn the enemy? We were also dictated to by the movements of our enemy. The convoy Jane had set her attention on was due back in the UK shortly. The time, therefore, was now.

The focus of our planned attack, this rest-stop, was miles from the base. Miles. Direct, it would have been three hours' drive over roads that were either too conspicuous or too damaging to the suspension at speed. We had no choice but to travel most of the distance at night, in advance of a dawn raid.

Our place to rest for the night was a woodland clearing. The half a dozen trucks were hidden amongst the trees and the heat from their engines was the only heat we were going to feel that night, apart from a few warming embers we were allowed to have across the small patch of rocky ground.

Like me, the women were all huddled up in sleeping bags covered with blankets. But they were asleep. I was shattered, but my brain couldn't shut off. The only thing heavier than my eyelids was the burden of my responsibility. I lay there, chilly, looking up into the night sky wondering how the hell it had come to this.

Only a generation ago the West had been the richest it had ever been. We had it all – health, welfare, education. Security. We had a future. And it had all evaporated.

We have no one to blame but ourselves. The signs were all there – the terrorism we fostered in the East, the liberalism we eroded in the West. The climate deteriorated as we squabbled over costs, and the solution to the global financial meltdown was left in the hands of faceless, revolving-door politicians.

Liberalism's greatest flaw was its selfishness. When the skirmishes started in the East, we said these were regional issues. And when the skirmishes turned to battles, we voted no. And when the battles turned to wars, we said it was too late to help those who were losing. And when the desperate turned up on our shores, we turned them back, angry and resentful.

No one was prepared to make a sacrifice for liberal democracy to thrive and survive. We defeated liberalism long before they did.

I turned on to my side, curling up in a ball to try to hold on to some heat. I exhaled several times under my blanket, trying to heat it up. Well, at least I was fighting now. Would my mother be proud of me? Would my father?

My father.

I should've killed him. It was only my own selfishness that stopped me. I couldn't do it. He was sick, very sick, with no chance of recovery. And the lack of drugs meant that those last days, when he wasn't unconscious, he was in pain.

I did that to him.

I should've killed him. Instead I let him fade away.

He asked me, one night, when the morphine was low, when the pain kicked in, to end it all. "I'm holding you back."

"You're not holding me back. I want to be here." That's what I said. Your truth is always selfish. His pain wasn't as important to me as my own fears. He was my last link to all I knew so I made him live, even though it was killing him.

My shoulder hurt, a jagged rock was digging in so I turned on to my back. The blanket of cloud above us had broken and I could see the stars, some of them. I breathed deeply and exhaled, the gentle mist forming from my lips. Was the air really safe? Had the contamination passed? Had enough of it genuinely been blown away? The State tells me that I'm not safe, RAZR tells me that I am. The State tells me that I am safe, RAZR tells me that I am not.

I took another deep breath. Either the radiation was still in the air or it wasn't. There was no point fearing death any more. If it wanted me, it was having plenty of opportunities to take me.

The chill was settling on my chest. I turned on to my other side to curl up again, but as I did, I saw her. On the edge of the clearing, not far from me. Sat on the ground, back up against a felled trunk. No sleeping bag around her or even near her. She just sat there, arms resting on her knees, lost in her thoughts.

Next to Jane was a pile of embers, the small source of heat that we'd been allowed. Fires without flames.

It was strange, seeing the leader alone. Awake but alone. There were no guards close to her. Even Helen, who was nearby, lay asleep. Shouldn't it have been the other way round? Maybe the rest all slept because they knew she was watching over them.

She was alone. She was vulnerable.

Jane sat, gun by her side, looking out into the night.

I lay still under my blanket watching her.

Occasionally her head would drop and she would stare at her hands, deep in thought. Sometimes her lips would move, briefly, momentarily in conversation with herself. Then she would raise her head again. It would nod of its own free will, gently, as if she was convincing herself, part of an internal debate.

Uneasy lies the head that wears the crown.

Observing greatness or observing tyranny? Depends who wins the war, I suppose. History is always written by the victor. And I had a say in that. I had a role to play. Jane, the wanted one. Poised on the verge of victory, on the brink of a suicide mission. If she won, would we learn to admire her? Or would we continue to live in fear?

Then the movement of her head and lips stopped. She was no longer talking to herself. Her head became still. Conscious awareness.

She had sensed I was watching.

"You stare a lot." Jane spoke, but her head never moved. In the shadows I wasn't even sure her lips moved. But I knew her voice.

I shuffled until I sat upright. "You think a lot," I replied.

I saw that rueful smile again, a nod of the head.

My cover blown, I got to my feet, wrapped a blanket around me and crept nearer. But not too close. Jane's personal space was an icy domain. And I knew where the edge was.

I shuffled to a large rock not far from her and crouched against it.

Jane said nothing, returning to looking at her fingers, at the woods, at her patrol.

I took a few breaths, thinking about how to breach the defences.

But it was Jane who broke the silence. "You're not sleeping because of anxiety?"

I shook my head. "No. I don't think so. Not about the attack. Maybe about the attack. Maybe about a lot of things." I paused, letting it hang. But Jane didn't fill the silence. "I find death traumatic. I'm not immune to it yet."

"Yet? Interesting term." Jane paused, then looked over. "You showed impressive skills, you know. For a hacker."

I held her gaze but I didn't really get what she was... Oh.

"With the women," Jane added. "Skills like a surgeon."

I waited. The game was still being played. "I had to learn fast," I said. "In the blocks, to survive. But even I can't abort an ectopic pregnancy with minimal damage to the woman's reproductive system."

Jane looked out. "Impressive skills with a gun, impressive skills with a scalpel... I'm lucky to have you."

My training. This was all my training. I was letting it show too much; it was becoming too evident. I had been clumsy. But I'd had to save those woman – it was the right thing to do.

"Don't mourn for them," Jane added. "Death is a welcome release. It's good that you've overcome your fear of blood though."

My head jerked towards her. How did she...?

Anne. Anne had told her.

I see.

I lowered my head. And that's when I caught sight of it again – Jane's gun. Lying by her side, close but not touching. I could get to it, if my movements were quick.

I looked at her. She was oblivious, focused on the troubling thoughts crashing through her mind.

I looked across at the patrols. They were nearby. If I were to attempt something here, would they get to me in time? Or would they be too late? It would be a suicidal attack, if nothing else.

But suddenly Jane broke the silence. "So, blood is OK when it's accompanied by violence?"

"It was adrenalin," I said. "I haven't... I don't have your ease with it."

I caught sight of Jane glancing over at me from the corner of my eye. "What's that supposed to mean?"

"They told a lot of stories about you," I said quietly. "The State."

"I'm sure you've heard many things," she turned to look back out over the camp. "Maybe some of them are even true."

"They say you killed all of those soldiers, our own soldiers." I looked over at Jane. Barely a flicker of concern passed across her face. "When we were fighting over there. The night you went AWOL from special forces. The night RAZR was born."

We both knew which incident I was referring to.

"You attacked our own forces," I said.

"It wasn't planned," Jane said. "Camp Guard was the closest camp we had to the caliphate. The squad I was leading had just suffered huge casualties trying to take out missile launchers on the enemy's front line. Successful but, well, our success had come at a price. My men needed attention and they needed it quickly. Guard was the nearest outpost. Do you think they should've been warned we were coming? Why? We were on the same side. I simply saw them in their true colours."

Now it was my turn to look away.

"We arrived in the dead of night," she said. "I had to carry one of my men five miles across enemy territory just to get him there. He had no legs. I thought they would be asleep, just the men at the guard posts, but the place was alive. They were all in a building on the edge of the compound. You could hear the noise through the walls. The whooping and the cheering. And the screams from the women."

Jane let that hang.

I didn't look up.

"I think I knew what I was going to see even before I stepped inside, but that still doesn't prepare you for it. I can still hear their screams. I can still smell their blood. And their mangled, bruised faces, I can still see them. But I can't remember the men."

Jane fell quiet and I looked over.

She was staring out into the darkness. "I remember my hand on my rifle and my finger on the trigger. I was completely calm," she said.

"No one in that building survived," I whispered.

"No."

"No one in that camp that night survived."

"No, they didn't." Jane looked at me. "Not even the man I carried across the desert."

We held each other's gaze. The silence hung between us for a long time.

It was Jane that looked away.

I looked down at her gun. A standard AK. Nothing tailored, completely generic. The strap was loose. No part of the rifle even brushed against Jane. It would be a clean grab. But her hand was close. Not that far. I could see her hands, resting on her knees.

She would get to the gun before me.

Then she said, "What I have told you is the truth, Laura. I am not the one who has lied to you."

One of the pieces of bark amongst the embers cracked and split.

Eventually, I whispered, "This is a revenge mission, isn't it?"

"That's what you think I have ordered?"

I shrugged. "Our odds aren't great."

"Which means more to you, the odds or the principle?" I sensed Jane looking at me but I didn't answer. Eventually she added, "The women wouldn't follow me if I was reckless with their lives."

"I think they would."

"I am not a monster, Laura. But to defeat tyranny, first you must become a tyrant. I do not want you to wear my scars. I don't want you to be like me, I don't want them to become like me. This alone is my burden. But trust my judgment."

"Then how do you break that chain if you've got to become what you're trying to destroy?"

"Because once I win, I will walk away. I will let others take my authority, a new Parliament. I have no interest in trophies. I am here because I will enforce change. We can never be free in a world that values us only for our ability to reproduce."

"But we need them too," I whispered. "We are not asexual. We cannot generate life without them."

"Them, them... That's an interesting term. I like it."

"I meant, men."

"Maybe. But 'them' is very revealing, you know this."

"But we do need them, don't we?" My voice was quiet.

"We do. That's what I struggle with."

Jane arched her back away from the trunk, bringing some movement into her shoulders.

Helen rustled nearby. Jane's head jerked quickly in her direction and she froze. Then, as Helen settled back again into her deep sleep, Jane slowly leant back again.

"Let's talk frankly about men." Jane looked at me intently. "About the State. You know, there's a reason why prostitution is the oldest profession in the world, because that's how systemic, how institutionalised the exploitation of women is. Was. Trading in women. A trade in women. That's what prostitution is. That's the legacy of men – our most enduring trade.

"One in three men has paid for sex," she went on. "Has paid, has exchanged money for access to the female body. Entitlement established. Access rights established. Control. Property that could be bought and sold.

"How does that make you feel? That a third of the men you ever met, ever worked with, that you ever took orders from, that you ever took in your arms as a lover or as a confidant, thought it was OK to pay a woman for sex? There's a one in three chance your father visited a sex worker, Laura. That he reduced a woman to lying there in silence, thinking only of the money she desperately needed, as he screwed her."

Jane shook her head and looked away. "It's exploitation. We cannot sit here any more and say this is OK. That we can work alongside, within, a framework that established this. This isn't about the women who were exploited. This is about men who value a female body in coins."

"But why a war?" I whispered.

"Don't place the blame for this war on me. Don't you do their work for them. Men have had five thousand years to right that wrong, and they never did. You cannot negotiate your way to emancipation, Laura. Why... How women took so long to figure this out, I don't know. But this is our one chance, our one chance, to break the patriarchy for good. And I will do so with my own bare hands by any means at my disposal."

"The world just isn't that black and white," I said.

The look in Jane's eyes... I thought she was going to grab my throat again, but she pulled back, the flash in her eyes reducing to a simmer. "You know what's black and white? Every man benefited from sexism. Every single one. And all men acquiesced, agreed with the system that institutionalised that control."

Thankfully Jane turned her gaze from me and looked out across the camp. "Twenty-four weeks. That's what they gave us, gave you. Every single man in this country. All men. That was the limit, the lawful period of time in which men would allow women to have an abortion. That was the limit, their limit. That was the line they drew in the sand. That tells you everything you need to know about men. All men. Your boyfriend, your father. Your boss. That's what they thought of your freedom."

She went on. "After twenty-four weeks, your rights were finished. After twenty-four weeks your impregnated body was no longer under your control. After twenty-four weeks your legal rights over your own body evaporated. At twenty-four weeks, legal ownership of your body passed from you to the government. We've always been vessels, chattel."

Jane snapped her fingers. "Just like that. At twenty-four weeks, they owned us. When people talked about protecting abortion term limits, it had nothing to do with life. It was only ever about control. And that was in a time of peace. Now, in war, you don't even have those twenty-four weeks.

"They don't want your love, your support, Laura. The State wants your obedience. They want you to hate me. They want you to fear me. But it's them you should fear. Think! Think about this. They want to control you. That's why I am telling you the truth because men never will."

I hung my head down, overwhelmed. I felt the chill. I felt a heat.

Jane leant back. "Any man who takes control of a woman's rights at any stage in her life is a terrorist."

"And you think you can end that?" I asked.

Jane turned to me. There was compassion in her. "Unequivocally. I don't fight for glory, Laura. There's no glory in war, no matter how noble the cause. I'm not going to go down in history. We're all going to be forgotten. But war is attrition on the heart and on the soul. I'm not cruel, but to win you have to be ruthless. And I am ruthless. I'm just another in a long line of civil rights leaders with blood on their hands."

I shook my head. "But then you're just a killer, just like men."

Jane sighed, the adrenalin starting to fade. "We're all descendants of murderers, Laura. All kings have been killers, since the beginning of time. It's weird, isn't it, how here at the end of days we've come full circle, how close we must be now in behaviour to men at the dawn of time?"

"I don't understand," I said.

"This is the state of nature," Jane explained. "This is proof of who we are. In a way it's surprisingly egalitarian. Men, women... Regardless of gender, we are killers. In a godless world without government, without authority, it is a matter of survival. And we survive by killing. We have returned to the beginning. Look around you – a dark, hostile landscape. No community, no family. No compassion, no love. Those who are angriest, survive. Those who care, lose."

Jane exhaled deeply. "This is the answer to the oldest philosophical debate of them all – what is man like in the absence of any rule of law? Does he murder his competitors for scarce resources to secure his own survival? Or does he come together in a community to share those resources, to find strength in numbers?"

Jane looked at her gun. "Hobbes was right. Man chooses to kill or be killed, irrelevant of the risk of mutually assured destruction. Man will choose to fight, not to share. Life really is nasty, brutish and short. It's kind of funny really, how you learn these things right at the end when it would've been so much more useful to know at the beginning."

"You think we're all murderers at heart?"

Jane looked past me, out into the distance. "Instinctively, innately. We are educated, educated to rationalise and reason so why have we not reasoned ourselves out of war? These are not reasonable times, you could argue, but we had our chance. This landscape, this war... It proves that when faced with mutual destruction, man will still choose to kill his enemy rather than create a peace with him."

Jane dropped her head, defeated as much by exhaustion as her words. "I am part of that, I know. But there is no going back. We had no other option."

The dying embers cast shadows on her face. I looked for signs of defeat, but Jane remained hard to read.

And she knew I was watching.

"Yes, we're all descended from murderers," Jane said again. "And we've returned to the same."

There was no anger, but a sense of resignation.

Maybe there was hope. Maybe I could persuade her.

"I've never believed Hobbes to be true," I said quietly. "We survived, the human race has survived against incredible odds, because we came together. If we hadn't, we'd have wiped each other out. None of us would have survived."

Jane smiled. She thought I was naive. "If you don't kill your competition for food, you will all die. That's what our ancestors knew – that if they were to survive, they had to eliminate the competition for the scarce resources. It was simple mathematics. Those who were prepared to kill the weak, they survived. Those who were prepared to crack another man's skull so he could rape his wife, those were the ones who ensured the human race continued. The veneration of male violence. Anyone who waited for female consent, well, they just died out. That's where we come from. That's what we've gone back to. Ashes to ashes."

Jane drifted into thought again.

"I just don't agree." My voice cracked as I said it. "If man had murdered to survive, we'd never have survived. We survived because of numbers, surely? Our odds against the hostile elements were too great. If we had killed each other, leaving only a handful of survivors, we'd have died out. To have survived against those odds we had to have reproduced in huge numbers."

"So you think there were rape sheds back then too, then?"

"No! No. And I don't think that now either. There are bad people, there always will be. But the human race has always survived because of love. The only way we survived was because we cared for each other. We came together, pooled our resources, as a community. Like we are doing here. That night, we saved those women. None of them can fight for you, many will die soon anyway. But you saved them. And in displaying that compassion we commit others to our cause. It's love that binds us together. It's love that gives us numbers. Strength in numbers. That's why I don't believe I'm descended from murderers. I believe I'm descended from enlightened people."

The cracks of the log splitting on the embers filled the silence that fell at the end of my argument. Some of the cinders sparked and landed just inches from Jane's boot.

"An individual act of compassion can save a soul but it cannot save the human race," Jane said softly.

I shook my head again. "If we're as bereft of compassion as you'd have me believe, you wouldn't be here at all. You've survived because somebody, somewhere, cared enough to protect you."

She didn't move. But she spoke. "I hope I'm not around when you find out how wrong you are."

"You must know the odds are against you," I said. "Even if we win here, the men overseas will attack."

"Nothing changes without struggle." She wasn't shocked or angry. She just looked out to the dying embers. "The odds don't matter. You must always stand and fight. We may not be able to stop evil but that doesn't mean we shouldn't try."

I sighed, "Well at least you'll die a hero."

Jane laughed. "Maybe. But I'm not going to die today."

And then she reached out and picked up her gun. "You can sleep peacefully, Laura. I'll protect you from the monsters."

CHAPTER TWENTY-FIVE
The Ambush

The trucks rolled to a stop. Still shrouded by the night, dawn not yet on the horizon.

In front of us, the rest-stop was brightly lit, its floodlights glaring against the dark sky. Its white searchlights swept over every under-manned gun turret, every hole in the fencing, advertising its weaknesses.

And its gates were open. The convoy had just arrived.

Jane was right; this was poorly defended.

We remained in the trucks, silent but craning our necks to catch glimpses of our target.

The men were in no hurry to offload any goods from the arriving convoy, nor were they keeping their weapons primed. Instead their rifles hung loose over their shoulders as they mingled outside, smoking and gradually decanting the supplies from the back of the trucks into the warehouses.

Sitting ducks.

I looked across at Andrea. She was in the zone – eyes wide, alert, staring into the near distance. Her fingers checking every part of her rifle, like a reflex.

Next to her, Helen was intense but present. She saw me look, she stared back, a smile of satisfaction, of anticipation, beginning to cross her face. This is what she lived for.

I took a deep breath.

Jane turned to the woman next to her in the front seat of the truck. "As soon as we've disappeared from view, give them the sign."

In the dark I saw the driver nod.

Jane turned back towards us. "We're on."

Helen pushed open the doors at the back and four of us jumped out, barely a muffle of sound as our feet hit the ground. Jane slipped out from the front. The other trucks around us were silent, deceptively dead. We ran past them, keeping to the shadows, staying out of the floodlights. Andrea in front of me, Jane in front of her. Alex behind me. And Helen behind her.

We leapt over fallen branches and side-stepped piles of accumulated debris. The five of us in this elite unit slipped along and past the side of the ring-fenced depot completely unnoticed. Occasionally Jane would halt us, letting a searching floodlight pass us by, but the guards in the towers were not alert. Few of them even had more than one person in them. Perhaps we shouldn't even have bothered going in from the back. With the right approach we could've walked through the front door unharmed.

The back of the depot was completely dark. Incredibly, the floodlights weren't working, or maybe not even deployed at the back. I couldn't see any searchlights either.

Jane pointed at Helen, nodding towards the roads behind us. And Helen and Alex promptly left our side.

It was quiet. It was dark. But it wasn't silent. We could hear the hum of activity, of life, from the camp. Slamming doors, raised voices. The occasional laugh, the odd crash of metal as supplies were tossed from the lorries into wire trolleys, the grind of the gears from the small forklift trucks.

Helen and Alex returned. Helen nodded at Jane. Jane nodded back and turned her focus back to the depot. We crouched there patiently in the dark.

Jane looked left, looked right. Nothing.

We waited.

Then there it was.

The shriek of the missile.

The vivid flash of orange lighting up the sky.

The deafening explosion.

The gush of the powerful back-draught swept through my hair and across my skin.

The judder ripped through the earth.

The shouts from the men inside the fence.

The hail of bullets from the women on the front foot.

The crash of metal on the far side of the camp – its defences collapsing.

The second detonation.

Without looking back, Jane said, "Go." And we did.

So quick I can't remember who it was who clipped the fence and pulled it back. I remember there being two doing that. I think Andrea was one.

But Jane was through the hole first. Leading and covering. Down on her knees, rifle up, securing our entrance until we were all through.

We were hidden by the darkness, the men pouring past us, drawn to the firefight at the front.

Another explosion. Another flash of orange.

More rounds of gunfire.

More shouts from the men.

The blows, the screams from the attack were terrifying the men rushing past us, oblivious to our presence. Their pace was fast, their panic palpable. "Formation! Formation!" they screamed as they sprinted past.

Dozens passed.

They opened fire. They were firing on our troops.

Andrea and I saw them, the group of men. Almost thirty of them, all within touching distance. A row standing while the ones in front of them crouched. All rifles up, all firing.

One man fell. Dead. Then another, his head blown clean off. Then another.

But still the rest of the men kept firing. Firing at our army.

Shouldn't we engage? I looked across at Jane.

She had seen them too. Her eyes – ice amongst the fire.

Why wasn't she moving?

I looked at the men, I looked at Andrea. She looked at me.

Then Jane stood straight, put the barrel of the AK into her left hand, and walked out till the row of the men's backs was in front of her.

And she opened fire.

Sweeping her AK from left to right, from right to left, from left to right.

The men fell. Shot in the back.

All the men fell.

Andrea yanked me out of my shock. "Come on."

Andrea grabbed my arm and dragged me into the depot. As she did, I glimpsed Jane lead Helen and Alex forward into the fire, shooting in the back all those who were shooting our women in the front.

"Guns up!" Andrea called. "There will be more."

Andrea ran ahead of me, running fast. We ran in formation, one behind the other, minimising the target. Me just running behind but to the side, so my sightline wasn't blocked.

Suddenly a group of men ran out in front of us. We shot them down in a hail of bullets.

We started running again.

At the back of the building, under the roof, was the loading bay. The trucks gave us cover but most of the men had been drawn to the firefight at the front. Not enough men left to cover a two-pronged attack. Jane had been right. This was a good target.

A metal spiral staircase was fixed to the wall at the back of the loading bay. It led up to a room suspended high up into the wall. The lights were on and it was manned.

This was the room we wanted.

Andrea stood out from behind a truck, cocked her rifle into the computer room and opened fire. The man at the top of the staircase was knocked sideways by the force of the bullets, causing him to smack his head on the brick wall behind him, then fall onto the metal staircase. Whether the bullet killed him or the broken neck, who knows?

One man in the room was still alive. Andrea saw him go to pick up his rifle. She leapt forward to get a clearer shot, opened fire again. The hail of bullets smashed the window but she got her mark.

"Watch the computers!" I shouted.

Then suddenly I saw a group of men come through the open door at ground level.

Andrea hadn't seen them but they saw her.

I stood out from the safety of my cover.

I shot them all.

I looked at their bodies. I had done the right thing.

"Move." Andrea was already racing to the staircase and bounding up the steps.

More explosions rocked the ground.

I followed her, bounding up the metal steps.

A body fell past me. I looked up to see Andrea drag another from the room and throw him out.

The gunfire out front was slowing. And I could hear the women shout. We were in the ascendancy.

At the top of the staircase, Andrea was pulling a man's body clear from the computers without even blinking. "Go!" she shouted as she dragged the body past me and threw him over the railings too.

I shoved the USB stick straight into the side of the nearest screen, wiped the table and woke the screen from its slumber. A program was running on the screen. "They've sent an alert."

"To who?" Andrea came to my shoulder. Then shot the light bulb above us.

I cowered under the shattering glass. The room was pitch black but it was a smart idea.

I scanned the screen quickly assimilating as much as I could. "Don't know. I don't think all the messages were sent. We interrupted them. But some have gone out, to a central command."

"What does that mean?"

I deleted the unsent messages and opened up the files on the USB stick. "It means we're out of time. This base is near a relief unit. Reinforcements will have been mobilised."

We heard an almighty smash of glass some way off. "They've started the fire," Andrea said. "Hurry."

I started the upload. The progress icon flashed up on the screen. Its blocks gradually, gradually turning to green. "Come on." I smacked my fist down on the table. I stood up. "Let's just go. We don't have to stay. Leave it to upload."

"No," Andrea said. "We'll make it. We'll make it. Stay alert."

I stood next to Andrea, facing out into the depot but constantly looking over my shoulder.

The green progress icon crept across the screen. I pulled the rifle forward, holding it in my hands. So plastic, so cold to the touch.

Andrea suddenly shot off a round towards the trucks on the ground. I snapped my head back from the screen to see two men in army fatigues collapse just feet from the bottom of the staircase.

My calm temporarily evaporated. My heart hit fast forward, a flurry of palpitations shot around my body.

I could feel the sweat.

"Laura?"

I looked at the screen. The green creep filled its last bar. "We're done."

"The virus is uploaded?"

The screen behind me was dissolving, scrambling into a myriad of pixels. "Yes."

CHAPTER TWENTY-SIX
The Assassination

The data was corrupted. The virus I'd written was virulent. It would destroy any record on the local network – erasing from history anything that hadn't been backed up. Given this depot was on the main route between the new Parliament and the coast, we'd gambled that this would include communiqués with the navy and army overseas – their logs, deciphers for their codes, confidential reports. Given time, maybe ten minutes or so, it would worm its way deeper and decrypt the path to the servers. And from there, anything was possible. Maybe it would erase every confidential file they had on RAZR and its soldiers.

But would it get that far? Reinforcements were coming. If they were properly briefed, they'd destroy the computer room first and worry about the men after.

As I raced down the metal staircase all I could feel was adrenalin.

I had landed a blow, a meaningful blow.

I was no longer just a cog in a wheel but a player.

The blood was pumping in my veins, my thoughts were racing but Andrea's mind seemed clear.

"Down here," she said, heading not back to the fence but into the depot itself.

"Wait. We're not retracing our steps?"

And then I saw them, out back. The men, dozens in retreat, pouring over the trucks, rushing not to us but towards the fence at the back, swamping the wire like a flood desperately trying to breach the dam.

The women pursued them like predators, vultures, killers. Leaping onto the trucks, the roofs, the bonnets, taking the high ground and raining bullets into the backs of the men.

I saw one of the men drop to his feet on the other side of a truck but he stumbled and a woman swooped on him like a hawk. She got him. I saw her lift her rifle and pound the butt down again and again and again. Whatever was left of the man was out of my sight.

"Laura!" Andrea was standing at the entrance, waiting for me.

"We should help them."

"They are fine. My task was to get you out. This is the way out."

I looked back at the women. One of the men had tripped up. Three women descended on him and one crushed her boot through his skull.

"Now!" Andrea shouted.

I turned, ran to Andrea and followed her at pace into the corridor.

I felt a rush of cold air coming through from ahead of us. The army must have blown out most of the entrance. "We're going through the depot, into the firefight?"

"It's the way out," Andrea replied.

The corridors were long, straight, dank and dark. Exposed

metal pipes hung in the galleys above us and the walls were close, really close. My shoulders brushed both sides and Andrea almost completely covered the way in front of me.

She was running fast, gun up.

Suddenly she stopped and opened fire.

I dropped down to my knees, saw the men she was aiming at through her legs, and opened fire from my lower position.

They all fell.

Andrea started running again, jumping over their bodies.

I scrambled up to my feet and followed. My fitness not quite as good as hers, my breathing hard, my feet less nimble over the dead men.

My heart was beating so fast, the pounding in my ears almost drowning out the gunfire from the front and back.

I could feel heat, though not just from within me. Heat. Fire.

And then it was in my throat.

Smoke.

There was smoke.

Not thick enough to force us to our knees but enough to make me try to cover my mouth with my sleeve.

Andrea came to a juddering halt.

I ran straight into her back.

Up ahead the corridor had fallen in, destroyed in the attack.

"Shit," Andrea said. And then she started running back, retracing our steps, taking another turn.

"How come you know where you're going?" I asked.

"I don't but there's no exit behind us."

BOOM!

The building shook.

My knees almost went from underneath me. Andrea fell to the floor.

The explosion was close.

Another explosion ripped through the air. Was that us? Were we still winning?

We got to our feet. Left into the next corridor. Right, around the next corner. Always running, rifle up. No idea what was in front of me. It was just corridors. Seemingly abandoned corridors.

Andrea turned sharply to her right as the corridor took a sudden diversion. And then she stopped and I crashed straight into her again.

Over her shoulder I saw what had stopped us.

And it was not a destroyed corridor. We were in a large space, a room glaringly bright from the buzzing fluorescent strip lights hanging overhead. And in the middle of the space was Jane.

Jane was standing in front of the rest of her unit, her pistol held out in her right hand.

And her pistol was aimed at point blank range at a person kneeling on the ground in front of her.

That person's hands were tied. Their head was bowed.

Oh God, it was a woman.

It was Helen. Helen!

Helen was crying.

But she was not pleading.

What the hell was going on? What the—

I stepped to the side.

Andrea immediately put up her arm, blocking any move forward.

I looked across at her. She was still facing forward, but her mouth was open.

She didn't know either.

Jane's arm didn't move. Still and calm.

Helen whimpered in front of her but no words were said.

The rest of the women stood there, silent. Obedient.

Jane simply looked down the barrel of her gun. Her lips not moving. Her eyes glacial.

And then she pulled the trigger.

She pulled the trigger.

A single shot.

One bullet.

Helen's neck jerked back as the contents of her head blew out and across the floor.

The rest of her body followed, collapsing back on her heels.

Oh my God.

I froze.

I felt my body slump.

Andrea, it must've been Andrea, picking me up, pushing me upright against the wall, bashing my rifle against the bricks.

Jane looked over to us and then back to the rest. "Let's go."

She turned her back to us, put the pistol into the back of her trousers and headed off towards the front of the depot, the rest of the unit falling into line behind her.

They vanished.

I stood there, gawping at the body.

Andrea grabbed my arm.

I shrugged her off and pushed her away. "What the fuck is this? What the fucking hell is this?"

I staggered to Helen's body.

I touched her neck.

I touched her chest, her arm. I was trying to find a pulse. I have no idea why. The contents of her head were pouring out over the floor. The flow of red was fast, quick. I had no idea what I was doing.

Andrea grabbed my shoulder, I shrugged her off again.

I leapt to my feet and pushed Andrea, shoving her against the wall. "What the fucking hell is this?"

"Let go, Laura, let go."

I gripped her neck, squeezing, tightening.

"Let go, let go!" she gasped, her hands flapping at my arms. Then she punched me hard in the side of my stomach.

"Aargh!" I screamed and let go.

I clasped my hands over my ears, around my head.

Looking at Helen's lifeless body, looking away again, looking at the red on the floor, looking at the body, looking at the walls, looking at the body, the lifeless body swamped in blood, looking at the floor.

I was spinning in circles.

"Not here, not here," Andrea gasped. "We have to get out."

She started to head off but my feet couldn't move.

"Did you know, Andrea?" She didn't look back as she staggered on. "Hey! Hey! I'm talking to you!"

Andrea stopped, leaning against the wall but still not looking back, either at me or Helen.

"Did you know?" I asked again.

I saw Andrea's head drop. "No. No, I didn't."

She turned, not to face me directly but I could see her profile. "Please come on, Laura. I told Jane I would get you out alive. I have to keep my promise."

Under the glare of the stark bulbs Andrea was pale.

"What does it matter, Andrea? You might as well just leave me here. This, this…" I pointed at Helen's body. "I'm not living for this."

Screams came through the corridor – behind us and in front of us.

"Not here," Andrea whispered. "Let's go home first." And then she looked at me. "Please."

Gunfire from out the back, behind us.

I bent down and pulled the rope off Helen's wrists. I don't know why. And then I stepped over her and headed with Andrea through the deserted corridors and out into the front.

Out into the battlefield, out into the warzone.

Dawn had risen over the carnage. Destroyed trucks on their backs, engines ablaze. The air was filled with the smell of petrol. Thick, black smoke poured out from the side of the building where the walls had been blown away.

And strewn across the battlefield were the bodies, the markers of every life we had taken as retribution.

And surrounding them, pools of dark red blood gathered in the mud.

The screams and gunfire were now intermittent and in the background.

Andrea was ahead of me, slowly clambering across the trucks, treading on the corpses as she stumbled towards the wrecked fence out front where the more alert, more nimble members of the elite unit were waiting.

As was Jane. Who was on the other side of the fence looking right at me.

And then I saw them, coming over the crest of the hill behind Jane. The trucks. One after another. I pushed my rifle to the air and shot off a couple of bullets and shouted, "They're coming!"

Jane spun round, saw the trucks.

She pulled a pin out of a weighted grenade from her belt and tossed it towards them. The grenade hung high in the air, as if floating. Then it fell like a rock through the windscreen of one of the oncoming trucks.

The detonation sent the truck sky high, flipping it, destroying everything inside. A string of explosions blew across the road where we had rigged it. The flash of orange, the thunderous boom of detonation pushed us back. But it also forced the trucks behind it to veer, to swerve.

One went straight into a tree.

Next to Jane, a woman shot off a rocket from a launcher towards the other trucks.

The rocket seared through the side of one of the trucks and blew it inside out.

Jane ran towards it, not a trace of hesitation in her as she left the rest of us in her wake.

I ran fast to catch up, as did the others. The other women were firing indiscriminately but above even that, I could hear the screams from the dying men within.

Jane jumped onto the door of the wrecked truck that was now on its side. She crouched down and reached in through the broken window, dragging out a bleeding man from the seat inside. She grabbed her dagger from her belt and jabbed it again and again into the man's neck.

I was just feet from her.

My blood went cold. I froze.

I could see the blood spurt from the man's neck and his body jerk as his battling last breath left his body.

Ashes to ashes.

"Laura!" Mandy grabbed my arm and dragged me to the doors of one of the other trucks.

I stood, inert, as Mandy started dragging out the barely conscious men from inside.

I watched her gag and bind them. I watched her pass the men to the women next to us who marched them to the road and made them kneel. And I watched her beat a man who stumbled. She pounded him again and again until Alex came and pulled the man away from her.

A screech of tyres behind us. I jerked my head round. Our vehicles had arrived.

I limply took the arm of one of the men Mandy had bound and guided him to the back of one of them, the doors of which Jane had flung open. I handed him to her, eyes down, and staggered back to Mandy.

"Quickly," Alex said as she came alongside me. "We may have beaten the rapid response unit but more will be following."

Becks and Rachel were doing the same at one of the other bullet-riddled trucks, dragging the men out and putting them in ours. But one of the men, an older man, was not going down quietly. "You call this justice? You call this a revolution?" he screamed. "You're murderers, all murderers. You think this will win the war, you'll win nothing!"

I could see his dark hair through the blood on his scalp. A big, broad man.

"Where is your leader?" he shouted. "Where is your famous leader? Huh? Where is she? Let her show her face. Let me see her. Or is she too scared for battle, huh?"

Some way behind him, we all saw Jane twitch and slowly walk towards the man.

He evidently hadn't seen her though because he didn't stop. "Where is she, huh? Oh, your famed warrior missing from the field of battle, is she? Or is she dead? Ha! Your fabled leader dead. Whatever she is. An absent leader. An invisible woman. A politician, a self-promoter."

Jane strolled up to the back of the man, out of his sight.

She pulled out her pistol from the back of her trousers.

"She's nothing more than that. A fucking terrorist. None of you have fucking balls. None of you."

Jane stood right over him, her gun aimed straight, directly at the man's head.

We held our breath. We knew what was coming.

But he didn't because he kept on. "Where is she? Where is RAZR?"

Jane circled the man, her pistol never wavering from his skull, and came to rest right in front of him.

The man, the whole line of men, drew breath.

Their eyes widened, their jaws dropped.

Jane placed her pistol right on the man's forehead.

It was touching his skin.

The horror in his eyes.

And then she said, firmly, "I'm right here."

And she pulled the trigger.

Then she turned to us and said. "We're done here."

And we were.

CHAPTER TWENTY-SEVEN
The Prisoners

Our trucks screeched back into base and they dragged the men out.

Jane must've heard them as she walked away towards the building. She knew they were in the vans, she'd told Andrea to lead their transfer to the "holding rooms", but men don't make that kind of noise unless they're in pain.

We must have had several dozen of them. Men we captured from the base, and those we captured from the cavalry that tried to save them. There were almost as many of them as there were of us.

I stood in a daze by the open back doors as Andrea, Mandy and the rest were only too keen, too willing to obey Jane. No one was talking about what had happened. Not that the trucks had been silent on the sprint back to base. Some of the men had tried to be heroes. It hadn't been a smart move. Mandy kicked the shit out of one who tried. No one stopped her. Andrea was too exhausted to try; I was too shocked.

Mandy and the others dragged the men away while Jane and her cabal headed in the opposite direction, into the building. And just as Jane disappeared round the corner of the school, Anne came rushing over from the same direction. No words or glances exchanged with her sister.

The others had already taken the rest of the men away by the time she got to me. Anne looked me up and down as she touched my arm. "You look OK. Any damage?"

I jerked my head towards the single crumpled figure left in the back of the truck. "He's worse."

I had been left with one that simply couldn't move. The others had been dragged limping or stumbling, or just simply dragged, into a set of buildings on the other side of the compound. But there was no dragging this one.

Anne looked into the truck. "We're going to need a stretcher." And with that she disappeared towards the back of the parking area.

I stepped inside the truck, putting the AK I'd been gripping solidly for three hours down onto one of the benches along the side, and headed towards the back.

The man at the back, in the shadows, was lying still. His head desperately damaged. I crouched over him. He was in a bad way. His skull had lost its shape; great bloody dents had crushed the smooth outline of his head. And the blood loss was bad. But the damage to his torso was worse. I could see it. And I could smell it. "Can you hear me?"

He was too scared to respond.

"OK, I've got one." Anne appeared at the door with a stretcher and clambered in with it.

"We should just treat him here," I said.

"No." Anne shook her head. "Prisoners have to be secured first. No exceptions."

"He won't make it."

"No exceptions."

The smell from the man's intestines was putrid. How he'd survived the speed and distress of the three-hour sprint back to safe territory, I don't know. If I'd been him I'd have just let go.

Anne picked up the man's legs. I stopped her. "This is an exception," I said. "Look at him."

"I know he's in a bad way but—"

"No. I mean, *look* at him."

Anne looked at his face. The man was older, thinner. His hair was greyer than when I'd last seen him on the news reports but his face was unmistakable.

And I saw the recognition in Anne's face.

"I need him to survive," I said quietly to Anne. "I need to talk to him. We operate here."

Anne looked at him, lifted his hand to look at the intestines underneath. In the dark it was hard to make out details but she looked up at me and gently shook her head.

"I'll wait inside," Anne said, then left, the truck gently lifting as she stepped out.

The man gasped and wheezed, his breath rattling around his empty chest. He looked at me. I looked at him. We sat in quietness for a few moments – long enough to play with his insecurity, short enough to ensure he didn't die first.

"Who are you?" He could speak. Just. Raspy, faint. But I could make out what he said.

"This is RAZR," I replied.

He spluttered. I made out just the edge of a smile cross his face. "I guessed."

And then the smile fell.

His skin was thin, really thin. And his hair was sparse on his scalp. He had aged so much since I saw last saw his face, before The Fall. His eyes were betraying him. I could tell he was weighing up many things in his mind, and weighing me up.

"Where are the others?" he eventually asked.

"The men or the women? Well, they're both in the same place. You know why we're not moving you, don't you?"

He closed his eyes then opened them again. "Kill me," he said.

I shook my head. "Do not assume I am merciful just because I have saved you from the others. I need information from you first."

I could make out the ooze from his intestines through his fingers. He had a blanket covering his legs. I had no intention of moving it.

The man nodded, at what I don't know. From the distant look in his eyes and the sudden twitches in his lips he seemed to be having a separate conversation with the ghosts in his head or perhaps those he could see. He was passing over.

"Where were you going?" I asked.

My voice snapped him out of his thoughts. He lifted his hand and beckoned me towards him with a small gesture. "Parliament." His eyes lit up. "The new one."

"The one in Manchester?"

The man looked surprised.

"I know more than you think," I whispered.

I could see the thought process in his eyes. He coughed, his chest wheezed. He tried to lick his lips. I grabbed a bottle from the floor of the truck, ripped off a piece of my top, spilt water on it then held the material to his lips. I let the damp soak into his mouth before moving the cloth.

"Don't believe the others," he said. "Go back home. There is a future there."

"They took you from the building, didn't they – the women? You were in the original convoy that had just arrived at that base, weren't you? Where were you coming from?"

The man said nothing, staring out into the darkness.

I looked out the back of the truck. I didn't have time for this.

"Kill me," he whispered.

"I cannot do that," I said. "Be under no illusions about the tit-for-tat that's being played out here. I'm not interested in torturing you but I want to know what you know."

"I know nothing," he said.

"Well, then you have nothing to fear from me, do you?"

If he weren't hanging on by a thread, my instinct would have been to kill him anyway. This man was too dangerous to hold alive.

"Where were you travelling from?" I asked again.

He shook his head.

I wiped the sweat off my forehead then leant in, resting just gently enough on his wounds to force a gasp. "Let me explain this to you, I am the nicest person you are going to meet here. If I tell them who you are, someone far worse than me will come to talk to you."

He looked at me.

"I know you're not afraid of death," I said. "Maybe you're not afraid of dying but I will keep you alive till you answer my question."

Tears started falling from the man's eyes.

"So let's start again. Where were you travelling from?"

"France," he whispered.

I eased off from his chest. "What were you doing there?"

"Peace deal."

"Peace? With who?"

"Daesh."

My heart stopped. "Daesh? They are in France? How can you deal with them?"

The man sighed, his breathing heavy. He closed his eyes.

Shit. "Hey, hey," I said. I shook him, gently, but it was no use.

He exhaled one last time.

I sat back on the bench. Shit. Shit. This was a whole new level of problems now. The Foreign Secretary abducted and killed returning from securing a peace deal with terrorists who were now on our doorstep. Shit. Daesh was close. They would exploit any weakness in a divided nation. Daesh would come for us. RAZR had to stop.

And how did Jane not realise he was in this convoy, that he would be at the rest-stop when we attacked it? Had she not been listening to the intercepts properly?

No.

Wait...

Of course she knew. Of course she knew this. She was sabotaging peace negotiations she knew all about.

I left his body on the floor of the truck and leapt out.

I thought they had taken the men to a separate building at the back of the school, close to the medical centre. But as I approached it, I heard shouts and screams coming from the kitchens in the building opposite instead.

I stopped and listened again. Yes, definite screams. And from male voices. I sprinted towards the kitchens.

I felt the heat on approaching the building. And, on the inside, the heat was so intense that the kitchen walls had become slimy.

From the far end of the corridor I could see the women.

And I could hear the men. The noise bouncing off the damp walls hurt my ears.

The door to the main room facing me was flung open. The kitchen was lit up from within by the bright flames from the stoves, which had to be raging to be that bright, that hot.

I could see figures walking back and forth across the entrance.

And through their legs I could see a pile of naked bodies on the floor in a heap.

Shit.

I heard Mandy shout, "I told you to get the fuck down so you get the fuck down! I'm not fucking interested in this you piece of shit!" and I broke into a run.

And the hell that unfolded in front of my eyes as I stepped into the room...

The pile of bodies on the far side.

The blood trickling out from underneath the pile.

Some of the bodies were still twitching.

At the far end, by the ovens, Becks, Rachel and a dozen others stood over a handful of men with limbs so charred that the smell of their burning flesh filled the room.

And in front of me, a stripped male strapped down over a work-surface. His damp, sweaty back had been cut a dozen times and the heat was making his torn skin so tender that his lacerations were tearing further apart. On his arm a tattoo – a winged dagger.

Shit.

And the woman holding the bloodied knotted rope? Mandy.

"What the fuck are you doing?" I said.

"What the fuck's it got to do with you?"

"Jesus Christ, Mandy. Untie the man."

"Fuck off!" she said, as she whipped her wrist, warming it up for another round. Then she cracked the whip across the man's back.

He screamed out in pain.

The bloodied rope fell off his back, revealing a new cut.

"Fucking hell!" I headed straight for Mandy.

Becks got up and blocked my way, but I pushed her away. "Get the fuck off me!"

Suddenly the others all stood up and faced me.

I stood there for a moment, stunned. And outnumbered.

I took a breath. "I understand your anger," I said, trying to calm the tension in the room. "But this isn't what we're here for."

Mandy stepped around the man on the table so she was facing me directly. "And what the fuck would you know about what we're here for? Huh?"

"This isn't payback."

"It's a fucking good start."

Mandy walked back behind the desk and flicked her hand with the rope back behind her. I leapt forward and grabbed her wrist. "No fucking way."

"Fuck off, cunt!" and she shoved me, hard.

I fell back against the row of desks behind me.

Mandy whipped her hand back and snapped her wrist. The rope cracked open another bloody line on the man's back.

I launched forward so quick not even Becks could get to me in time. I punched hard through Mandy's jaw.

Mandy's head flung back – but the hit hadn't been enough to fell her. She stumbled, then she launched herself at me. I felt a knee in my stomach, my hair being pulled out of my scalp.

I punched her hard in her ribs. Thrust my kneecap between her legs and bit her arm.

I felt her elbow crash straight into the soft part between my neck and my shoulder. "Aaargh!"

I punched down again and again on to her chest. I heard her splutter.

I pulled away and punched her again in her jaw. The blood spurted up from her mouth.

The pack of women descended on us, pulling us apart.

I grabbed Mandy's top and kicked her in the thigh as she

landed a blow around the side of my head.

The hands pulled me back but I still staggered to my feet. "What are you trying to achieve?"

"I'm trying to hurt them!" Mandy screamed, the blood oozing out of her mouth.

"Why don't you put your fucking brain to work and talk to them!" I shouted back, pushing the women off me. "We need answers."

Mandy shrugged off the women holding her back. She gripped her jaw, holding it in place long enough to spit out, "I don't have any questions for him."

Then she moved towards me again.

Quick as a flash I pulled the gun free from the back of my trousers and pointed it at her head.

She recoiled.

A sudden whirl of clicks from the women surrounding Mandy and half a dozen rifles were aimed at my head.

I didn't flinch, not breaking eye contact from Mandy once. "We are not monsters. We are not monsters."

I didn't dare drop eye contact. I didn't dare.

The only sound in the room was the wheezing and gasping of all those who desperately needed medical attention – whether they would survive it or not was open to question.

Nobody moved.

Mandy held her jaw. I could feel the throbbing in my ribs.

The air thick with the smell of burning flesh.

I sensed a movement out the corner of my eye. The man behind Mandy, at the feet of her cohorts, writhing in agony. His flesh was charred and its smell filled the air. But none of the others moved, none of them even looked at him.

All eyes were on me.

It was Anne who broke the impasse, of all people. Suddenly rushing in, throwing a wet towel over the man they had been burning. And no one stopped her. Mandy didn't even look at her.

I took some steps towards Anne, and as I did, Mandy and the other women took steps in the other direction.

Moving like hands on a clock, the closer I got to the flames and to Anne, the closer the others got to the door.

Our guns never dropping.

I watched them step around the men, never treading on the bodies of either the dead or the dying as they made for the exit.

And Mandy never stopped watching me, the last of the torturers to leave the room.

I dropped my gun.

"They need water," Anne said.

I looked down at the charred bodies beneath my feet. "They need a miracle, not water."

I turned the stoves off, the flames disappeared. The sudden rush of cold that comes from vanishing heat.

Anne cradled a man's head in her hands. He coughed and spluttered. Both his arms were burnt up to his elbows. They were black, withered. He'd need them amputated.

And the man by me with his burnt leg. That would need to go.

And the dead one, or unconscious one, whose arm had burnt and shrivelled.

Some bodies were still twitching under the pile on the other side.

I went over and started to pull the hot, wet, naked bodies from the pile.

"Careful!" Anne shouted.

My adrenalin was still pumping too fast. The slithering sound of peeling flesh. I took the body that was lying on top, back up, in my arms and as I turned him over, I saw the cuts on his thighs, his chest. And the gaping wound over the left side of his head where his eye used to be.

I lay him down. "Where's Andrea?"

"She's gone to see Jane."

A new battlefront was about to be opened up in the main building. Mandy and the rest would have gone straight there too.

The man I had laid at my feet didn't seem to be breathing. I caught sight of more twitching in the bodies. I went and peeled off the next body, to try to free those that were moving but when I saw the man's face, or what was left of it, I almost dropped him.

I turned away and nearly threw up.

Anne, though, could handle it. I watched her soak more towels, lay them over the burns.

I pulled myself upright. "You haven't asked me where Helen is. You didn't ask your sister either, when she passed you."

Anne kept her head down, her hair covering her face as she continued to press a piece of gauze down on the face of one of the men in front of me.

"I know you can hear me," I said.

But still nothing.

"Talk to me." I grabbed her arm, but Anne shook me off. "Did you know?"

But my shouting just seemed to make her cowering worse.

My breath was so short. I was in pain. My ribs hurt. My back hurt. I wasn't helping her, Anne fumbling with the sick man by herself. Her back was to me. I couldn't read her.

I took a breath, leant against the wall. Breathing heavily, I put my hands on my hips. "What is going on, Anne?"

"My sister believed there is, was, a spy in the ranks. That we'd been infiltrated."

My heart stopped.

Anne went on. "That there was someone close to her playing both sides."

My mind suddenly hit the throttle.

Pins and needles shot up the side of my face.

Fuck.

"The attack on the centre, when they were trying to save the women," Anne added. "It wasn't a surprise attack. They knew we were coming, that's what she told me."

"That's paranoia," I said. "It was a last-minute attack. Maybe the recon wasn't perfect. Maybe it was just better defended than we—"

"No." Anne stopped and looked across at me. "Jane said they were ambushed."

"There's no way it was Helen," I said.

"Why?" Anne gasped. "You think it was someone else?"

"You think it was Helen?" I countered.

"I didn't know it was Helen. I didn't know that."

I paused. "Who did you think she meant then, when she told you?"

Anne turned back to the man. "I don't know. I don't know."

"But you knew your sister was going to kill someone tonight?"

Anne went on to another man. "Did he survive, the man in the truck?"

I didn't answer. The change in subject was unwelcome.

Anne looked back at me. "What did he tell you?"

I looked at Anne closely, trying to read between the lines. "That we're fighting the wrong battle."

Anne and I managed to hold it together long enough to tend to every man in the room. Every single one.

The dead I sorted into a new pile on the other side of

the room. The rest we killed. We had nothing that could save them. Anne had some fentanyl. The two of us filled up syringes and injected the arm, the neck of every single man that was still clinging on. These are the decisions you have to make in war.

CHAPTER TWENTY-EIGHT
The Revolt

I wanted to record every single life the women had taken. So I cut off the ID tags from around their necks and passed these to Anne to collate before I dragged their charred remains, their legless torsos and blackened arms, outside.

In truth, I don't know why I was dragging them outside – I hadn't excavated any pit and the movement often detached the limbs from their bodies – but the air inside was just so bad.

But outside, it was the trucks that caught my eye. The trucks, our trucks, were still out in the open. Exposed. And their doors had been flung open. And there was movement – some of the women were filling up the backs of the trucks with equipment, with boxes.

I went back inside to tell Anne but she was no longer alone.

I had wondered who Jane would send to get us. I thought it might be Andrea. I had hoped she would come herself because I wanted her to see the horror, to see it with her own eyes.

But Jane hadn't come. Nor had she sent Andrea.

She had sent Winter.

Winter was frail, damaged. Still not recovered from the raid to free the women. Her torso still tightly bound and she had to lean against the wall. It was a shock to see her upright. Anne was quite worried but Winter's explanation of "I wanted to see them for myself" worried me more.

"I could smell them from out there," she said. "That smell... It makes me sick. But I can't deny that it makes me happy."

A gust of cold air came in through the open door behind me.

"You need to get in the warm," Anne said to Winter.

Winter nodded, adding, "But we need to go. I need to take you."

"We haven't finished with the men," I said.

Winter shook her head. "I have my orders."

"Is she going to tell us why she killed Helen?" I asked.

Out the corner of my eye, I caught Anne dropping her head.

Winter looked away, away from the men, and turned her back to lead us out. "I don't know."

The hall was packed. As Anne, Winter and I walked in, I could see the balconies above us were standing room only and the floor was full of familiar faces.

But none of those faces wanted to stand near me. Even Winter took steps away from me, despite the fact that I'd just pretty much carried her almost all the way to the hall. I didn't blame her, though, for moving away from me. Hers was an understandable reaction if you live your life in fear.

The tension in the air was like a surge of electricity through my body. The room was on edge, barely containing its emotions.

On the other side of the room was Mandy. Mandy, Alex, the sisters and the rest. None of them looked me in the eye.

The doors opened and in she walked. Flanked by Andrea. The new hound, the new guard dog. A perverse version of battlefield promotion.

The voices fell and the seas parted.

A clearing appeared in the middle of the floor, and Jane walked into it.

There was a shuffling of feet as the rest backed off, giving her more room, even though the space they'd cleared for her was huge.

She put her hands in her pockets and stood for a moment, looking across all those in front of her and above her. Around the room, each and every face was waiting with baited breath.

I looked across at Andrea. She didn't see me though. She didn't see anyone. She was half looking at Jane, half staring into the distance. And she was carrying a rifle – the only one in the room.

Jane started to speak. "You are all heroes. Each and every one of you. What I have asked of you and what you have given, I can never repay. What you have endured and what you have witnessed, I can never erase from your mind. You have given all you have and I am the most humble of recipients."

And then she paused, just for a moment.

"But let me be clear on this – violence matters. Only violence brings change. Don't ever let anyone tell you otherwise. I am not afraid of my anger. It is legitimate and valid – as is yours. What we are committed to is a revolution. And revolutions are never easy. No struggle, no progress. Elites do not share their power. The oppressed will always remain oppressed unless they are prepared to revolt. Power cannot be obtained through petitions and conferences but through the violent assault and overthrow of those who seek to keep us suppressed. There is no alternative. There never has been and there never will be."

Jane looked down at the floor momentarily. Then looked up again. "And elites do not fight fair. The closer we get, the more violent the thrashing of the dying beast. They fight us, they discredit us. And when they fail to kill us in open battle, they send assassins into our nest to kill us while we sleep."

Whispers bounced around the room. Feet shuffled.

Jane let the noise rise, and waited till it fell.

"I know to all of you she was a comrade but that's not the same as a friend. I had been monitoring her for some time, that's why I held her close to me. My loyalty, my commitment is to you and I knew a point had been reached where, not my, but your safety was in danger. So I eliminated that danger for you. We are spared for now. But they will try again."

Jane took a few steps towards the centre of the room. "That is why I have ordered an evacuation. We are moving. I cannot be sure of the security of this base any more and I feel..." She paused. "I feel that it would be good to leave behind those experiences, those actions, that we all want to move away from. We can move forward cleansed and secure."

Jane turned her back and headed back towards the door.

"Is that all you're going to say about it?" I said. I heard the words escape my lips before I even had a chance to think. They just burst out.

Every head turned to me. The drawing of breath across the hall was audible. Jane turned back towards me, slowly. Head first, feet following.

And then she stood, hands in pockets, looking at me.

All eyes on me.

"Is that all you're gonna say?" I asked again. "When the hell did we get into the business of summary executions? Where's the evidence? Where the hell is the evidence against Helen, 'cause let's at least give her her name back and not hide behind this 'she' shit? You executed Helen with no evidence, no trial, no chance for her to defend herself."

"Did you see her protest when she was in front of me?" Jane asked.

"She worshipped you, for fuck's sake. Her head was so fucked up she thought that if you wanted her death, she'd give it to you."

Jane didn't move. Hands still in her trouser pockets, shoulders back and down. But her look was increasingly frosty. "I've never demanded idolatry."

"Bullshit."

The sea of faces drew backwards, like the tide pulling back from the shore, drawing all the breath out of the room.

"I am not the enemy, Laura," Jane said. "Direct your anger towards men, not me."

"Men?!" I shouted. "Yeah, let's talk about how we project this fucking anger out at men. Look at my hands! Look at my hands!" The room gasped as I held them up. "Look at them. This is not my blood. This is not my ash. This is not dirt from the earth on my hands. Those men we took at gunpoint are dead. We murdered them. We tortured them and then we killed them. What are you gonna say to them, huh, the women who adore you?" I pointed towards Mandy and her cohorts. My jab wasn't welcome. "Nothing?"

Jane said nothing.

Nothing.

I dropped my hands. And waited.

An icy chill swept up my spine.

"Well, now you have the floor, Laura," Jane eventually

said. "So why don't you share with me what I've been doing wrong. How should I have addressed this collateral damage?"

"Collateral damage?" I took a breath. "Jesus. You should, I mean, we should punish those who torture others. No, *you* should. You. You have the authority here. You cannot condone these acts. This wasn't war, this was murder. You, we, have to make a stand about this, we have to be bold, be brave enough to punish those who commit these barbaric acts."

The whispers raced around the room.

"And what makes you think that I haven't?"

I looked over at Mandy. I looked back at Jane. "You've said nothing and the perpetrators are still in this room."

"As opposed to where? A cell?"

"If you do not punish them, you stand with them," I said. "If you do not punish them publicly, you condone them. We are not men. We are not murderers. And when you executed Helen, you robbed yourself of the moral high ground."

The audible draw of breath again.

Jane let the gasps hang for a moment. "I'm not into the humiliation of my army. Every single woman in this room has fought bravely." And then she slowly started to walk towards me. "And I will not tolerate any betrayal of them, any betrayal in the ranks. I will defend all of these women until my death."

She continued to walk towards me, not stopping, not deviating, but coming straight at me until she was so close I could feel the heat of her breath. She leant in closer. I could see the fire in her eyes. "Do I make myself clear, Laura? I do not tolerate any betrayal."

I looked deep into her eyes, not flinching.

Every word now was loaded. I knew it. She knew it.

Jane stepped back, addressing the hall again. "Our new base has to remain confidential until we get there. The risk of interception..."

As Jane spoke I looked deep into my heart. I had nothing left to lose.

I took a breath. "I haven't finished yet." I stepped forward into the ring.

The room gasped again. I saw hands jump to mouths.

"My judgment is sound," I said. "My judgment is that leadership is about knowing what is right and having the guts to call it out when it is wrong. And on this, you have failed."

Jane's attention turned back to me, almost in slow motion. The icy front had become a glacier.

"You hate men," I said. "Whatever your reason, whatever's happened to you, you hate men. There's a part of you that agrees with what they did, Mandy and the others. You turned your back after we razed them to the ground. You walked away when their blood was still up. You knew this could happen, you knew this *would* happen. If you believe this, if you believe that what they did was fair, was justice, and if you believe that your actions were fair, the justice in this movement has gone. Violence begets violence. Word gets out we torture men, they will torture us a hundred times over. And if word gets out that you execute suspected opponents in front of your army to ensure the terror and fear in the ranks remains, we have become the very violence we seek to replace."

Silence.

The fire in her eyes was ablaze.

I could see her chest heaving.

The glacier was melting. And fast.

"Don't you ever claim to know what my judgment is!" Jane shouted with a force I'd never heard.

The heat rushed to my cheeks. I fell back, just a little, from the force of her words. I could feel my hands tremble.

"This is war," she said. "And you can never win a war with clean hands. I lead this army, I inspire them. And I stand by every action they make. Their actions are my responsibility."

I found my feet. "What they did was a crime!" I cried.

Jane started circling the edge of the ring. "Those men were in the business of murder. If they could've killed me, they would have. If they could've murdered you, they would have. Helen was sent to kill me, I got there first. I shed no tears for any of them. You live by the sword, you die by the sword."

"We are invoking a war."

Jane stepped forward. "No! They started this war!"

"Then we must end it!" I shouted. "We cannot build a future with just women, we can't. There's no future if it's just us. This, what we're doing, is mutually assured destruction. We want to live, right? We want to survive, yes?" I looked around the room. So many eyes staring back at me, quizzical, not hostile. "Well, what the hell are we doing? If *we* live by the sword, we too will die by the sword. That rule cuts both ways."

Jane looked around the room. Did she sense a shift? "You are free now, Laura. Freer now than you have ever been your whole life. For the first time in history you are in a space where you have complete freedom over yourself and over your body. What we are creating is true liberalism, true equality."

"There is no liberalism when you carry a gun," I jabbed towards Andrea. "Freedom with a gun will always become tyranny. We need men, we need men for this to work." I watched Jane, her pace increasing on the far side of the ring. "We have to win men over."

Jane stepped further towards me. "Women have lived, loved, worked and died alongside men for generations. And where did that get us? I will not let the State rebuild itself with the same oppression of women."

"You are replacing one tyranny with another. You have become what they always said you would. You are fulfilling *their* agenda, not ours. We need to talk to them."

"Power is not given, it is taken."

I stepped forward.

And immediately Andrea stepped in, her rifle up.

I threw my hands up. "Whoa, what the... I'm not trying to kill her. I'm not here to hurt her."

"You're wrong," Andrea said. "You're wrong on everything."

I saw Jane take a few steps behind Andrea, the orchestrator slipping into the shadows.

"You've got no fucking idea what we've gone through in this army, what we've seen." Andrea's voice was shaking. "And you're fucking naive if you think men are different out of combat than they are in it. They're not. They're fucking not. It's the opposite. War is just man with their fucking restraints off."

Shouts of "Yes!" came from across the room.

Andrea looked around the crowd around us. "Do men hate us?"

More shouts of "Yes!" came back.

Andrea looked back at me. "They hate us. I don't know why but they do. The abuse, the raping, they constantly kicked the shit out of us. Why, when we were raped, why did they put us on trial?" Andrea was getting hysterical, playing more and more to the crowds. "Why did they take away our abortion rights, huh? Fucking hell, why were they even allowed to dictate how we use our body?" Jabbing the air with her forefinger. "Why did they hate us all the fucking time?"

I watched Jane as Andrea unravelled.

And Jane looked at me. Andrea, her dog let off the leash. How that suited her.

"Andrea, Andrea," I said. "I understand, I understand but for you to portray all men as rapists betrays us all."

"Why did they laugh at us, mock us, grab us, abuse us, humiliate us?" Andrea wasn't listening to me. Her tornado of emotions out of control as she whipped herself up into tears. "Why do men fucking hate women?"

Andrea suddenly pushed me. "And you want to criticise *us*? You want to criticise my friends? Why? Why do you hate us?" Andrea thumped me again and again.

I grabbed her hands. "Andrea, I don't hate you, I don't hate you."

"You saw those women. You fucking saw them." Andrea's fists thumped my chest again and again. Punching hard, punching deep. "I'd kill every last fucking one of those men who did that to them. I hate men."

Suddenly Andrea swung her fist.

I saw it and dived but it still connected and I fell to the floor.

The room gasped.

My nose, my lips were throbbing.

Jane's feet ran up to Andrea and I saw her dragging her back from me. My hand instinctively rose up to my face. I wiped my top lip. Red.

The room fell into a shocked hush, a hush broken only by Andrea's sobbing.

I staggered to my feet. No one ran to help me.

Jane had her arm around Andrea. "It's OK. She's not a threat to me." She handed her over to Mandy.

And then she walked back over to me.

She reached out. I flinched, but Jane's hand didn't move. I looked down at it, then, tentatively, let her touch my face. She turned my head, looking at the damage. Her fingers were warm. Her touch tender. "You'll be fine."

Jane dropped her hand from my jaw, stepped back and looked up at the hall, her audience, her crowd. "Men don't realise how much they hate women, how much they fear us. That's why they cannot change – because they cannot, *will* not face up to that. And those who don't learn from history are condemned to repeat it. We will break that cycle. There will be no peace offering from us. I am not merciful."

Peace offering.

My brain twigged.

Jane took the cheers of the room.

She had her back to me but as she turned towards me, she realised I was not finished.

"At what point are you going to realise that we have no option but peace?" I said.

A flash of shock, surprise, crossed Jane's eyes. She shook her head, just once. Her eyes narrowed. "Why would I concede at the point of victory?"

I touched my jaw. "Because worse is coming. And you know that, don't you?"

The room fell silent.

"That wasn't a random attack, was it?" I said. "That wasn't a random depot. That wasn't a random convoy that was arriving at that rest-stop." I looked out to the room. "That convoy was transporting the Foreign Secretary back from negotiating a peace deal. A peace deal with Daesh." A murmur went round the room. I looked back at Jane. "Daesh is in France. And if we don't work with men to defeat them there, they will come for us here. And they will treat us far worse than the enemy we are trying to destroy from within."

The murmurs moved up to whispers but not once did Jane shift the intensity of her gaze from me.

But she said nothing.

My throat was dry. I wiped my nose again. It was still bleeding but it wasn't broken. I looked up to the balcony, then slowly down to the crowds, careful not to jolt another flow of blood from my nose.

"I know the men have done terrible things to you," I said to them all. "To us, to our friends. But what is coming is worse. Those men will turn us into slaves." I took a breath. I swallowed down a trickle of blood that ran down the back of my throat. "I know I'm asking you to choose between two terrible choices, but only one of our enemies promises us a future."

The room was silent.

I went on. "We attacked that base last night to scupper the peace deal." I took a moment, looking down at the floor, trying to find the right words. "I understand why, but we cannot lose to Daesh. We just cannot. And if that means we have to join with men, then we should face that."

Jane came to life. "What would you like to do? Look at your options – would you rather be raped by a British man or one from overseas? Tell me, Laura. I'm curious to know."

My brain was racing, trying to come up with the right words. I looked up to the balconies and out across the sea of faces. "Look at it this way. If, as you say, our wombs are the most valuable commodity left in this world then the cards are in our hands. They need us more than we need them. We can bargain with them."

Jane started pacing back and forth again. Her body language said 'pull back', the fire in her eyes said 'I'm gonna claw your eyes clean out of your skull'.

"I'm going to say this as calmly as I can," Jane said, her chest heaving deeply but quickly. "Your womb means you don't have rights, not that you have a bargaining chip. You are a young woman, a young menstruating woman, with at least a decade of childbearing years ahead of you – if you live. You are a precious commodity, so precious, so understand now that the last thing they are going to allow you to do is sit back and pick and choose. Let me make this clear to you." Jane didn't look up or around. This was all on me.

And she was closing in. "The survivors are short of numbers and short on time. As soon as you step foot onto their territory to negotiate, they will get you pregnant. The only choice you're gonna get is whether they rape you or inject you. And that'll be if you're lucky enough for there to be some spare embryos knocking around."

Jane was standing only a metre or so from me. "I refuse to buy into your darkness," I said. "This world you have in your head... That's damage done to you. I don't accept that that is my future." I took a breath. "I choose to leave."

I looked at her, standing still in front of me. Staring deep into me.

I repeated, "I choose to leave. I'm going to take my chances."

Jane let it hang in the air.

My heart wasn't beating. I couldn't feel it. I felt hot. I felt ice cold.

Then she said it. "I can't let you leave. You know that."

"I would never betray you, any of you. I wouldn't tell them where you are. I would never do that."

Jane shook her head. "You can't promise that. They will make you talk."

"What difference does it make? You're moving."

"You know too much. They'll break your mind and piece together the fragments. I will not let you leave."

"You cannot stop me."

"Yes I can."

The chill raced through my body. My blood froze to ice.

Jane didn't move. She meant it.

"No, you can't." My voice broke to a quiver.

Jane raised her finger. "Arrest her."

"What!" Anne shouted out. "No! Jane, really. She's just tired out."

"I said, arrest her." The finger of the executioner aimed straight in my direction.

"You cannot arrest me!" I shouted. "This isn't a court. What the—" I felt a grip on my left arm. It was Andrea. "Let go of me. Let go." I shook my arm, trying to shake it violently, but Andrea just tightened her grip.

Jane turned her back to me.

I shouted out. "You are fucking lost!"

Even I didn't see it coming. Jane swung her fist so fast I just about heard the whoosh of air as she spun round and smacked her iron fist into the side of my head.

And the smack of my head as it hit the floor was the last thing I heard before I blacked out.

CHAPTER TWENTY-NINE
The Cell

In the absence of light, darkness prevails. Behind bars in my own country. I would never have imagined this, never imagined it was even possible. But these are new days. And they are not good ones.

The floor I had been laid out on was cold. My head was on fire but my back was ice cold. I could feel a pain in my hip, a jarring stiffness, probably from where my body had smacked the floor in the hall.

My vision was still shaky and the room was dark, but I could make out glints of light bouncing off the tall metal bars, just inches from my face, that ran from ceiling to floor.

The bars were screwed well into the floor. I focused in on the screws of the metal plate nearest to me. They hadn't rusted at all. They were shiny. They were new.

Slowly, painfully, I brought my head and chest up, pushing up on my elbows until I was seated. I was still in the school. I had to be. I could make out the sounds above me of an army preparing for a move.

The room's only entrance was via a locked door on the other side of the bars. There was a window in the door and the corridor outside was brightly lit, its brilliant yellow light such a stark contrast to the dark of my cell.

An armed guard was on patrol outside – I could see the back of her head through the window. I remained alone in my cell. I guess my mind was too dangerous to have her on my side of the door.

Would they leave me here when they moved on? Would she kill me before she left? Jane had to do something. I was now a ball and chain around her ankles, an enemy within. You can't carry prisoners. It cripples any attempt to stay nimble, hinders your flexibility. If they kept me alive, they'd have to watch their backs as well as their fronts. That was the only thing in my favour. That was the only advantage I had in this position – that I would force an action.

And all actions have consequences.

I didn't have much time. Jane would make a decision quickly. Great leaders always do. But so soon after Helen, would another killing strengthen or weaken her?

I took one deep breath, then another. Just trying to get the oxygen in, inflating and deflating my chest. I tried gently to move the jaw but it wasn't great. I was worse off now than when I left the block of flats. And I had failed in my mission.

"The status quo is changing rapidly." That's what he had said to me, the man in the suit, when he called me into his office. "We are expecting the announcement to be made tonight in the Prime Minister's address."

The deafening judder of a Chinook flying low over the building and across the river filled the room. He crossed his legs and folded his hands together, waiting for the noise to pass. "And that means your responsibilities will change too."

I nodded. Any more would betray the wave of fear and excitement that shot up my spine. You can prepare for a moment for months but still, the excitement when it finally comes to pass is hard to control.

He studied me closely before adding, "Is there anything more you need from us? Anything at all?"

I made the necessary eye movement – down to my left – to show I was thinking about it. Though thinking about it now, how on earth I thought that would fool him, I don't know. "No," I eventually said. "I understand what is expected of me."

"OK," he said. "Good luck. And you will hear from us, when the time comes."

I nodded and turned to leave.

"Agent," he said. I turned back. "We wouldn't have asked this of you if we didn't think highly of you."

"I know," I said. "Thank you."

I left his room.

I never saw him again after that meeting. He wasn't even in the building when the Prime Minister went in front of the cameras to announce the state of emergency. I don't know what happened to him, or to the Prime Minister in fact. Their fates lost in the darkness.

But I got the sign. A note stashed into the rations left at the foot of the tower block, along with the gun. That had been months ago. I had chosen not to obey, not immediately. My father was ill. I had to look after him first. I had to wait for him to die before I could act. I was all he had left.

And with him, went all that I had left.

A key turned in the lock to the cell. My head jerked round. With the open door came a flood of light. And Anne, carrying a tray.

She shut the door behind her. "Are you OK? Come over. I have food."

A dagger of pain shot through my hip as I staggered to my feet. I stretched it out gently and found my way to the edge of my cell.

Anne passed me some rough bread through the bars.

I took the bread but I couldn't eat it. My head was pounding. It hurt. I touched my jaw with my right hand. It was swollen and sore.

"I think it will go down." Anne pushed a bottle of water through the bars. "Here."

"I'm surprised they let you come to see me."

The harrowed look on Anne's face was all the response I got to that.

"Nothing in this place is on camera, or recorded." She leant against the bars. "Maybe whatever has happened down here was never meant to be recorded."

Anne's head was slack on her neck. It seemed too much effort to hold it up straight. "I'm tired of running," she said. "There's a few of us, we're tired. Many just want to sleep. Some for a very long time. We don't want this any more. You've started whispers. Jane knows it. She's created a tough schedule for our move."

"Anything to stop you talking."

Anne nodded. "You've only just joined. You've seen London. But if you could get out of here, would you know where to go?"

The guard's face came into view at the window. I started eating the bread. Anne caught what I was doing and started clattering some things on her tray deliberately.

The guard's face went away.

"We would head straight for the nearest main road," I said. "Jane would guess that but it's still our quickest route to safety. I know where we are. We need to get to the main road. From there, we can find safety."

Anne's face never broke from the sorrow it came in with.

The guard's face came back again.

Anne caught my eyes looking over her shoulder again. "I've got to go."

"Anne—"

"I'll be back later." Anne turned, knocked on the door and left.

She didn't look back.

Had I said enough? Had I said too much? I felt sick.

The minutes passed.

Many minutes passed and the door never reopened – I had said too much. Anne was Jane's sister, not mine. She was a trap, she was the bait. And I had bitten.

Shit.

Jane knew, of course she knew that Anne and I had talked. All the time we had spent together. The medical centre, the men, even my injections... I had been set up. Entrapment. And I had walked straight into it. The shame of my naivety. I had trusted that Jane did not know about me. I had been a fool. The summary execution was coming. I had picked the wrong action and now the consequence would be all mine.

I curled my head down to my chest and started to cry. Why had I stepped forward? Why? I could have stayed silent. I should've stayed silent.

Eventually they came for me. I saw the movement through the window in the door. I saw the hushed whispers as another person joined the guard at my door.

I stood up against the wall of my cell. I was going to face this head on. Maybe I could overwhelm them. How many would she send? Maybe she would come in person and execute me here. Or maybe I would be bumped off in the dark by an unidentified executioner.

If I were Jane, I would do the latter. The army couldn't take another public execution. Even an army can only take so much murder.

My legs were too full of adrenalin to remain still.

The new guard peered through the window more than once. My movement made her jittery. It made no difference. I continued to move.

Then I heard a slump, the dull thud of an unconscious body hitting the cell door. And another.

I froze. My body went cold.

The key turned in the lock.

And in walked Anne.

With Alex, Becks, Rachel…

And Mandy.

Mandy.

Anne started unlocking the door of my bars. "Let's go. We have about one minute to get out of the building."

I flew out of the door, following Mandy out of the room as Becks shoved a gun in my hand. "It's loaded."

"Where's Andrea?" I asked, stepping over the guards' bodies by the door.

"She's just unconscious," Becks said as we looked down at the body.

"Are you sure?" She didn't look just unconscious.

"She was a No," Mandy said. "We put it to her, Anne did, subtly. But it was a No."

"Yet you're a Yes," I countered.

Mandy looked at me as we strode on. "You can trust me."

"That wasn't what I meant."

Mandy grabbed my arm, causing us all to stop. "It takes a lot to stand up to Jane. And a lot to stand up to me. What I did was wrong. I don't recognise this person that I've become."

Alex started us moving again. "Come on. We don't have long."

"Jane will know we're escaping anyway," I said. "How many of us are there?"

"Two dozen. About that," Alex said. "Outside."

"That many?" I said. "Why didn't you all speak up? There's no way Jane could have withstood that level of dissent." None of them responded. "Sorry – I didn't mean... Let's just focus on getting out of here. I know how to get us where we have to go."

In truth, I only had a vague, unsure idea of how, practically, we were going to get there. But I had to get out.

At the end of the corridor, on the other side of the doors, was the loading bay – the exit. We rushed up to it.

"Wait." Rachel put out her hand as we got to the doors. She got out her pick to unlock the alarm.

"No need." The cold air hit me as soon as I pushed open the doors. "The alarm would have been deactivated on loading the trucks for the move."

And there in the bay was the convoy of trucks ready for the evacuation.

The others flew past me, towards the exit. I stood staring at the trucks. This was odd. The silence was odd. There was no one around. No one. An evacuation without any evacuees.

That meant only one thing.

They were ready for us.

CHAPTER THIRTY
The Splinter

We stood at the edge of the field. The sky overhead was dark, as was the field in front of us. And the lights were off in the buildings behind us.

Something was up.

The field was silent. Completely silent. The sound of the gravel under the feet of the women coming to a halt behind me was all that could be heard.

Many had been hiding in the shadows of the building, waiting for me to lead them across.

Next to me Mandy muttered, "We're surrounded."

I looked around, furtively trying to catch a glimpse of movement amongst the trees.

Nothing.

Not even the glint of reflected light or the rustle of a leaf.

Complete silence.

Mandy was right. We were walking into an ambush.

The trap had been set. This was going to be my Helen moment.

"OK, we need to split up." I pointed Becks down towards the main drive out of the complex. "I want you to—"

"Split up?" Anne's snap was so quick I couldn't tell if it was from anger or fear. "No way. We are stronger if we stay together."

"No. We're not," I countered. "We don't have time to discuss this."

We really didn't.

I turned to Becks. "Take half the group with you. We need to spread them out. The greater number of exit routes we take on, the more chance we have of getting to the road. Once we get to the road they can't touch us. They'll be too exposed. We need to split up to improve our chances."

Becks nodded.

"You mean, draw their fire." Anne was speaking but way too loudly.

I snapped. "Anne, we are going to have to shoot our way out of this either way, whether we stay together or split up."

Anne's eyes watered up, but she nodded. "OK. She won't shoot us though."

I looked at her, briefly, and then got back to the mission. "OK, Becks, take them. You guys, follow her and head down the drive. It's obvious but they might be calling our bluff."

Becks looked beyond me, out into the field. "They're in the woods?"

"Probably."

"Where will we meet you?"

I couldn't give her an exact place, she knew that. No locations, no links. Instead I said "I will find you. Just get to the road."

I had no idea whether she believed me, but I meant it.

"Come on. Follow me." Becks jogged off, taking half the group with her. It was the right thing to do, to take half of the group. It was the less risky path. But that doesn't mean there wouldn't be a welcoming party for them near the gates. We were right out on the edge now.

I turned to the remainder. "Whatever happens behind us, keep moving forward." Some of them nodded. Anne wasn't one of them, but she stepped forward to stand next to me.

Rachel gave me the nod then she peeled off to the right, taking most of the rest of my women with her. There was a path through the woods, overgrown as it was. Maybe it was foolish to send the women down an obvious route out but I sensed that Jane was more likely to be after me.

Maybe Anne was right. Maybe Jane wouldn't shoot at them.

But she would shoot at me, for sure.

And Jane knew, as I knew, that as leader, you take on the most difficult task yourself. My path was straight ahead, across the open field that had no cover, then into the woods on the other side that had no trodden path through it. Through to the road.

There were just four of us left – me, Anne, Mandy and Alex.

Both of my hands on the rifle, I led them out into the field. We jogged. There was no point walking. They were probably already watching us. Let's just get this over with.

We jogged quickly. Running an impossibility in the darkness. I could hear the others behind me, our boots on the turf.

Then.

Suddenly.

A flash of white lit up the sky.

BOOM!

The ground underneath us shook.

We jerked our heads around.

The drive. The drive away from the school had been mined. Or the gates had been rigged.

"Oh God, no." Anne almost dropped her rifle.

But there were no screams.

A crack of gunfire flew out from the trees.

The field around us cut up as the bullets pelted down.

They were in the woods.

"Get behind me. Single file." They did as I told them. They crouched in a single line behind me as I fired off a round to my left, a round to my right. And then straight ahead. "Do the same."

The women fired off blind rounds in to the woods.

"Forward."

We ran forward, alternating in rounds as we went. Anne shot to her left, Mandy to the right.

Their bullets continued to fly at us.

I cried out. "Is anyone hit?"

"No. Not hit." From Alex.

I could hear the concentrated gunfire behind me, down the drive. Gunfire meant some at least had survived the explosions.

"Forward." I shot off more rounds in front of me.

Anne shot to the left, Mandy to the right.

Another hail of bullets cut up the grass around us. But we weren't hit. They weren't hitting us. The bullets were being fired short.

"Do you think they're dead?" Anne, I could tell from her voice, was not coping.

"I don't know. Keep moving forward."

Round to the left, round to the front.

Then we ran – Anne shooting to the left, Alex and Mandy to the right.

BOOM!

The sky flashed again.

But I didn't turn round.

"Keep moving forward," I shouted and I meant it.

This time the white light in the sky was accompanied by screaming.

No, wait, shouting. These weren't screams of pain. I could hear shouting – orders, warnings. But I couldn't work out the voices.

"Keep moving forward."

"We should turn back." I could hear the break in Anne's voice.

My answer was resolute. "No."

Round straight ahead, round to the right.

The woods were only metres from us now.

Suddenly, an overwhelming concentration of gunfire burst into life behind us, back by the building. Near the overgrown path.

The others. They had found the others.

The gunfire was being diverted. There was a break in the bullets aimed at us.

I turned to see my women distracted, looking back towards the gunfire. "In." I dragged them into the woods.

The woods were cool and quiet. We leapt over stumps and fallen trees, nipped in between trunks to get further, deeper into the shelter, into the darkness. We needed cover.

A giant log blocked the way in front and I came to a halt.

Anne grabbed my arm. "We need to go back."

"No," Mandy said.

Behind her, Alex was still gripping her rifle. But Anne, her head was constantly shaking, her arms trembling. Her head twitching.

Anne shook me. "We need to—"

"No," I said, but it wasn't well received. "Look, we can't retrace our steps. We need cover. We can't recross the field.

When we get to the road, we will head towards them."

"We need to draw their fire." Anne was jumpy. "That's what Jane would do, she would draw the fire away from them."

"But Anne, that's what we did when we ran across the field." The three of them looked at me, an awareness falling across their faces. Yes, ours had been the most dangerous path.

There was no sound.

No gunfire, no explosions, no shouting.

"Listen," I said. Silence had fallen again.

And that meant one thing.

"We need to run." I started to pull them together.

"The guns have stopped." Anne started to wander back but I grabbed her arm.

"I know. That means we need to move."

Alex grabbed Anne's other arm and together we ran round the log, up and down some ditches, deeper into the woods.

Then I saw her, out in front, standing on the crest of a mound.

Jane hadn't seen us. She was surrounded by a division.

Some of her women were on the floor of the woods. She had taken casualties.

In front of her, others had their guns up, pointing out to the field.

She was partly obscured by the trees but I saw her.

And then she turned and saw me too.

I saw her open her mouth.

"Run!" I pushed the others with me in the opposite direction. "Run fast."

And we did.

If she wanted to kill us, she'd have to shoot us in the back.

CHAPTER THIRTY-ONE
The Surrender

We ran without stopping for an age, not once looking back. Running through trees, fast over mounds and ditches. We ran on and on and on. None of my makeshift brigade asked me or challenged me. They just followed.

Feet quickly over logs, trampling leaves.

I couldn't hear any other feet behind us, just the sound of ours.

And the heavy breath of exhaustion.

"Stop. I need to stop." Anne was cramping up. "Oh God, my legs. My legs are hurting."

The rest pulled up pretty quickly. The excuse to catch breath was grabbed and soon we were standing around, hands on hips, breathing heavily.

"They're not following us." Mandy was right. She also had a deep cut on her arm, which she caught me looking at. "It looks worse than it is."

I looked back out towards the woods.

Nothing. The odd rustle of some leaves, but nothing else.

Alex joined Anne in leaning over, resting her hands on her thighs, gulping in the air. Mandy couldn't stand still, shaking out the lactic acid in her legs. But all of them kept looking back towards the woods.

Maybe they wanted to go back.

"OK, let's move on, to safety," I said.

The three of them turned back to me in unison and we marched on.

Rachel and her division found us more than us finding them. Both of our groups had still been in the woods, heading directly to the road, but Rachel had been leading her women more along the perimeter, closer to the road.

"But we didn't want to take to the road itself," she said. "They're watching the roads like hawks. They would've found us."

Rachel and I talked closely, quietly, as our two brigades mixed once again – the fitter tending to the wounded and the calm appeasing the scared. It wasn't a joyous reunion. Thoughts of those not with us were heavy in the air.

"A couple of them were hit with bullets but they were just grazes." Rachel was whispering her casualty report to me. "The bullets flew past them, singed the skin. Must've hit trees or flown off behind them. None of them seem to have lodged. Charlie over there has two sprained ankles just from tripping on roots but she ran on."

"Adrenalin?"

"Adrenalin." Rachel took a few breaths before carrying on. "The others, a few scrapes from trees but we took no fatalities. Laura, I don't think they were shooting to kill."

"No, I know. But don't tell them that."

"Why not?" Rachel asked.

"I don't want them confused," I said. "That was still live

274

ammunition they were firing at us. And we still don't know what's happened to the others."

Rachel nodded. She hung her head.

I couldn't think of any comforting words to say about her sister. I just stood, inert and uncomfortable.

Then Anne came up to us. "We have to go back for them."

I looked at Rachel – a light had come on in her eyes.

"No," I said.

Anne shifted her weight from one foot to the other. "I'm not saying all the way back. Not to the school. But we have to retrace our steps. We have to see that they made it out alive. And if they haven't…" Anne looked over at Rachel, then back to me. "Well… Then we have to bury them."

I shook my head. "I can't."

"Jane would go back," Anne snapped.

I glared at her.

Suddenly the chatter in the background stopped.

I took a deep breath and silently reminded myself that everyone was tired.

Anne dropped her gaze away from mine. We weren't going to go back and she knew it.

I looked up at the others, now all staring at me. And I spoke. "We cannot go back. If the others did survive, Jane has got them now. If we go back, it's either to find them dead or to be dead ourselves. If Jane refuses to bury them, that is her call. I cannot risk you all to honour civility. We don't live in that kind of world any more."

Anne hung her head. I had no interest in flogging her for it. Anne's was the correct thing to do but mine was the right.

The other women showed a defeated acceptance. We all understood the limits of compassion.

"We move on," I said. "This way to the road."

"No," said Anne. And the group drew breath at her refusal.

275

I sensed the shift.

I looked at Anne. "We only need to get to the road," I said.

"No. We move on."

"Why?"

Anne was adamant. "They, the men, the State, can rescue us but I will not let them destroy my sister. Where they pick us up, they'll assume she's nearby."

Around us, the rest of the twenty or so defectors were gripped.

Behind her Mandy nodded. "Jane's not evil, just misguided. We're not offering her up."

I looked back at the other women, then beyond them back into the woods. It was true, the further we ran, the more time Jane had to evacuate. She was slipping through my fingers. She would melt away again before reappearing somewhere else to push on to final victory.

Anne's look at me was glacial, like her sister. I had hesitated too long. "Of course," I nodded. "Let's run up further."

And so I turned my back on the road and we went on, deeper into the woods.

We marched on. Rifles in hands, always looking anxiously out into the trees. We walked in three lines of single file – I led the one in the middle, Alex to my right, Mandy to my left.

It's funny, the ones who end up staying by your side. Never the ones you expect. I thought of Andrea, true, but I also thought of Anne. Did Jane expect loyalty to her to divide in that way? To keep my friend but to lose her sister?

And what about my other women? Had they made it out alive or had Jane killed them? Could she, would she, kill her own? Surely even Jane had limits. And even if she'd caught them and they'd pledged reconversion to the cause, could she believe them? Would I?

I kept having to snap myself back into my body. My mind constantly wandering into these thoughts. I had to concentrate. The woods were dangerous. Poor light and no knowledge of the terrain. Jane knew the woods; she may even have mined them.

Our pace had either been quicker than I thought or my mind had wandered too often but, either way, the light from the break in the trees ahead of us came upon us before I had expected.

We all saw it.

In unison, we broke from a march to a jog.

And then a jog to a run, bursting out of the woods on to the deserted road.

The relief that we had made it was palpable. Mandy smiled and hugged Rachel. Alex looked up to the heavens and opened her arms. Anne started fanning out the back of her top, drying out the rivers of sweat pouring down her spine.

I looked left and right. No cars, no sign of men. No sign of women either. "OK, let's shelter here and wait," I said.

I knew we wouldn't have to wait long. The tarmac under our feet was springy, fresh. This was a new road, a road in use.

The women were tired, a few of them shivering. Mandy would need attention for that cut, it wasn't healing. I looked up and down the road, back and forth. Then I caught sight of the anxiety as they watched me.

"They will come," I said. "They will come for us."

Anne looked at me, unconvinced.

"We're precious cargo," I said to her.

It was enough to placate her. She nodded and wandered off to encourage the women to rest. I stood separate from the others, looking out onto the road, looking for the vehicles.

And we didn't wait long.

It wasn't even a passing convoy that picked us up. Instead, not more than an hour after we first came to a stop, a convoy of armoured vehicles turned the corner at the bottom of the track, way off in the distance, and started coming at us full pelt.

All of us got to our feet.

And all the others pulled out their rifles.

"Get off the road." Anne started flagging the women to vanish into the shelter of the woods.

"No," I said. "That will scare them."

I strode out into the middle of the road.

The trucks didn't slow their pace.

I dropped my gun to the road.

"Laura!" I could hear Mandy to my right. "Get off the road!"

I didn't look over. I just kept focusing on the trucks. "No. We're not here to fight them."

The women recoiled. I could sense them shrink further back into the woods.

The trucks kept coming.

They flanked out. Three abreast, thundering towards me.

I heard the grind of the gear changes.

I put my arms in the air, not once breaking from my focus on them.

They were going to stop. They were going to stop.

Then with an almighty screech of the brakes, the trucks skidded to a halt.

The plumes of dust rolled like waves towards me.

The bangs as the doors were flung open.

The thud of boots hitting ground.

The cracks of rifles being loaded.

As the dust particles lost their momentum and started falling to the ground, lines of men appeared in front of me – all dressed in army uniform with goggles and packs and shields.

A dozen kneeling on the ground. Another dozen standing above them. All of them had their rifles aimed at me.

They had come for a fight.

Another phalanx of men burst out from behind the lines and headed into the woods.

"Stop!" I shouted.

And they did.

"We're not here to fight you," I said. "My name is Laura Lewis. I am here to bring us in."

CHAPTER THIRTY-TWO
The Arrival

I watched the terrain change through the smears on the clear plastic in the doors at the back of the truck. The fresh road laid through the woods eventually gave way to a motorway. The roads were empty except for us. Occasionally we'd pass an overturned car or a burnt out vehicle but fewer than I'd expected. Most had been taken away – along with all foliage. All trees, all hedges, all plants that once lined these roads, the screening, had been ripped out. There could be no place to hide. No cover for terrorists in the grass.

We were heading north.

We had already gone through two military checkpoints and we'd go through more before we got to our destination. But no matter how the security patrols swelled as we neared our destination, I didn't feel any safer.

I looked down at the chains cuffing my wrists.

And then down to the chains around my ankles.

The chains around Mandy's ankles opposite me caught my eye.

As did the ones on Anne sitting next to her.

I glanced down the whole line of ankles of the women on the bench opposite me.

And then their wrists.

I looked straight back out the window, too afraid, too ashamed, to make eye contact with any of my women. Women who had followed me in good faith.

It wasn't supposed to be like this.

Two armed men on either side of the doors, three men up front with the driver. And men made up every single member of the army that had picked us up.

"Where are the women?" Anne had asked them as they made us lie down on the road as they cuffed us. "Where are the women? Why haven't you got any women in your army?"

As she did, Mandy had whispered to me, "How did they know to have extra trucks with them?"

I didn't have answers for either of these questions.

There was not one woman in their ranks, not one. Anne's fears were the same as mine. And when she voiced them she unleashed a contagion of fear through our ranks. Some struggled and fought with the men. One man kicked Alex in retribution. At least I had stopped that but they refused to treat Mandy's arm.

Where were the women? The army, the State had been pluralistic when it all went south. What the hell had happened?

The sound of Chinooks overhead meant we were closing in on our destination. Armoured vehicles protecting goods lorries started to pass us, going in the other direction. The depth of security barricades on either side of the road increased and the speed of our vehicles slowed right down.

"Is that it?" Alex's voice broke the silence in the truck. "Is that the enclave?"

I snapped my head round and, like everyone else, jostled to get a view through the windscreen.

"No," said Mandy. "This is the new government headquarters. This is the centre of everything."

We were approaching a huge perimeter wall, like something you'd only ever seen on the Korean borders or photos of 1950s Berlin. A solid barrier that towered up into the sky. But it was not yet complete. Parts of it were still being built.

Its guard towers were manned – each turret had two or three gun-wielding men within. And each turned their rifles towards us as our convoy approached.

I had seen early designs for this new government zone back in the day, but that was a long time ago. Publicly, of course, we would not be moved. Privately, the need to move London up north was already acknowledged. But it wasn't supposed to be militarised. Not to this extent. That development had been borne out of unexpected necessity.

On the other side of the wall, in the lion's den, our convoy finally pulled up and out we shuffled, the prisoners in chains.

Anti-vehicle trenches were being dug at the foot of the wall both by hand and by machine. The chain gangs in army fatigues glanced up at our convoy, but gazing at my women earned them a swift rebuke from the guards and they soon returned to the grind.

The barbed wire was there, along the top. But not all the way around. There were gaps. The State was not organised. The State was behind schedule. RAZR had destroyed the rebuilding schedule.

As I turned towards the main buildings, I saw one of the soldiers doing a handover with an administrative official who'd come out to greet us. The official looked at me and nodded. I looked away.

The women, all of them, were looking in the other direction, facing the huge complex that the wall surrounded. Most of them seemed quite shocked. They'd obviously not been here before but the buildings were familiar to me.

The fountains at the base of the huge steps were no longer overflowing with water and the pretty trees had been taken down but the Greco-Roman architecture was unmistakable. For at the top of the steps stood the new parliamentary building of the State. Its white columns were brilliant, even in the dank drizzle. And alongside it, the gothic turrets and domes of the old Town Hall were now offices for the State.

"Lewis, Lewis." It took me a second to realise the administrative official was talking to me. He was wearing beige and had a big stomach. "You are coming with me."

He gesticulated at my chains and one of the armed guards started unlocking them.

I looked at the women. Some were hopeful, others were terrified.

"And the others," I said to the man.

"No," he said. "They are going another way."

I stood and watched as those who had trusted me with their lives were marched away from me.

And I let them take them away. I don't know why I hesitated, why I didn't shout, why I didn't rage at the men. But the look on Anne's face as she turned back to me before they pushed her on will haunt me till the day I die.

CHAPTER THIRTY-THREE
The Interview

The men had brought me to a bare, windowless room. Nothing on the walls, nothing on the high ceiling, and nothing on the table in front of me. And it was locked from the outside.

"We had to abandon London. Too difficult." The official with the stomach remained with me. No name badge, no introduction. He had directed the soldiers guarding me to this room. The soldiers had left but the man remained, and he hadn't stopped talking since we'd arrived. "You can't lock down areas where the buildings are on top of each other."

It was just me and him in the room but he wasn't sitting in the chair on the other side of the table from me. He just stood and talked. "Too many places to hide. All that door-to-door... You can't take control of an area. So we had to, not withdraw exactly, but transform the status quo, so we changed our base. A proactive solution."

He kept looking at me oddly, then down at his hands. His palms were glistening.

My balance was off. The plan was that I would be greeted

by a team from the agencies. I should be being debriefed by now. Where was everyone?

The guy looked at me, awkwardly, and shuffled his feet. "How were we to know RAZR was actually an organised army? That she'd been recruiting people for years? Afghanistan, Ukraine, Kurdistan, the Baltics..."

My ears pricked up. Instinctive whenever Jane became the subject.

The door opened and in walked a new man. He looked at me, briefly, then to the official. "You can leave."

The official nodded and left, but his replacement wasn't in military uniform. This was no general. He wasn't much taller than me. Hair closely cut. Not military standard to the scalp but short. Balding at the top. He looked old. Forties, fifties... Hard to know for sure in this day and age. We were all ageing fast.

He sat down opposite me and opened a folder of papers on to the desk, a thick folder. As he shuffled through them I recognised the watermarks on the papers – MI5.

This was more like what I was expecting. I leant forward in my chair.

Then, just as I did, the door opened again and in marched about a dozen men. All in army uniform.

I leant back again.

The men formed a perimeter around the desk and stood to attention, backs to the walls. The man at my table was unmoved. He didn't even look up.

He'd been expecting them.

None of the soldiers looked at me – all looked ahead.

The man looked up from his folder to me. "My name is Owen. I'm here to debrief you. You're—" Owen suddenly stopped, looked towards the closed door. He was listening for something. But there was no sound other than him.

He turned back to me. "Three years, two months and fourteen days ago you were assigned the task of infiltrating the, then, small but increasingly influential and violent terrorist group RAZR, the Resistance Against State Reformation, with the intention of both a) retrieving significant data on the terrorist cell, its locations, its activities and its funding mechanisms, and b) if possible, bringing in its known and wanted leader operating under the chosen pseudonym Jane. Last confirmed photo, this one."

Owen slapped a black and white 10 x 8 image in front of me. The photo wasn't in focus nor was it recent. But there she was, at the back of a small group of men. All in camouflage gear. Jane – younger, thinner. Less of the Amazon but her arms were still strong. It was her. I would recognise her from the stance alone, let alone the features. Gun in one hand hanging down by her side, her other in a pocket. Weight evenly distributed on both legs.

Where was the photo taken? I couldn't tell for sure. The two-point plug in the wall said Eastern Europe, but the features of the two men nearest her were more Russian than Slavic.

How had I not seen this photo of Jane? I had seen every photo, had studied every trip. Why had I not seen this one? Where was this? Jane was never in Russia. Or was she?

Owen had stopped. I looked up. He had been watching me as I studied the photo.

We held each other's gaze for a moment. Then he went on. "And if that wasn't possible, for whatever reason, to bring us evidence of her assassination."

Owen paused again. This was no debrief. Here, in this room, we were teetering on the brink of something else.

The men around me remained static, unmoved. But I could sense them.

I said nothing. Why would I? No question had been asked.

Owen calmly placed both his hands on the folder. "Our last known confirmation of your whereabouts was four weeks ago, when you arrived at the filtration centre for classification. Later than expected. But, as per the plans, you were placed in a high-risk convoy the next morning, which was duly intercepted. An interception which led to us being inflicted with twenty-three casualties, two destroyed heavily armed militarised vehicles and the loss of one key hard drive."

Hard drive? What hard drive? I was meant to be the only asset in the vehicles. Maybe those had been my files, the ones Jane had seen.

Still I said nothing – no questions, no answers.

The men around me didn't even stir.

Owen took a deep breath. Not of anxiety. He was trying to calm a swelling anger. "And now here you are, four weeks later. We've had no contact from you, no data leakage as requested, and you have brought us no head on a platter. Yet, in that time, we have experienced the loss of 289 men, including our Foreign Secretary, the sabotage and wilful destruction of a significant part of our security data, including the loss of vital scientific work on a cure for the virus, the theft or destruction of crucial armoury, including materials that were due for dispatch to the forces fighting in the Lebanon, the abduction and murder of almost one hundred pregnant women, and the destruction of a peace deal secured with the moderate splinter group from Daesh, a loss which has prevented the cessation of hostilities on the southern Mediterranean coastline and has led to the loss of more lives as that pointless part of the conflict continues to distract from the rampage of the fundamentalists through into Turkey. So…" Owen snapped my folder shut. His blazing eyes fixed on me. "Let's start with your version of events and go from there. The convoy you were abducted from, it was RAZR?"

I didn't drop my gaze from his. "Me and the eleven other women who were travelling as passengers in the convoy were abducted by a heavily armed female-only unit. They never gave their name."

Owen looked at me. The temperature in the room was rising all the time. "This woman..." tapping on the photo in front of me. "This woman that you spent seven months prior to the dismantling of your intelligence unit studying and following, learning every detail, every habit, interrogating every previous known contact... Was this woman the leader of the *unit*..." Owen sneered on that last word "... that intercepted that convoy?"

"Yes."

Owen took another long, deep breath. "Right. When you were intercepted, when RAZR murdered twenty-three officers who were protecting your life, you were still within a zone where, had you sent out a flare, an alert, we could have found you."

"No I wasn't." Owen froze, my bluntness catching him by surprise. I went on. "How did I know that? Not because of any cartography or landmarks but because we were so effectively and decisively intercepted. It wasn't a drawn out protracted ambush, it was overwhelming force. And I knew enough about RAZR to know they wouldn't expose themselves like that."

"What do you mean, 'expose themselves'? They take risks regularly."

"Calculated ones." And as I said this I realised—

Owen leapt on this. "What made you think this was a calculated risk?"

I'd said too much.

Owen kept on. "RAZR intercepts our convoys all the time – or they try to – but they usually wait for easier moments."

I said nothing.

Owen tilted his head, just slightly. "Are you saying Jane knew what was in that convoy? That you were in that convoy? That she knew who you were?"

I said nothing.

And his eyes narrowed. "Forgive me, Laura, but I feel I am questioning you, dragging information from you with immense pain. Just to clarify, you are still of the State, for the State. Am I right? Or should we be looking at a different set-up here?"

"I'm not defending her."

"You're not?"

"No. She tried to kill me. And I witnessed her killing many people, including some she believed to be traitors in her own ranks."

"Did she try to kill you because she thought you a traitor?"

I paused. "No. But I consider that a reflection of the work, the preparation, I did, to ensure I had her confidence, to earn her trust."

"Yet so quick to lose it. I mean, that's what's happened, right? Because why else would you walk in here with some of the most wanted yet without the ace?"

Think, Laura, think. Warm up here. "My assignment was to infiltrate RAZR at the highest level, to patiently but deliberately build up a significant degree of trust from the highest echelons of the resistance, to build up a detailed list of the movement's personnel, strategy and operational activities. There was no way I could do that by ringing an alarm as soon as—"

"Or for that programme to be abandoned if an opportunity presented itself to have Jane captured or killed," Owen said.

I replied calmly. "And at the moment my convoy was intercepted, I judged that there was none. And at that moment, I did not know it was RAZR."

Owen leant forward. "But Jane was part of the armed assault on the convoy."

"I didn't recognise her immediately."

"No?"

"No. Which is why I did not know it was RAZR and which is why I did not raise an alert."

Owen looked down at his papers. "Six hours after your vehicle was attacked, we picked up two women, an Abigail Harrow and a Gail Talloy, who confirmed they were with you in the convoy."

Shit, I'd forgotten.

"They were with you to go on to the enclave, but were abandoned by you, their sisters in the so-called female resistance movement, because they didn't fit the bill."

I bit down on my tongue. Breathe, Laura, breathe.

Owen lifted up a piece of paper, bringing it closer to his face. "They confirmed to us that you were in the convoy and that this woman—" Owen jabbed at the photo again, "—was in your convoy also. They recognised her."

"They were mistaken."

"They were mistaken in their recognition of a woman you admit was in the convoy but you didn't recognise? Maybe we should have recruited them instead."

"I do not know if there was pressure put on those women to placate you, to give you the answer you're looking for but, at the time, it was impossible to know Jane was in the convoy and, at that time, Jane had not revealed herself." My eyes never left Owen's. "The two women you are referring to are confusing Jane with a decoy. Jane was using a decoy. I wasn't deceived but they probably were. I mean, they looked similar but then it can't be hard to find someone of her height with long brown hair. It's not an unusual look. And this is an old photo of her. And, as I know from my own work, Jane made a deliberate, concerted effort to wipe her DNA and all images – or rather as many as she could – from government databases before she absconded. It's a pretty blurry image."

Owen nodded. Slowly.

"There is a reason why you are sat behind a desk and I am in the field," I added.

"I apologise." Owen placed the photo of Jane back in the folder. "Let me step back here. You went dark for four weeks on an assignment of critical importance, during which time the terrorist group you infiltrated continued to wreak a terrible trail of destruction across the UK. Let me make this clear to someone who's not been at a desk for three years – RAZR is winning. We are very vulnerable. If RAZR choose to align with our enemies, they will win. And then hell knows what would come from that."

"I was never under any illusions about the importance of my mission."

"Thank you, Laura." Owen closed the folder again. "Give me the location of RAZR."

The blood drained from my face. "I cannot give you that."

"You can't?"

"Not for sure." For the first time I sensed a twitch, a reverberation, across the men that stood guard around me. "Not exact map coordinates. Only a few were ever allowed to know location and I wasn't one of them. My role was data retrieval from State networks during raids, then analysing this data so others could identify targets and make assault plans for future missions."

"Only you uploaded as well as downloaded." Owen pushed his chair away ever so slightly, and crossed his legs.

"Now, now, Laura, let's not be shy. You corrupted a lot of the data within our systems. Given your skills, I would argue that you did that deliberately."

"Like I said, winning Jane's trust was hard." I made a conscious effort to breathe slowly. "She was smarter than the obvious fawning." And clearly even smarter than I had realised. I had been blinded on both sides.

"Well, maybe if you won't talk, or maybe if you can't talk, perhaps one of the others will."

Owen's words hit me like a truck.

I felt my heart stop.

"Like the decoy that came with you," Owen said. "Was she the one in the convoy?"

Pins and needles shot all the way up the left side of my body.

Anne. They knew they had Anne. Was she being harmed?

"Oh, come now, you think we didn't see the similarities straight away? Her sister's face is etched into everyone's minds, whether we want it there or not."

Owen was staring at me intently. If I averted my eyes either up or down to the left, that's a giveaway sign. Manage the body language, Laura, manage the body language.

And these men that surrounded me... Did a similar group now surround the women who had followed me, who were now in my care?

"You've gone very quiet all of a sudden," Owen said. "Can we encourage you to talk a bit more?"

Owen looked at me, proud and in control.

We are less evolved from animals than we think.

A survival tip in the jungle has always been: don't look a lion directly in the eyes. The lion wants to dominate you. If you are looking straight into his eyes, it's defiance. It's a sign you're not broken, not intimidated. And if a lion doesn't think he's scared you, he'll kill you.

It's all about power, it's all about territory. It's all about control.

And men are no different.

I looked down at the table. "Anyone can say anything under torture. I have no reason to lie to you. Last night, I led the women you have through hails of bullets and rigged explosives to safety on the basis that the resistance offered them no future. There's nothing waiting for those on that path other than extinction – ours as well as their own. If I believed even for a second what RAZR is promoting, I wouldn't have come back, let alone bring women I'd fought alongside."

There was a tap at the door.

No one moved.

Owen's gaze never left me. "Dark waters get murkier when loyalty becomes entangled. You may have formed emotional attachments that your brain cannot rationalise. You may have vested interests you are protecting or, worse, you may now be a double agent seeking to destroy us from within."

Silence.

No one had answered the door.

My heart was thumping.

Owen leant forward, his elbows resting on the table. "And you turn up here, with no head on a platter, no details on where we can find RAZR, and a reluctance to speak directly."

Now I understood why the men were also in the room. They weren't just here to stop me running but to hold me down.

Owen gently ran his fingers along the top of his folder. "So, let's talk now, shall we, Agent? Tell me something I don't know about Jane. Surprise me."

There was another knock at the door.

I looked at the door, but no one else in the room even twitched.

I looked back at Owen.

Owen raised his eyebrows. "No? Nothing?"

Smack!

My forehead was smashed into the table.

Men leapt forward and grabbed my arms, tied my wrists to the armrests. My head was spinning. I'd been hit from the back.

One of the men yanked my head back.

I heard Owen say, "Let them in."

Even in my daze, I could make them out in the blur, the men who wheeled the trolley into the room, up to my chair, and then left.

The trolley.

I couldn't focus. I didn't have to.

My head was throbbing, my vision askew. I was tilting forward in my chair but I saw a black soldier hold down my left arm, hard in the straps, as a white guy slid the needle in.

Prepare yourself, girl – you will fade, become woozy. They will slam your head again or slap your face to keep you conscious. Then they'll ask you questions. Prepare the reflex automatic statement.

The sharpening image of Owen looking into my pupils faded out again into blurred lines. My fist loosened, my jaw unclenched.

Owen was talking. I remember bits, fragments but I was focusing on my constant internal affirmations. "You know what this is… You know what you need to say…"

It was truth serum, in the needle. In my arm. Sodium amytal, probably. The CIA had sent us a case-load for prisoner interrogation at the start of the war because we had already shipped most of ours to Erbil.

The serum itself is nothing to fear. It only works if you're scared.

I was hit again. The slap was so hard I almost fell off the chair.

I was yanked up on my right-hand side.

"Let's start this again, Laura." Owen's voice again. Queen's English. Important I focus on details. They tell you this in training – disconnect yourself from the pain. It's hard to do, it takes practice. But it can be done. Your answers aren't relevant, try to remember the details. They could come in useful later.

"Where is the last known base of RAZR?"

I closed my eyes and let my head drop. This was no time for defiance. Defiance is just pride, defiance is just pride... I kept repeating it to myself, silently, as the man went on and on.

"Did you meet the leader of the RAZR resistance movement known as Jane?"

Oh, how I would like to have looked him in the eye. Oh, how I would have loved to prove, unequivocally, that we could not be broken, that we would not comply.

"Were you an active participant in raids coordinated and led by RAZR on State facilities and assets?"

But I had to swallow it down. I needed to get out of this room alive.

"Did you kill on the orders of Jane or any other member of the RAZR resistance group?"

Keep your breath calm, Laura. Keep your breath calm.

"Did you at any time act on your orders to terminate the life of the wanted terrorist leader known as Jane?"

I needed to get out of that room.

I'd made a terrible, terrible mistake.

CHAPTER THIRTY-FOUR
The Intervention

I had no idea what was left of me.

My smashed head was on the table. I could feel the cool plastic surface on my forehead. That sensation was a constant but everything else was floating in and out.

Barks from the man circling around me. Or was it more than one voice? I can't remember. It was hard to tell.

I was still sitting in the chair, or at least slumped in it, but I'd disconnected myself completely from my body. It was the only way.

Focus on the lights, focus on the lights.

My eyes were closed and I was following every brief shard of light that fell across the back of my eyelids. Gold blurs singed with red floating across, left to right, then evaporating. Focus the mind, escape the body.

The table shook, jolting me back into my body.

The pain.

The heat in my head.

The man pounded his fist down on the table again.

He said something.

He smacked the back of my head.

"Where are the terrorists?" he shouted.

My head was suddenly yanked back off the table. The sudden brightness scorched my eyes. I winced under the glare. But as I tried to lift my hands to cover my eyes, the sensation came back to them. They were still strapped to the armrests.

"Where is RAZR?" Owen snapped.

"I don't know."

The man standing behind me slammed my head back into the desk. I just about had it in me to ensure the forehead took the blow not the jaw. There is no agony like a broken jaw. The skull is a lot tougher to break.

"Uncuff her hands."

And they did – but freeing up only my left hand. The right remained strapped down. I can't be sure what any of the men looked like. I don't think I saw any of their faces. And the memory plays tricks on me even now. It creates faces in my recollection when, in truth, I remember none.

But I remember their hands.

This one's hands were rough and scabby. A meaty palm with thick, stubby fingers. And strong. The force with which he pushed my left hand down into the table was enough to make my metacarpals crack.

My head was yanked back again.

"Laura, Laura, Laura…" Still Owen. Still the same tone in his voice, still the passive aggression. "You are an intelligent woman, brilliant intelligence, wonderful assimilation skills. So don't think for a second that I'm going to believe that you don't know where you've been the past thirty-two days, so let's not play games."

My sight was a mess. The smacking on the desk had shaken me. My legs couldn't take any weight. I was trying to covertly press my heels into the floor, to see if they could handle any opportunism, but there was nothing there.

The pressure on my hand was replaced with a brush of heavy cold metal. The chill shot through my body, up my spine to my lips.

"I don't know, I don't know!" I cried out.

"You don't know, what? The names?" Owen was close to me. His voice was near. I could feel the heat from his breath. "Well, that's OK, Laura. Describe it to me. Describe them to me, describe what you remember – the places, the people – and we can go from there."

The fear, the fear. That cool metal on the top of my middle finger of my left hand. Resting, waiting.

"I... ah... ah..." Desperately stalling, desperately trying to rationalise what I could say, what, if anything, I could confess, that would lift the weight from my middle finger, that would lift the hands from my left arm.

The school flashed through my mind. The army training on the fields. Jane standing underneath the cross. The gun just inches from my hand as she spoke by the campfire. Helen's head bowed just as Jane pulled the trigger. Jane stabbing the fleeing men through the neck like a Fury. Jane executing the man. Jane the tyrant. Jane the murderer.

I opened my mouth.

But before I said a word, the women flashed through my mind. The women who came to free me, the women who marched through the wood, behind me. Anne's face as they were marched away.

I closed my mouth, shook my head and closed my eyes.

The object lifted from my fingers as a sweaty palm crushed my left hand deeper into the table.

I heard the whistle of the hammer as it passed my ear.

The smash of my finger, the crushing of the bone.

I passed out.

Under torture there is no such thing as truth. The tortured mind is in shock. Synapses are confused. Thinking is muddled. So why do it? They were either desperate or they were hurting me simply because they wanted to.

A yank of my head brought me round.

My face was slapped repeatedly, hard.

My mind was groggy, my sight, as I peeled open my eyelids, was poor. I could make out figures but I couldn't hear what they were saying. The ringing in my ears was so loud.

But I felt the head of the hammer resting on the knuckles of my left hand. Lifted briefly, then gently touched on the skin again.

Then up again and

Smash!

"Aargh!"

Another finger was smashed. The pain, the pain...

The shots of agony surged up into my brain in milliseconds.

I whimpered, trying desperately to gain control of my mind but the throbbing in my hand... I slumped into my chair praying to what was left of God to just have them kill me quickly.

"So what's it to be?" Owen was in my face now, though I wasn't looking, my eyes still closed. "Still nothing in the memory banks?"

I opened my mouth. My throat was dry but my mouth was full of saliva. I could feel it covering my tongue and spilling over my lips. Or at least I thought it was saliva. But I managed to get my words out. "You shouldn't believe anything I say."

"Laura, Laura." I sensed Owen take a seat on the table in front of me. His voice was coming from that direction. "Perhaps you've been brainwashed into thinking that men are blunt in their stupidity but, you see, there's a reason that it's your left hand, or what remains of your left hand, that we are focusing on." And then he came in close. "We need you to use your right hand."

I shook my head, trying to work out what I could feel as much as saying no. "You've not—" I choked a bit. "—shown me any confession."

Owen laughed. "No, no Laura. We don't need you to sign any confession paper. Justice is a vague concept in a time of war. We dispensed with those niceties some time ago now. No, you'll need your right hand to spell out where RAZR is as you won't be able to tell us after we've cut your tongue out."

And that's when I cried, briefly. Quickly. Just choked a cry. Then swallowed it back down.

"OK, wheel it up." That wasn't aimed at me. Owen was talking to one of the other men in the room.

I could sense movement – the draught from figures walking around me, the opening and shutting of the door, the screech of trolley wheels out and then in.

A new trolley.

The new trolley.

I couldn't hold my head up. I dropped my chin to my chest and just swallowed in as much air as I could.

A serrated crocodile clip was snapped around a finger on my left hand.

I knew what that clasp was connected to.

"Oh, look," Owen gasped. "The fingers aren't in a good state, are they, Laura? Can we even attach the next wire? I don't know. What will we do?"

I choked up again.

"What's that? The sound of self-pity?"

You probably think I should have said something, anything. Surely saying at least something would've changed the course of this story. But I cannot agree. We had passed the point of this being an information-gathering exercise. And I didn't want to accidentally tell them any truth. To lie effectively requires calm conviction. And I was bleeding.

"So, one more time," said Owen. "Where is RAZR?"

I exhaled, kept my chin to my chest and just accepted what was coming.

The electric shock jolted through me.

I convulsed and threw up.

And blacked out.

I don't know how much time had passed before I came round. I was still in the same room but not on the chair. I was lying on the floor and as I moved my legs I couldn't feel any table legs either.

The room was filled with noise – the sound of men hollering and cheering. Hand slaps, back slaps and whooping. There was a lot of movement. I immediately lay still again, discreetly trying to open my eyes. All I could see were boots, constant movement. I couldn't sense any order or chain of command in the room. Almost impossibly, I feared the absence of Owen's voice. He wasn't in the room.

Shit.

My right hand was pain free. I could feel the floor, I could feel the wrist on my left. I tentatively slid my fingertips on my right hand up to the back of my left hand. As I brushed my fingertips along I felt the bones underneath start to pervert from their smooth lines. I chose not to slide my fingers on any more. I could feel my thumb still on my left hand so at least that was still there.

I gradually moved my right hand down to my waist.

My trousers, they were still intact. My trousers were still intact. I breathed a sigh of relief but my movement was seen.

"Hey. She's moving, she's moving!"

I heard another round of whistles. I heard another round of cheers.

I knew what was coming next. In man versus woman, it is the ultimate weapon.

But I had only one thought: if this is what was happening to me, only God knows what was being inflicted on the women who came with me.

I had to get to them.

The first soldier threw himself on top of me. "Yeah. She's conscious. Ha! Ha!"

The room whooped and cheered. I could feel the weight of his body pressing into my hips and chest, the heat of his breath on my face and I knew that I couldn't face it.

I had to get out of the room.

He ripped open the front of my trousers.

I had my eyes scrunched closed.

I could feel his hands between my legs, trying to pull them apart.

But all I was feeling was the side of his hip, tentatively. I tried to make out that I was squirming. But I was actually only after one thing.

And I found it.

He was still carrying his gun.

His hands pushed against my vagina. His gun was still clipped down.

"Come on bitch, open up." He tried to push my arms up, then he punched me in the face. My hand dropped away from his hip.

He pushed apart my legs.

I had to get the gun. The next punch could push me into unconsciousness and there was little chance of me coming back after that. I had to get the gun. My mind was blanking.

Orientation was gone. The darkness was coming.

Then I felt it.

It hurt as he forced it in.

The pain brought me back to life.

I went for the gun.

Quick. Clip flip, pull out, flick the catch.

BANG!

His head blew clean off. My eyes were half closed, vision blurry. I didn't see it, I felt it. He had made the mistake of putting his head into point blank range. Failure impossible.

The men roared.

But then

BOOM!

The whole room rocked as the explosion ripped through.

It shattered the walls, debris flying through the smoke.

The men screamed in pain.

I felt the heat, like a rocket of fire shooting across the left side of my face. My bullet must've triggered a self-destruct mechanism.

But then gunfire filled the room. The bleeding headless corpse on top of me meant I couldn't see anything but, wait, the bullets were hitting the other men.

Their bodies fell like cannonballs.

And then the bullets stopped.

The corpse was hauled off me.

The bright white light scorched my eyes. I flinched. But then I saw a blurry figure framed by the white light come into view.

And I heard her voice.

"Laura? Are you alive?"

All I could do was gasp. The hazards of the light and the blood in my mouth, blood I couldn't be sure was my own. But it was enough for Jane. She grabbed me and lifted me clean off the ground. Her arms around my legs, I flopped over her shoulders like a baby.

And all I could see, as Jane sped us out of the room, was the collateral damage of the dozen bloodied bodies underneath her feet.

CHAPTER THIRTY-FIVE
The Firefight

Out in the corridor, Jane dropped me to my feet and leant me up against the wall.

I looked left – more bodies. Men blown apart littered the corridor, its walls decimated in the explosion.

Jane grasped my shoulders and looked closely at me. "I know you've been drugged, I know you're hit, but I need you to carry your weight. Can you do that?"

I felt sweat pour down my forehead, throbbing in my arms. I nodded. "Yes."

"OK." Jane pushed a rifle into my right hand and over my shoulder. "I'm going to get you out of here. I will lead but I need you to cover me. Do you understand?"

"Yes," I muttered again, barely able to hold my own head upright. "You came back for me," I said. "You came back for me."

"Not alone." Jane strapped down the ammunition belt around her chest and checked the bullets in her guns.

I looked right – more bodies, more burning embers.

And Becks.

Becks.

Lying crumpled by the security door. Almost folded in half. Oh God.

Jane ripped a section from the bottom of her top, tying half of it around the tattered waist of my trousers, to hold it together, and the other half tightly around the stumps on my left hand.

"Look, I want to talk to you," Jane said, grabbing my shoulders again. "I want to make sure you're OK, but right now, we have no time. Do you understand?"

I nodded.

"OK. Can you see me?"

I nodded. The drugs were fading.

"OK. Can you move?"

"Yes." I took my own weight as Jane dropped her hands. She pushed my pistol into the back of my trousers. My gun. My own gun.

"You left it behind when you ran out on me. Now seems as good a time as any to give it back." And she looked deep into me as she pulled me off the wall. "I know this will not be easy but use your adrenaline, do you understand me?" I nodded. "OK, let's go."

And we started running.

Running away from the room, away from the bodies.

And away from Becks.

"Where are the others?" I asked as I fell into step behind the leader. "I've got to get the others."

Jane didn't even turn to face me, she just kept running on.

"Your sister," I added. "And Mandy, Alex and the others."

Jane came to an abrupt halt at the end of the corridor, at the foot of a staircase. "Those others," she said. She turned to look at me and I finally had enough in me to see that look, to feel that ice again. "I sent Andrea to find them."

Jane pulled her rifle forward into her hands.

I stood back.

Jane looked at me, not moving, the rifle aimed at me.

I took another step back.

"Stay behind me and keep focusing on securing us from the back," Jane said. "I will handle anything that's coming our way."

Jane sprinted up the stairs to the small landing in the middle but I was too far behind.

Looking up, I saw the boots and I saw Jane open fire.

Bullets hitting the boots like hailstones.

The men fell like rubble down the steps.

I struggled up the stairs, taking refuge behind her.

But as soon as I had, Jane leapt up the rest of the stairs, kicking the head of one of the soldiers as she rushed past.

I followed her, staggering over the bullet-riddled bodies.

The staircase opened up into another corridor. A brighter building with high ceilings, large windows that flooded the corridor with natural light.

Jane slowly stepped out and looked around.

There was no sound of boots, no sound of men.

I could feel the sweat pouring down my face. My breathing was heavy. I gulped in the air.

Jane looked left, looked right, listening. Then she said, "You used my sister as your cover."

"No I didn't."

"Yes you did."

Jane checked left, then right again, then checked her guns. "You kept her with you. One stray bullet on a moving line, it would've hit her, not you. You knew that."

I didn't know that. Did I know that?

Jane looked straight at me. Not a glare, just cold.

I stood there at the top of the stairs. "I didn't know that."

Jane reloaded her rifle. "I wouldn't have killed you anyway so it makes no difference."

Jane looked down the corridor, to her left, just listening.

I leant against the wall, or rather fell against it, as I tried to come back to life. I watched her. She was always looking, always listening.

"Do you know what they were asking me in there?" I asked.

Jane didn't look at me. "I knew even before you stepped into that room, even before you absconded from the prison," and then she did. "Before we even intercepted your convoy."

A shiver shot up my spine. "Then why didn't you... I don't know, expose me?"

"It wouldn't have achieved its purpose. And anyway, my greatest failing is that I want to win the battle as well as the war. I wanted to win the argument." She looked at me. "I wanted to change your mind."

"If you knew who I was, who I am, why did you come and get me, in the convoy?"

"I wanted to keep you where I could see you."

"So you got it wrong with Helen? Helen should have been me."

A rueful smile crossed Jane's face. "You were not the first. And they will come for me again."

"But Helen?"

Jane's face fell. "I'd known for some time. I'd guessed. Blind devotion is always suspicious. I thought I could change her mind, like I have with you." My cheeks flushed. "But it wasn't to be. She was the one who'd warned them we were coming for the women. At the art gallery, she left a message with the two women we left behind. A password, a link of some kind, to a secure communication channel between her and the State. She told the State the target after I told her."

A rewind flashed through my mind, the images from that time in the gallery – me leaving Abby on the floor with Gail, leaving with Helen, then turning back to see Helen squeezing Abby's hand, the words whispered in her ear. I never saw Helen interact like that with anyone else, ever. I looked closer at the playback in my head. I saw a passing of a note into Abby's hand as she leant in.

Jane was right.

I looked at Jane. "Are you going to kill me?"

Jane paused. She didn't react, not initially. Then she shook her head. "No," she said, softly. "I knew you would never betray me."

Tears rolled down my cheeks. "I'm sorry."

"It's OK."

Then we heard a muffled sound – faint explosions from the far side of the building.

Jane's head jerked left.

The piercing shrill of the fire alarms filled the air.

And then a secondary explosion closer, louder.

Jane's ears pricked up like a hare's, and we were off. Running towards the explosion.

"Keep your gun up!" Jane shouted. "Look behind us."

I spun round just as a squadron came into view behind us. But I saw them first and my spray of bullets brought most of them down. My accuracy not great but the adrenalin gave me enough.

I saw the grenade as it flew over my head towards the men. Jane's grenade.

The explosion was so fierce it blew the rest of the men clean off their feet and split their limbs from their bodies. I was blown backwards.

"Come on." Jane yanked my arm and pulled me up from the floor. We ran on.

Around one corner.

Then another.

Then another.

My legs hurt. I was exhausted.

"Run," Jane hissed.

Rifles up, running hard down the endless corridor.

Explosions ahead of us getting louder.

Running.

Ahead.

Fast.

My legs hurt.

Lactic acid or unnoticed bullet hit?

I couldn't see any marks on my legs.

We turned a corner, puddles of blood covered the floor.

Another explosion rocked the building.

The ceiling cracked open above us and heavy clouds of dust fell on our heads.

I choked on the ash.

I could smell burning.

The sound of gunfire.

Then a sudden rush of cold air.

I turned the corner and there they were – at the blown out entrance to the building – an army of angels.

Angels with guns.

And suddenly every single one of the women aimed their rifles straight at my head.

I gasped.

"It's OK, it's OK." The guns lifted. "It's who we came for." And at the front of the army was Andrea.

The whole entrance to the building had been blown out. Light debris was still falling from the night sky like snowflakes, the trucks were outside and, covering the steps and the roofless entrance between me and them, were hundreds of women.

The true scale of Jane's army was awesome. She must've drafted squadrons in from the secured areas. They were swarming all over the entrance to the compound. They were vast.

A rocket shot off from one of the trucks.

Another explosion rocked the building.

My knees almost gave way as another section of the compound was destroyed.

Jane grabbed my arm and pulled me back up.

She had brought the whole resistance with her. To get me. To save me.

Andrea looked at Jane. "Becks?"

Jane shook her head. "The others?"

Andrea hung her head.

Jane looked away and sighed.

"Do you think they'll kill them?" Andrea asked.

"We can only hope so," Jane replied.

"There's so many of you," I said, not to anyone in particular.

"Not enough to hold the territory though." Andrea came over and held up my left hand. I looked in the other direction, both away from her and from my hand. Andrea dropped it. "We have to go."

Outside a squadron of women were cuffing and dragging dozens of men into the trucks.

"Get off me, you fucking bitches." The men were so loud, shouting, screaming.

Winter was wrestling with one that refused to stay still as the rest were cuffed on the floor. Another prisoner wouldn't kneel so she kicked away his lower legs and the man collapsed head first. She didn't pick him up.

Half a dozen men, though, were being held in kneeling positions in the middle of what was left of the entrance hall.

Jane nodded towards the men. "Who are these?"

"We captured them trying to escape," Andrea said. "They were all trying to get in the same convoy, an important one. They're generals."

The men had their backs to us, all kneeling, all cuffed, one by one being dragged out to the trucks. But one man, one man...

Slowly, step by step, I walked away from Andrea and started to circumnavigate the man.

"You call yourselves freedom fighters?" he spat.

I knew him. I knew his voice.

I knew the frame of the back of his head. I knew the thinning hair.

And as his profile steadily came into view, oh, I knew that face too.

"You're murderers, you're all just fucking murderers," Owen hissed. "Huh? You call yourself the fucking future? You're all going to fucking hell. Fucking hell!"

Winter wasn't sure what to do with him. She looked up at Andrea and Jane who were behind Owen and just shrugged her shoulders.

He still hadn't seen me, at the side. His face was puce, his chin had dribbles of blood running down it. But still he didn't let up. He grunted, he snorted. "You're all just fucking soldiers. You think things will change for you because there's no men to lead you? Huh? You fucking gullible bitches. Your leader's no different from all the ones that've gone before. Oh, she waves the flag, commands your loyalty, but where is she when the battle needs to be fought, huh?"

Jane twitched.

"You." I whispered the word without even realising it.

Jane straightened up. "You know this man?"

Owen, though, hadn't seen or heard me. "Yeah, your fucking glorious leader's just a coward. Huh? Where is she then, huh?"

Jane came up to me but I couldn't turn my head away from Owen.

Jane looked at me, then looked at him.

Jane pulled her gun from the back of her trousers and placed its barrel at Owen's head.

Owen felt the gun. He stopped.

Jane walked around until she was facing him and her gun was at his temple.

His face was frozen with horror.

The men all gasped.

"Come here," Jane said.

It took me a moment to realise she was talking to me. I went up to her.

With her spare hand Jane grabbed my left hand and held it in front of Owen. "Did you do this to my woman?"

Owen was frozen with fear. He didn't move.

All the sound, all the movement in the room ceased.

Jane dropped my hand and aimed her gun at the floor towards Owen's knees.

She clicked the safety catch.

And then pulled the trigger.

Bang! Bang!

Owen shrieked in pain as Jane blew out both of his knees.

And, just as he collapsed to the floor in agony, Jane stamped her boot straight through his jaw.

"Everybody, to the trucks!" Jane shouted.

The women did as they were told, retreating from their positions at speed, out through the shattered doors into the night.

Owen was shrieking on the floor and as he was pulled away, his limbs dangled, barely attached to the stumps of his legs. The trail of blood coming from him was immense and his cries were unbearably loud.

"No," Jane said. "Leave him. I'm not listening to that noise."

And so Owen was dropped.

The women poured towards the trucks. A wave of darkness tumbling back towards safety.

And that's when I saw the soldier. His head covered with blood, torso shattered, foetal on the floor, twitching. Cuffed, bound, he was waiting to be shoved into the trucks, like all the rest.

I wish I hadn't seen him.

If somehow I could turn back time, I would change what happened next.

I would bite my tongue and look away.

I would just have got into the truck and run with the rest of them.

But I didn't. My instinct was immediate.

And in that moment, it all went wrong.

I stepped forward. "I know you. You were in the truck with us. You took them away."

Jane turned. She'd overheard.

She looked at me, looked at the man and then leapt on him, grabbing his collar and dragging him up from the floor. "Is this true? Did you take my sister? Where are my women?"

The man was twitching violently, shaking. He was not long for this world.

Jane lifted her rifle and shoved its barrel into the split in the man's side. The barrel went in deep. The squelch was audible and the blood started to pour. "If you tell me I'll put you out of your misery."

None of us stopped her.

I looked away as the man's twitching increased in ferocity. I scrunched up my eyes as I heard Jane dig her barrel a little deeper into the man's flesh.

He squealed. But I heard him. "The facility. The building... Outside."

And then I heard a muffled round of bullets and looked up just as Jane dropped the body to the floor.

Andrea stepped forward as the last of the women behind her fled out the exit, retreating to the waiting trucks. "Jane, you can't go. We have to leave now."

Jane looked at Andrea. "Take the women, get them safe. Leave one of the trucks in the shadows. If I make it, I make it. If I don't, just leave. You." Jane pointed the bloody barrel of her rifle at me. "You're coming with me."

CHAPTER THIRTY-SIX
The End

Behind us, on the other side of the walls, the trucks were pouring through the destroyed gates and racing out to the secured areas, to safety. We could hear them – the engines, the tyres on tarmac. But instead of being in one, Jane and I stood in a pitch black and chilly remote outbuilding.

We waited, not moving, listening both to the interior and the exterior. The trucks were leaving to the sound of chasing gunfire. A rear-guard action from the men.

I looked at Jane. In the darkness I could make her out, head tilted, listening. Listening intently. The gunfire wasn't coming in our direction. It was following the trucks.

The trucks had covered us; we had been lost in their escape – as Jane wanted. But all I could think was, with them went our support, our own back-up.

The sound disappeared.

We were alone.

Our eyes had adjusted to the absence of light. In front of us there was what seemed like a large glass screen. You could make out the odd reflection and refraction of what little light there was in the room on its surface.

Jane walked forward, rifle loose in her hand, until she was right in front of the glass.

She lifted up her hand to the glass and leant forward, looking through it into the darkness on the other side.

I stood silent, too concerned to make a sound. My attention was as much focused on any noise from outside as it was on Jane. I couldn't hear anything though. My mind was conflicted about whether this was good or bad. I hate silence.

Jane stepped back. "I want the lights on."

"We can't," I whispered. "They'll know we're in here."

Jane turned back to me. "The lights are going on."

She pulled out a torch from her belt and scoured the room. But this was no empty entrance hall – this room had a purpose. There were empty desks and dead computer screens on either side of us. And the walls were covered with shelves packed to the brim with pots, bottles and endless books.

Jane walked past a table near us without any thought but as she did I saw them, huddled under the desk. "Jane."

Jane followed my sightline. She put her torch light back in that direction and she saw them too. She leapt forward and dragged the two terrified lab technicians from under the desk. One of them was female.

"Who the fuck are you two?"

They were shaking, mute, too frozen with terror to answer. Jane threw me the torch and I kept it on them.

She grabbed the woman by the collar of her white coat. "Have you touched any fucking alarm?"

The woman was shaking, dribbling, holding her hands up in the air.

Jane pushed her to the floor and went up to the glass. I walked over to the two technicians and stood over them, my gun aimed at their bodies.

"How the fuck do we turn on the lights?"

The captives said nothing. Jane headed to the wall. I could hear her hands smacking everything they could touch. Then a whirring, a buzzing as the bulbs hummed into life.

Brilliant overheads scorched the eyes.

And then we saw them.

Beyond the glass screen, which we could now see had a set of doors in it, was a ward of beds. Dozens and dozens of beds. And in every single bed was a body. A female body. But though bright bulbs had come to life above them, nothing in the room stirred.

Jane stood at the glass doors, rifle in her hand, back towards us.

She said nothing.

"Jane, we can't save them," I said. "We need to leave."

Jane looked around, searching the walls. "When you lead, you have responsibilities."

"They're not even conscious," I said. "They might not even be alive. We can't wake them up and march them out of here."

"Are they alive?" Jane snapped at one of the cowering technicians, but there was no response other than a pathetic whimper.

"They're behind alarmed doors, Jane. We can't shoot the glass. We can't get to them without letting everyone know."

My mind was racing. I was torn between guarding the technicians and pulling Jane physically back from the brink.

But Jane was not for turning.

I looked through the glass to the drugged wombs chained to their beds. Then back to the terrified pair cowering by my feet.

Jane slung her rifle over her shoulder and pulled out her knife from her belt. She came back to me and grabbed the man by my feet. "Open this door or I'll cut off your hands."

I bit my lip and turned my head away, just a bit.

"Do it," Jane hissed.

The man staggered to his feet. Jane grabbed his shoulder and held the knife to his neck, pushing him towards the desk.

The woman was still trembling underneath my rifle butt.

I looked across at Jane and the man. He held out one of his shaking arms and put his hand over a palm reader. A light swiped across his palm.

Then the palm reader and the lights in the room suddenly flashed red, and a piercing alarm rung out.

Jane pulled back her knife and struck it deep into the man's neck. He slumped on to the floor.

Jane put her dagger back into her belt and pulled her rifle forward. "Well, I guess they know we're here now."

"What the hell happened?"

Jane turned her rifle to the glass doors. "Heightened pulse alert." And with a hail of bullets she shattered the glass.

She leapt into the ward, scouring the beds, lifting up one unconscious head after another.

I walked forward, slowly, in a daze.

The metal beds, the unconscious women... A couple of them were stirring. One of them was visibly pregnant. And she was attached to a life-support machine.

The shattered glass crunched under my foot, the piercing ring of the alarm in my ears. "Jane..." But I wasn't sure what I wanted to say, or what I was trying to say. I came to a stop and stood, frozen.

"Come and help me." Jane was frantic, racing around the beds, but it was clear that she couldn't find what she was looking for, who we were looking for.

Oh God, where were they? I was terrified that I'd find them in the beds, and I was terrified that I wouldn't.

"Oh, fucking hell!" Jane screamed. She looked up at the ceilings, into the corners of the room. She pulled out her rifle and took one quick shot at each of the three alarms above us. The silence fell like a cannonball.

I stepped forward slowly, looking at the women in the beds. Their bodies lay strewn under distressed sheets, some of which were bloodied. I couldn't hear any breathing from some, no sound. The blonde in the bed nearest to me... Her hair was all I could see. The mess of straggled hair covered her face. Her body inert.

None of them were our soldiers.

"Maybe they're not here," I said. "Maybe the State has—"

"Oh, for fuck's sake! Stop talking about the fucking State!" Jane shouted at me. "Stop being so fucking naive. There is no State, Laura. There is no State. This is a military dictatorship. The politicians are gone. The world they told you was going to exist never fucking materialised. It never fucking materialised, do you hear me? Look around you. This isn't the fucking Parliament. It's a military barracks. We are ruled by the army. These women are kept for the men. That's their purpose."

My hands dropped to my knees. My throat retched but nothing came up.

I pulled myself upright again and looked at Jane but she wasn't looking at me. Her head was tilted again, she was staring out into the distance.

And then I heard it too, the sound of boots outside.

Jane checked her rifle. "They're encircling us."

"We need another exit."

"But we need that exit to be secure." Jane stepped forward, past me, back towards the entrance. "We'll rig the front of the laboratory. We have the explosives. It will give us time, if nothing else."

She stepped over the woman still cowering on the floor, pulling the explosives from her belt and lacing the front of the building with them.

My failure was complete. I had failed those women. I had failed myself. And I had failed Jane.

Finished, Jane stepped over the woman and back into the ward. I put my rifle to my hands, waiting to hear her plan. How were we going to get out?

But Jane said nothing and did nothing.

She just came to a stop amongst the beds. Then she walked over to the pregnant woman who was tied to the machine. Jane ran her hand along the woman's arm and then placed her palm on the woman's forehead.

Around us the enclave was preparing for the final war but Jane, I don't know, was she in shock? Was she taking it in? She passed from bed to bed. Occasionally her arms would twitch towards one of the beds, as if she was thinking of trying to free one of the women, but then her arm would just drop.

The futility overwhelmed her.

She walked back towards me and came to a stop in front of the bed of the pregnant woman again, just staring at her comatose body.

The silence from outside... Deafening. I had no idea whether Jane was aware of that. Or if she even cared. I took a step forward, hesitated. I wanted to reach over, to save her, to tell her to let it go and find an exit. But I hesitated, fearful of breaking the trance.

Jane gripped one of the metal bed frames and just cracked. I heard a cry, a yelp. She was gripping that metal frame so tightly.

There was silence outside this room. No gunfire, no explosions.

Silence only meant one thing.

"We have to leave." The words just leapt from my mouth.

I could hear the crack, the sound of suffocation as she tried to hold it all in, to not completely fall apart.

I took a step forward.

And another one.

She sensed my encroachment. She stood up and faced me. She pulled out her gun.

Oh God.

Jane's face was tear-stained but her voice was clear. "Leave none behind."

Then she turned to the beds on the other side and opened fire.

She waved her rifle across every single one of the beds. The bullets flew across the room, into every bed.

I could only watch in horror.

The blankets twitched and moved as the bullets riddled through them. The bodies underneath jerking from the force of the firepower.

The horror.

Jane's rifle swept back and forth as she sprayed the women with gunfire.

And then she turned back to the woman, the pregnant woman in the bed. Jane dropped her gun to her side, went round the side of the bed and yanked the cables clean from the life-support machine in a single powerful jerk of her arm.

The dull tone that accompanied the flat line.

The scorched earth policy.

Only in death would we be able to deny men.

BOOM!

The walls blew in.

The explosions ripped through the laboratory, shattering what was left of the glass doors and the walls around it.

They had triggered the explosives.

Jane grabbed my arm and dragged me towards the back, as far from the entrance as possible.

A second round of detonations swept a back-draught through the room.

I looked back. "Jesus."

The clouds of dust suffocated the first room, the laboratory, and swallowed up the woman we had left alive behind us.

We raced on to the far end of the ward but there was nothing but a wall. Jane pulled out a grenade from her belt. All I could do was stare at it. "I'm sorry," I said.

"For what?"

"Everything."

We could hear the men making their way towards us. The boots on crushed glass getting closer. Jane pulled me back to behind the beds. "Stand back."

She pulled out the pin and threw it at the wall.

It exploded inwards, rocking the floor and throwing bricks and dust through the room.

Jane leapt forward as I was still coughing and spluttering on the floor.

She came back and grabbed me. "Come on."

We were outside. The building was right up against the vast wall of the enclave. I looked up. The only way was to go up. I looked down. I only had one hand.

Jane put her fingers in her mouth and whistled. Then grabbed my arm and dragged me into a crouching position, hiding in the shadows.

I heard the whistle first. The whistle of a speeding object approaching us...

BOOM!

323

The ground shook, the blast deafening, as a vast section of the enclave wall near us was blown out. The detonation was catastrophic, bricks and concrete following the rocket as it blasted out into the centre of the enclave.

We heard the men and their gunfire as they recovered and headed straight for the attack point. Then we saw them, in their masks, come round the side of the building.

Jane grabbed my hand and we dived into the clouds of debris.

Jane's feet were moving fast but I was coughing, struggling to breathe. Jane dragged me on. I couldn't see anything.

But then I tripped, stumbled over some debris.

Jane pushed her arms under my shoulders and started to drag me through the hole in the wall, pulling me on as I coughed, wheezed, struggled to breathe. As my feet clambered over the bricks.

Blurred figures in the mist started getting sharper. Heading towards us. Men. Jane dropped me and leapt at the figures. I could feel the whooshing of her blade.

I tried to get to my feet. Jesus, my ankle had twisted. But ahead of me I could see the truck, I could see Andrea.

"Jane!" I shouted.

"Run!" I heard her shout. "I'll cover you."

I crawled as fast as I could to the truck. Breathing hard. I struggled to my feet desperate to flee whatever was behind me, the adrenalin killing the sprain in my ankle.

I fell against the back of the truck. Andrea gripped my left arm and dragged me inside, my head just missing the rocket launcher.

I turned back.

Jane wasn't behind me.

She hadn't broken free.

The cloud was settling and I could see her.

Oh God, the men had her. They had her.

The men descended on her like a wave, dragging her back, pulling her further into their clutches. She was thrashing, trying to fight them off but they poured all over her, clutching her hands, her wrists. Gripping her legs and lifting her clean off the floor.

"Shit," Andrea said.

They clawed at her, their gloved hands grabbing at her limbs, her body. Her clothes ripped in the frenzy. She was being swallowed as they swarmed over her.

She fought them.

I could see her, thrashing her legs, convulsing and contorting her body as they lifted her up.

I moved forward. Andrea grabbed my arm. "We can't."

"We don't have a choice," I said.

They lifted her clean off the ground, grasping at her.

"We are losing her!" I screamed. "Give me a grenade."

Andrea shook her head. "There's none left. We have nothing left."

I looked back at the hell. We were out of time.

"Jane!" I cried out.

The men turned to us.

"Engines!" Andrea yelled at the driver.

"We can't leave her!" I screamed.

"We have no choice," Andrea shouted back. "Jane gave us our orders."

"They'll kill her!" I screamed.

The engines roared to life.

Andrea had tears in her eyes.

I turned back to the wall, pulling my gun out from the back of my trousers.

I aimed it at the melee.

The men were pushing in, moving constantly. The aim was almost impossible to get.

And then suddenly the crowd broke.
There it was, through the dust, a direct line to Jane.
I pointed the gun straight at Jane's head.
I closed one eye and took aim.
Then she saw me.
She saw my gun.
But she didn't move her head.
She closed her eyes and I pulled the trigger.
One clean shot.
Her head snapped back and she fell lifeless to the ground.
Our truck pulled away at speed.

Andrea collapsed down onto the bench but I stayed standing, looking out behind us at the collapsed body getting ever smaller in my sights, the truck racing me away from my past and headlong into our uncertain future.

Acknowledgements

Darkness was born from anger – that, I suspect, is obvious. But anger cannot be sustained for any length of time. This book, this story, was shaped over many, many months. Months that then became years. A long period of angst and hard work, and of calm consideration and careful thought. But for all my work, this book wouldn't have made it into your hands without support from those close to me.

Writing is an unbelievably hard career to pursue – so many knocks in the pursuit of only a remote possibility of fleeting success. My closest friends and family have been amazing in their belief in my abilities. One day I hope to be as good as they think I am.

I also want to thank my editor, Gillian Holmes, and the team at Whitefox Publishing for their support and sage words of advice.

Finally, to Twitter. Social media's reputation as a platform for hate and abuse is pretty much well deserved. But for me – and for many others – it is also a place of incredible support and encouragement. My friends on Twitter have galvanised me and given me the strength to carry on during those many moments when my motivation and resolve felt like they had walked out the door. I thank you for that. Really, I do.

About the Author

Victoria is an arts and culture writer based in London. She is a graduate of the University of Manchester and the LSE and, prior to writing, worked in the City. Her experience there led to Victoria's first book, *Banking on Burlesque*, which charts a period of her life when she worked as an investment banker by day, and a burlesque performer by night. *Darkness* is Victoria's second book. And it won't be her last.

And, yeah, Victoria is a feminist. No ifs, no buts.

www.victoriasadler.com
Twitter: @victoriajsadler